Be sure to read the first book:

Forces of Evil

by Trish Kocialski

Forces of Evil takes place in New York state in a small Catskills resort town. As the story unfolds, two female undercover agents from separate agencies meet, and join forces to try to decipher and stop a diabolical plot of world domination from reaching its climax. As they find themselves falling helplessly in love, adding a new dimension to their jobs, and another set of priorities, the team races to a cliffhanger conclusion.

Available through your favorite local or online booksellers.

"This isn't Nancy Drew, and thank God for that! It's about time someone wrote an exciting action/mystery with strong female characters, and Trish Kocialski has done just that. The character development is solid. These are interesting and competant female agents involved in an exciting tangle of politics, secrecy, love, and danger of global proportions. There is enough detail to make the setting (Catskill Mountains in New York) and the personal lives of these two women very real and engaging. The storyline is completely plausible, and the unraveling of the layers of the mystery held my attention and kept me reading late into the night. The ending is very satisfying. I want to see more books with these two agents."

—Cynthia R. Knowles,
Dansville, NY

Blue Holes To Terror

Blue Holes to Terror

Trish Kocialski

QuestBooks
a Division of
RENAISSANCE ALLIANCE PUBLISHING, INC.
Nederland, Texas

ISBN 1-930928-61-0

First Printing 2001

9 8 7 6 5 4 3 2 1

Cover art and design by Mary A. Sannis

Published by:

Renaissance Alliance Publishing, Inc.
PMB 238, 8691 9th Avenue
Port Arthur, Texas 77642-8025

Find us on the World Wide Web at
http://www.rapbooks.com

Printed in the United States of America

Acknowledgements

I want to thank my friends and family for their constant encouragement, and especially Linda Mullen, who is the best taskmaster anyone could have. I would also like to thank Daylene Petersen, my editor, Barb Coles, my division director, and Cathy LeNoir, CEO of RAP.

Dedication

To my soul mate Carol,
I am truly blessed to have you in my life.

Chapter
1

There was a firm knock at the door. Lieutenant Colonel Deanna Peterson had been rocking in her oversized leather desk chair, looking out the window into the courtyard. The chair was the only luxury she allowed herself in her large, but spartan office, at the Pentagon. She swiveled her chair around and straightened the papers that were scattered about her desk before she called out, "Enter." A brilliant smile quickly replaced her formal military countenance as she recognized the individual entering through the doorway. It was her long time friend, Tracy Kidd, with whom she had recently been reunited while on detached assignment in the Catskills of New York. That was an assignment she would remember for the rest of her life, for it was where she finally reconciled with her past, and took a bold step into the future.

"Hey, Colonel," came the quick salutation from Tracy, "how about lunch?"

"Tracy. It's good to see you. Are you here alone? Where's Colleen?" Stepping from behind her desk, Dean greeted her old friend with a barrage of questions and a fierce hug instead of a handshake. Not allowing Tracy time to answer, she added, "So, what brings you to Washington?"

Tracy grinned at her friend's obvious delight at seeing her. "Oh, just one of the perks of being Director of Parks and Recreation. We brought a busload of senior citizens down to see the sights for the weekend. We just got in. I left them in Linna's capable hands and hopped the first cab over here to see you. Colleen couldn't make this trip, but she sends her love," Tracy said, answering all of the questions as Dean waved her to a chair by the desk and returned to her own. "We haven't heard from you in a while, so I just took a chance you'd be here and not out on assignment in some backwater. And before you ask, I ran into Captain Jerral at the Information Desk, and he got me the visitor's pass and directed me to your office."

"Good old Jerral. That's right, you were posted together at Fort Sill. Yeah, I've been here plowing through paperwork for what seems like eons." Dean motioned at the stacks of papers littering her desk. "I was just rocking in my chair and contemplating how bored I am, when you knocked. I really hate paperwork. Much rather be out in the field."

"So, why aren't you?" came the direct question from Tracy.

"Well, with the loss of General James, the higher ups decided that his replacement, Brigadier General Carlton, needed an aide who was well versed in intelligence work in the field, and guess who they picked?" Dean pointed at her chest with a sad smile.

"Carlton? Is that Mary Carlton? She's a one-star now?"

"Yep. Nice to see a woman progress to such a good posting, but it's sure cramping my style. General Carlton was always a top-notch administrator, great with budgets, proposals, planning, and staffing, but unfortunately has never been in the field herself. So now I get to help her make those assignments, track their progress, recommend changes, etc., etc."

"Hey, it can't be that bad. At least you get to see Katie, don't you?" Tracy offered this comment with a broad smile. "How are the two of you doing, anyway?"

Here Dean brightened visibly. Katie had become the stable force Dean needed in her life, and they grabbed every chance they could to be together. However, working for different government agencies was not helping their relationship to develop on a normal track. Katie was often out in the field, while Dean was swamped with paperwork. She filled Tracy in on the latest assignment Katie had in El Paso, knowing full well that nothing she said to her friend would leave her office. "She'll be here this weekend. She's just finishing up the paperwork on the case and will be arriving at National on the red eye from Dallas late tonight. I know she'll be glad to see you...and Linna too.

What's your schedule like with the seniors?"

"Not too bad. We bought a packaged tour this time. The company is providing a tour guide for the whole weekend. Linna and I came along just to participate and see whether it's a good deal or not for future reference. So I can slip out any time, but Linna will be available only in the evenings. What'd ya have in mind?"

"I know a great restaurant down by the river. Best crab cakes you've ever tasted. Maybe we could all get together there. It's called The Crab Pot."

"Hey! That's where the tour has us scheduled for tomorrow night. Dinner is at seven."

"Great. Katie and I will meet you there at seven."

The two friends talked a bit longer and were about to leave for a short tour of the Pentagon when they were interrupted by an order for Dean's presence in General Carlton's office. "Guess I'll have to bow out on the tour, but we'll see you at the Crab Pot tomorrow." The women rose from their chairs and hugged again before they left Dean's office, each heading in a different direction.

One thing about Ronald Reagan Washington National Airport, it was almost always busy. Dean parked her SUV in the short-term lot and ran into the airport, scanning the monitors for Katie's arrival gate information. *Damn! They're early. Must have caught a good tailwind. Okay, Dean, let's see how fast you can sprint down to the gate.* As she hurriedly turned from the bank of monitors, she ran right into Katie who had been quietly standing behind the tall woman and was just about to tap her on the shoulder.

"Ufff. Sorry, I didn't—" Dean said, as she reached down to assist the traveler she had just laid out on the floor. "Katie! Why didn't you say something?" Dean sputtered as she lifted her lover into her arms.

"Yeah...I'm glad to see you, too." Katie said, reveling in the warmth of Dean's embrace.

Releasing Katie, Dean put on her very best puppy dog look and started to apologize for being late, explaining that she had a very long meeting with the general, then had to run home to give Sugar her medicine, and then the traffic on I 95.

Katie reached up, smiling, and placed two fingers on Dean's lips to stop the litany of excuses. "It's okay, Dean. We got in early. I slipped the pilot an extra $20 to floor it all the way home, 'cause I missed you so much." This said with a wink and a smile. "I've got my bag, so let's just go home." *Home,* she thought, losing herself in Dean's eyes. *That sounds so good, and after this weekend, it'll be even better.*

"Hey, love, penny for your thoughts," Dean said, pulling the blonde out of her reverie.

"Mmmm, I was just thinking about how nice it is to be home." The tall woman gave her lover another hug before walking out into the warm October night towards the SUV.

"Are you hungry?" Dean asked, as she pulled out into the southbound traffic on I 95.

"Do birds fly? Of course I'm hungry...but, no beef or Mexican food, okay? I've pretty much hit my limit on those." Katie reached over to hold Dean's hand. "How about some Chinese, or Thai, or Indian, or—" Her list of suggestions was cut short as Dean shouted for her to hold on, and made a quick defensive move to the right to keep from being sideswiped by a limo coming up quickly on her left, zigzagging between their SUV and the vehicle just in front of them. "Holy Horse Puckey! Where the heck did he come from?" the blonde exclaimed, as she felt the strong restraint of her shoulder harness keep her from bouncing around on the slick leather seat.

"Damn!" snarled Dean, carefully controlling her SUV on the loose gravel of the right hand shoulder. Looking into her rearview mirror, she noted that the vehicle that had been in front of her was not as lucky. It had pulled violently to the left to avoid the limo and wound up sliding sideways into the median, kicking up a spray of dirt and grass before it came to an abrupt stop. "We'd better check on the people in that other vehicle. Make sure the driver is all right."

The two women got out of the SUV and checked for traffic before crossing the highway. When they got to the unlucky car, they found it occupied by two elderly people who looked to be in their early seventies. The male driver was slumped over the steering wheel, and his female companion was holding the right side of her head and mumbling what they assumed was his name, but was unrecognizable at the time. Dean noticed they both had their seat belts on, so she hoped any injuries would be minor.

"Check her out. I'll check him," Dean instructed. Katie

nodded and hurried around to the passenger side. Each worked quickly and skillfully, assessing their charges. Katie called over that the woman had hit her head on the passenger door, but seemed to be all right otherwise. Dean carefully checked the man for bleeding, pulse, and breathing. Though she found no sign of physical injuries, he wasn't breathing and had no pulse. "Quick, give me a hand. I've got to start CPR." Katie rushed back to the driver's side, and together they unhooked his seatbelt, carefully moved him to the grass, and began CPR. Dean performed chest compressions while Katie provided the breaths.

By the time they finished the third round, a few other vehicles had stopped to lend assistance. Dean shouted to the gathering crowd, asking if a cell phone was available and directing that a call be made to 911 for assistance. A young teenager who had stopped, quickly pulled out his cell phone and dialed for help, while his date went to check on the elderly woman. A truck driver helped the teen with the woman, who was now becoming hysterical as she watched Katie and Dean work on her husband.

By the time the ambulance arrived, the two women had managed to get the man's heart beating, and he had recovered sufficiently to breathe on his own. A Virginia State Police vehicle arrived at the same time as the ambulance. One officer went to interview the woman, while the other crossed over to where the EMT's were taking over from Dean and Katie.

"Excuse me," called the officer, as the two women turned over the care of the man to the ambulance crew. "May I have a word with you two?"

"Certainly, officer," Katie nodded, as they walked over to him.

"I'm Sergeant Dooley." He identified himself as he offered his ID for their inspection. "May I have your names, please?" The question came as he pulled out his report pad.

"Deanna Peterson," Dean said, then motioned towards Katie, "and this is Katherine O'Malley."

The officer made a notation. "Do you have any idea what happened here?"

"We were on our way from Washington National when a silver stretch limo, I believe it was a Lincoln, sped between my SUV and the Mercedes these folks were driving. The car had to be going at least ninety miles an hour when he cut between the two of us."

"Did you notice the plate or get the number?" Pen at the

ready, he calmly waited for their reply.

"At ninety miles an hour?" Katie asked incredulously. "We were lucky Dean was able to keep control of the car."

"Yes, ma'am, but did you notice anything significant about the car? There's got to be at least two hundred silver stretch limos in Washington alone. Anything that could identify this particular one would be a big help."

"It had embassy flags," Dean answered. "I can't be sure which embassy...went by too fast, and it's too dark."

"Well, that narrows it down a little; but if it was an embassy vehicle, we might as well hang it up now, 'cause we'll never see justice done." He jotted a few notes in his pad before closing it. "Well, thank you, ladies. Is there somewhere we can reach you if we need to?"

Both women took their business card cases from their coat pockets and handed their cards to the officer. He took them, reading the information, then whistled. "Well, thank you, Colonel Peterson, Agent O'Malley. If you think of anything else, please give me a call." He handed one of his cards to each woman and returned to his squad car.

As they walked back to the road, Katie asked a contemplative Dean, "You actually saw flags on that limo?"

"Mmhmm, and I think they were Algerian, and I may have seen the guy in the passenger seat before. If I'm right, he's a mercenary named Scott Gentry."

"You could get all that and still keep the SUV under control?" Katie shook her head in wonder. "So why didn't you tell the officer?"

"Like he said, if they were embassy flags, you might as well forget about it, it's a lost cause." Dean shrugged. "C'mon, there's a break in traffic, let's get back to the truck." She grabbed Katie's arm and steered her across the highway to where the SUV was parked.

Once the vehicle was back on the road, the young blonde turned in her seat to face her partner. "Dean?"

"Mmm?"

"Why do you think the limo was in such a hurry that it would risk cutting us off like that?"

"Don't know, love. Could be they were late for a meeting, or maybe the driver just likes to speed. We'll probably never find out." Dean glanced over at Katie, winked, and gave her a crooked smile before adding, "I just need more time to process what I saw. But if there's a way to figure it out, I will."

Katie smiled at her lover and put her left arm behind Dean's neck and began a gentle massage on tight neck muscles. "You know, hon, I just bet you will."

Chapter
2

1900 Hours, 21 October

Dean and Katie pulled into the parking lot of the Crab Pot restaurant at precisely 7:00 p.m., observing the tour bus unloading its passengers by the door. Linna and Tracy were holding the door open for the last of their seniors when Linna spotted Katie exiting the SUV. Insuring that the last person was clear, Linna let go of the door and began waving at her. "Hey, Katie!" Linna shouted.

"I'll go get them all seated and make my rounds with the group. Why don't you go over and say 'hi' to Katie and Dean? I'll meet you inside in a bit," Tracy told Linna before she followed her last senior inside. Linna smiled her thanks, then walked briskly over to the SUV and gave each woman a heartfelt hug.

"Jeez, it's good to see you two. How the heck are ya's?" Linna exclaimed exuberantly.

"We're good, Linna," came Dean's simple reply. Katie, on the other hand, immediately began to quiz Linna on their tour so far. Dean just smiled as she listened to the women chatter as the three made their way into the restaurant. *Damn, I really owe Linna big time. If she hadn't been so damned curious, Katie would be dead, and the whole Catskills case would have turned out quite differently. Tracy sure has one heck of a secretary in that woman.*

"Oh, it's been really great," she began enthusiastically, "but

I can see we're going to have to take several trips here before we can see all the sights. There's just too much to see and do in this town. We must have walked twenty miles today alone."

"Yeah, there's certainly a lot to do here," Katie agreed. "What have you found most interesting so far?"

Linna began a dialogue on all the sites they had visited that day while Katie listened in earnest, nodding at the appropriate times and making comments on her visits to the same places. As the two women conversed, Dean walked over to the hostess desk and waited in line. When it was her turn, she gave her name and another hostess came forward to lead the three women to their reserved table overlooking the Potomac. Katie and Linna talked the entire time until Tracy made her way over and sat down.

"I see Linna's filling you in on our tour so far," Tracy said with a grin, and then in a soft aside to Dean she added, "I think this trip is a winner already. Linna is definitely impressed, and that's the real battle on these trips. She demands the best for our people and doesn't stop 'til she gets it."

"Hey, if I were a tour operator, I'd be doing everything I could to keep that woman happy." Dean chuckled softly. "I certainly wouldn't want to be on her bad side." The two women chuckled in agreement, then turned their attention back to their tablemates.

"What's so funny?" Katie asked, raising an eyebrow at Dean.

"Oh, nothing, love. Tracy and I were just enjoying Linna's enthusiasm for the trip so far," Dean commented quickly, then winked at Tracy.

Linna looked over at her boss and gave her one of her stern questioning looks, to which Tracy quickly responded, "It's the truth, Linna. Really!" Then all four of them burst out laughing.

When dinner was finished, Katie tapped her water glass with her spoon to get the attention of her friends before speaking. "When Dean told me we were going to have dinner with you two tonight, I decided to wait until now to make my announcement." Dean raised an eyebrow at her partner, surprised by her secrecy. Katie had a terrible time keeping things from Dean, so she was truly curious about what was coming next. "After our little assignment in the Catskills, I started to re-think some of my goals with the DEA. And I made a few discreet inquiries. Yesterday, before I left El Paso, I received confirmation of a new assignment I requested." She paused for effect and found three sets of eyes totally focused on her. "Starting the first week in December, I will be assigned to the DEA's new Justice Training Center in Quantico as an instructor."

Dean was the first to break into a huge grin, knowing that this would mean that she and Katie would be able to spend more time together. It took a little longer for Tracy and Linna to realize the significance of the assignment before they, too, joined in with smiles of their own.

"Wow! That's great Katie. What will you be teaching?" Linna asked excitedly.

"Well, hand-to-hand combat methods, small weapons training, and some classes on surveillance and undercover techniques, for starters."

"They sure picked your strong points," Tracy commented, reaching over to give Katie a pat on the shoulder. "The new recruits will be getting the very best." They all lifted their glasses and toasted her new assignment. "Guess that means you two will get to see each other a bit more, eh?" she added with an even bigger grin that brought a nice rosy flush to the young woman's cheeks as well as to Dean's. "Well, this calls for some kind of celebration, and I think I have just the right thing in mind." Tracy smiled broadly at her two friends. "How much time off have you two accrued?"

After a brief moment for thought, Dean replied that she had about forty-five days, and Katie figured she had twenty-one. "Great. How would you two like to join Colleen and me at our condo in the Bahamas for the middle two weeks in November?"

Before they could answer, Linna jumped in and started raving about the great time she'd had there the year before ending with, "...so you just gotta go."

Dean looked over at Katie and immediately recognized that her young lover was already picturing herself on the beach. Slipping into that visualization, Dean pictured Katie in a bikini stretched out on the sand. That thought alone led her to quickly accept the offer. "That's really generous of you, Tracy. We'll have to check our calendars and make sure we can get the time cleared. When would you have to know by?"

"Any time before we step on the plane to leave is good with us. As long as you can get there, we'd love to have you."

"Okay, we'll check into it and let you know as soon as we can," Dean finished with a smile, as Katie gave her leg a squeeze under the table.

Before long, it was time for the tour bus to load and for the old and new friends to part once more. Of course, all of the seniors wanted to know who the two women with Linna and Tracy were, so there were many introductions and handshakes in the parking lot before the groups finally went their separate ways.

The ride back to Dean's house outside of Occoquan, Virginia took less time than the ride into D.C., as most of the traffic was still heading north on I 95 into the greater D.C. area. Dean really enjoyed the privacy her house afforded them. It was located on a dead end street, just across the water from the southeastern tip of Fountainhead Regional Park on the Occoquan River. Although a fairly large home, considering some of the houses her neighbors had, it was not too big.

Dean had designed it herself in the style of Frank Lloyd Wright's famous *Fallingwater* home in Pennsylvania, only she omitted the boulders in the living room and by the hearth. Other than that, she tried to stay true to his style, while blending in some of her own innovations as well. The lot was perfect for the design, and the seclusion at the end of the road was great. It was a labor of love, and the finished product showed it. She was glad that it was finally completed, having just moved in two weeks previously. Dean was looking forward to furnishing it beyond the essentials she currently had, putting off any major purchases in hopes of getting Katie's input.

The place already had the seal of approval from Katie's three cats, Sugar, Spice and Butter, since they had been staying with her while Katie was on assignment in El Paso. The trio of felines had totally taken over in the two weeks since they moved from the cramped apartment Dean had occupied in Georgetown. Katie had not yet seen the finished product, because they slept Friday night in Katie's old apartment in Arlington, then spent almost their entire Saturday cleaning it and storing the rest of her furniture, before they left to meet Tracy and Linna.

As Dean slowed for her exit off I 95, she looked over at her napping passenger and smiled. "Hey sleepy head, we're almost home."

"Mmmmm" the young woman protested, "did you have to wake me just now? I was having the best dream."

"Well, sorry I woke you then. Was I in it?"

"No," Katie began with a mischievous twinkle in her eye, "but, there was this drop dead gorgeous redhead in it. And we were making mad, passionate love on the beach—" Her words came to an abrupt halt as Dean reached over and gave Katie a playful smack on her arm. "Ouch. What was that for?" Katie's response was as exaggerated as the tap was soft.

"That, was for the big tease you are." Dean winked as she turned off the exit ramp onto Route 641. "I hope you like the way the house turned out. There's not much furniture yet, just the essentials. But it certainly looks a lot better than when you saw it before you left for El Paso."

Katie had been in El Paso on assignment since the last week in July and only saw the rough design of the house, leaving Dean to play architect and general contractor. Dean knew she was in for a surprise, and hoped that Katie liked the finished result as much as she did.

"I can't wait to see it. I went on-line to check out Wright's *Fallingwater* house, and that one looks spectacular."

"Well, I just hope I did him justice with the adaptation of his design to my lot," Dean replied, starting to get nervous about Katie's reaction to the surprise she'd left in the bedroom. Dean had already asked her lover to move in when her El Paso assignment was finished, at least until her next assignment took her away again. They had both agreed that it was foolish for her to pay for an apartment that sat empty most of the time. Now, with the instructor's position coming up in December, well—things were looking better and better.

"Do you think you'll be able to swing a vacation in the Bahamas?" Katie asked her partner as they headed down the road.

"Probably. It would be nice to be on a warm beach when it's cold back here."

"Unhuh." Katie shivered at the mere thought of snow, having had her fill the previous winter in the Catskills. "Oooo...that would mean you'd have to wear a bathing suit most of the time. Like that nifty little bikini I made you buy the last time I was here. Oh, yeah, I definitely want to go to the Bahamas."

Dean turned the corner onto her street as she thought about Katie in a bikini and smiled. *Yeah, I think a trip to the islands is in order.* Soon they pulled into the long winding driveway that was cut through the woods. "Well here we are, home sweet home." She hit the garage door opener, pulled the SUV in, and turned off the ignition. When she hit the button once more, the garage door closed behind them. The spectacular view of the house was now waiting on the other side of the small side door.

"Home. That's such a nice word." Its implications only served to emphasize Katie's uncertainty, and she knew she should take this opening to try and resolve that. In a hesitant voice, she asked, "Are you sure you want me to move in with you?"

Dean looked over at the young blonde, giving her one of her best, raised eyebrow, I-wouldn't-have-asked-if-I-didn't-mean-it looks, before pulling Katie into her arms.

"Yes, love, I do. I've been waiting for this moment for a very long time. Besides our house is located just right. The perfect commute for both of us." She lowered her head, stealing a kiss from the woman she'd lost her heart to nearly a year before. "You'll go south and I'll go north. Of course, I have to deal with more traffic on my commute, but then I drive a bit more aggressively than you do. C'mon, let's go inside." Dean walked over to Katie's side of the vehicle, taking her love's hand as she led her to the side door of the garage, opening it gallantly to display the house—illuminated in beams of soft light coming from the outdoor receptacles.

"Oh, Dean. It's absolutely breathtaking." Katie whispered as she caught her first full view of the house. She gave Dean an appreciative look before she continued. "I can't wait to see how the inside looks, but I think we need to talk about something first." Katie's voice quavered on the latter portion of the sentence, exhibiting obvious anxiety about something. "How about we take a little walk down by the water first?" Katie requested nervously as they exited the detached garage, walking on the slate path towards the house. *I need to get this out before I walk into that house, just in case I have to walk out of it,* she thought glumly.

Okay, love, what's on your mind? the tall woman thought before saying with a flourish, "Whatever madam wishes." They took the intersecting path that led down the steep embankment towards the river. The two women walked quietly, arm-in-arm, enjoying the Indian summer that had descended on the area. When they came to the river, Dean led Katie over to the teak-wood bench on the flagstone patio along the riverbank. As they sat listening to the gentle waves lap along the shoreline, Dean waited for Katie to break the silence.

"Dean?" Katie began hesitantly.

"Mmm?"

Katie rested her head on Dean's shoulder and sighed before she began to speak. "I probably should have talked to you about my re-assignment. I guess that was kind of a bomb I dropped at dinner. I mean...I...I just assumed it would be all right." She looked searchingly into the eyes of her lover, then continued, "It is all right, isn't it?"

Oh, so that's what's bothering you, you're afraid I'm not ready for you to be here full time...only when you're in between assignments. "It's more than all right. It's perfect." The tender response was followed by a sweet kiss as Dean wrapped her arms around Katie. "I miss you so much when you're not here, and you can't imagine how I worry about you when you're on assignment." She felt Katie tense a little in her embrace. "No, no...I know you're an excellent field agent. I just can't help but worry. I don't want to lose you...ever."

"And I don't want to lose you either," came Katie's reply. "I want to be close to you...all the time...not just between assignments. That's why I did it." Katie laid her head back on Dean's shoulder and began idly tracing a pattern on the woman's strong thigh.

Concerned that Katie was making the change just for her, and that it might not be the most appropriate use of her lover's skills, Dean asked, "Are you sure you'll be satisfied just teaching? You'll be missing a lot of the action, and teaching can become boring with the repetition of information from class to class."

"I'm not worried about that. I know it will be a big change, but it will be for the better. For us." Katie reached up and placed her hand over Dean's heart.

"Well, I probably won't get a field assignment any time soon, but there may come a day when I do, and I'll have to go." Dean shifted to look into Katie's eyes. "How will you feel about that?"

The young woman closed her eyes, took in a deep breath and exhaled slowly before she opened her eyes again. "I see what you mean about worrying. I guess I'll have to cross that bridge when we come to it. Let's just hope it doesn't come too soon. I'd kinda like to get my fill of you before they ship you off to Timbuktu."

"Mmmm," came the soft reply as Dean reached up with her free hand and caressed Katie's cheek. "What say we head up to the house and start working on that 'getting-your-fill' thing now?" Dean finished the statement with a radiant smile and a raised right eyebrow.

"Mmm, sounds good to me," Katie answered as she turned her head and kissed the palm of Dean's hand. Then the two women rose and walked back up to the house—Dean with her arm around Katie's shoulder, and Katie with her arm around Dean's waist. As they approached the house, Dean's thoughts turned to the bedroom filled with white roses and she smiled, no longer nervous about her partner's reaction to her surprise.

Sunday morning was spent exploring every detail of the new house. Dean was thrilled to see Katie's reaction to her dream home as she watched her lover bounce from one room to the next. The young woman was totally in awe of the way the house and its surroundings seemed to meld together. The combinations of rough and soft, dark and light, wood and rock, blended together in the three levels of the house to make a spectacular statement of form and function.

"This is truly magnificent." Katie said as they returned to the kitchen. She couldn't help touching the walls and counters as she danced around the room. "You must be really proud of it."

"I am," Dean replied simply as she began scrambling eggs for their breakfast.

"Thank you, Dean, for making me a part of all this. And thank you again for the roses. That was the sweetest thing I've ever experienced in my life." Katie slid up behind the tall woman and put her arms around her in a gentle hug, resting her head against the strong back. They stood that way for a long moment, enjoying each other's closeness until the sound of the door chime broke the spell.

"Now, who could that be?" Dean wiped her hands on the kitchen towel before she walked to the front door.

Katie, having released her hold on her beautiful lover, joined Dean at the front entrance. Looking out the window, they noticed a flower delivery truck in the driveway. Opening the door, Dean gave the young deliveryman a quizzical look.

"Deanna Peterson?" he inquired.

"Yes."

"These are for you." He handed her the heavy basket and was amazed at the ease with which she took it from his hands. "Umm, I have another basket in the truck for a Katherine O'Malley, but the address is incorrect. They said you might know where she lives."

"I'm Katie O'Malley." Katie stepped out of the entrance and smiled at him, then looked at the huge basket of flowers Dean was holding.

"Great." he responded with a big smile. "Saves me a trip trying to find you. Be right back." He dashed to the truck and returned with another basket of flowers. "Have a nice day, ladies." He tipped his baseball cap and walked briskly back to the van.

The two women took their flowers into the house, closing the door behind them. Looking at each other in surprise, they each set their gift down on the bench by the door and withdrew the gift card. Both cards had the same handwritten note:

Thank you for being good Samaritans and coming to our aid Friday night. Without your quick response, a night of joy would have become a night of tragedy. Sincerely, Arthur and Gwenevier Lyons

"Wow! That was really nice. Wonder how they found your address?" Katie looked up at Dean with a big grin. "Hey...Arthur and Gwenevier...like in King Arthur and Queen Guenevere?"

"Nah." Dean laughed as she picked up the baskets and returned to the kitchen, "They were much too young to be that Arthur and Guenevere." Which provoked more laughter before she got serious enough to answer Katie's question. "They probably got our names from the police, then traced me here through the Pentagon. They couldn't find you because I didn't leave a forwarding address at your apartment when I moved your personal stuff here."

"Well, that sure was nice of them. I wonder how Arthur is doing," Katie said thoughtfully.

"He must be doing fine or we would have gotten a different message on the cards." Dean replaced her card in the envelope

and put it on the table next to the basket.   "C'mon, breakfast is
ready."

Chapter
3

0600 Hours, 23 October

Monday morning found the women sharing a commute to Arlington, Virginia. Dean was dropping Katie off at the Washington headquarters for the DEA on Army Navy Drive. The DEA building happened to be located just a stone's throw from the Pentagon. Katie was pulling duty working in the Intelligence Division until her new assignment started in December. She knew she'd be stuck doing paperwork for the next two months, but she resigned herself to the fact, knowing that it wouldn't be forever. And, she had the extra bonus of commuting with Dean every day.

After dropping Katie off, Dean quickly proceeded to the Pentagon, anxious to get to her office to do a little investigating on her own regarding the limo incident Friday night. She was almost positive that the passenger in the limo was Scott Gentry, a really nasty mercenary, and the hairs on the nape of her neck had been twitching all weekend; this was not a good sign.

Logging on to her computer, she ran a quick check on Gentry's whereabouts. The records showed that he was last seen in Nassau, in June of this year. *Hmm, no luck there. He must be lying low for some reason. Well, let's take a look at his file, and see what Mr. Gentry has been up to lately.* She hit a few more keystrokes to pull up his file. *Oh yeah, he's a foul one all right. Yep, he was linked to Saddam during Desert Storm, Qadhafi on several occasions, all sorts of nasty things in Mozambique, Colombia, Mexico, Iran, and Algeria...hmmm, Mr. Diversity eh?*

Let's see, his strong points seem to be no scruples, a willingness to get his hands bloody, a mastery of armaments, and an engineering background with a good dose of computer programming. Oh, great. He was trained by good old Uncle Sam until he earned a dishonorable discharge. Dean went on reviewing his military record, which detailed several Uniform Code of Military Justice charges—ranging from theft, disobeying an order, unauthorized absence, and so forth—finally leading to time at Leavenworth. Next, she went on to review his civilian records. *Well,* Dean concluded, *compared to his civilian record, he was a good boy in the Army. Wonder what he's up to now?* She closed his file, but not before hot flagging it first as a potential threat, listing herself as the point of contact if he should be seen. *That'll alert the boys on the streets to keep an eye out for him.* Dean swiveled her chair around to look out the window and did what she did best when thinking—she rocked. She realized that doing just that little bit of investigating got her adrenaline flowing, and it made her even more aware of how much she did not like what she was currently doing as aide to General Carlton. Only now, there was Katie to consider. She sat there rocking and twirling a pencil in her fingers until her intercom brought her back to the present.

"Colonel?" came the voice of Sergeant Major Tibbits.

"Yes?"

"The general would like to see you at 1030 hours."

"Fine, I'll be there," she said as she tapped her pencil on her desk pad. "Anything in particular?"

"I think it's something about a car accident on Friday night," he responded in a hushed tone. Sergeant Major Tibbits had been General James' office aide, and he had always liked Colonel Peterson, so he felt very protective of her since the general's passing. "Is there anything I can do?"

"No, Sergeant Major, this shouldn't be a problem. Thanks for the offer though," Dean said with a smile, fully aware of his protective inclinations. *Now how would the general know about that? Guess I'll find out soon enough.* Dean looked at her watch and noted that it was only 0930 and decided to get a cup of tea in the cafeteria—and maybe a honey bun, too.

Katie barely settled into her cubicle on the second floor,

Intelligence Section, then sighed when the section secretary came in with a pile of old case folders for her to review. Y2K didn't have the dreaded effect that was publicized for years prior to January 1, 2000, but there were a few minor glitches that the agency was still straightening out. Her job, for now, was to make sure the files on the computer matched the hard copy files before they were sealed and sent to storage. The Intelligence Section, being what it was, had to triple insure that all the little snatches of information didn't get lost in the black hole of cyber-space. After all, a minor glitch in the intelligence field could result in huge errors on the playing field.

Oh boy, she sighed heavily, *am I going to be able to handle this until December? What was that line in one of those "Rocky" movies...keep your eye on the prize?* The prize to her was Dean. *Oh yeah, that helps.* She smiled to herself and cheerfully tackled the stack, one file at a time.

About halfway through the second stack, she came upon a file jacket that made her scalp itch. *Okay,* she thought as she flipped open the file to his vitals, *so this is the guy Dean saw in the limo on Friday. Not a bad looking guy. Tall...6'2", 210 lbs., dark brown hair, brown eyes, no distinguishing marks except for a very thin scar extending from just behind his left ear, under his jaw to his chin. Wonder how he got that one. Let's see why the DEA is interested in him.*

Then she flipped past his statistics and started to read his rap sheets. Reviewing his folder, she found pretty much the same information that Dean had located on her computer that same morning. *Not a nice boy, are you, Scott? Too bad the locals couldn't pin that drug charge on you in Nassau, but I'll just bet you were dirty.* She turned back to his picture and studied it a bit longer, committing his face to her memory. *Well, if you are working for Algeria now, I wonder which of your skills they're interested in?* Checking the jacket against the computer, she found that all of his information was up to date, so she set his file on the finished stack and went on to the next jacket.

Dean entered Brigadier General Carlton's office at 1025, still curious as to how the general had found out about the limo incident. "Morning, Sergeant Major," she called to the general's aide as she closed the door behind her.

Looking around from the file cabinet, Sergeant Major Tibbits turned and came to attention.

"As you were," came the command as she smiled at him, and he relaxed a bit.

"How do you do that?" Tibbits asked as he resumed filing the folders.

"Do what?" came the innocent rejoinder.

"Come into an office without anyone noticing," he said, shaking his head. "I didn't even catch the change in noise level when you opened the door."

"Oh, that's 'cause there wasn't anyone near the office when I entered," she said, smiling at him. Dean loved playing this little game with the sergeant major. Whenever she had the chance, she'd go into her stealth mode and try to catch him off guard. Most of the time she succeeded.

The sergeant major filed the last folder then returned to his desk, tabbing the intercom button. "Lieutenant Colonel Peterson is here, ma'am."

"Send her in."

"She's all yours," he said as he opened the door to the general's office. Dean walked past him giving him a warm smile, then changed to a more formal expression before she entered. She liked General Carlton and respected her, but her working relationship was not as comfortable as it had been with General James. Upon entering, she came to attention in front of the general's desk.

"Lieutenant Colonel Peterson reporting as ordered." She stood at attention until the general finished her task, raised her head, and commanded her to be "at ease."

Brigadier General Mary Carlton was in her early fifties, about 5' 9" tall, slim, dark hair, coal black eyes that sparkled with intelligence, and a medium complexion for a woman of African American heritage. "Have a seat, Colonel," General Carlton began, and indicated a chair next to her desk. "I understand you came to the aid of two elderly motorists on Interstate 95 late Friday night."

"Yes, ma'am. That's correct."

"You were with a young woman, a DEA agent, I'm told," the general continued. "Is this the same agent you worked with on the UN case?"

"Yes, ma'am," Dean replied, tensing a bit, unsure of where this conversation was heading. She knew the general couldn't ask any personal questions with the "don't ask, don't tell" directive, but was wondering what was coming next.

"Relax, Colonel," the general smiled. "I'm not going where you think I am. In fact, I couldn't care less, as long as it doesn't interfere with your work here." She got up from her chair behind the desk and joined Dean in the other visitor's chair. "Care to tell me what happened?"

Dean visibly relaxed, before going into a concise recounting of the event, including the information she withheld from the State Police officer, and concluded at the point where the elderly couple was taken away in the ambulance. "I believe Mr. and Mrs. Lyons are recovering from the incident. I received a 'thank you' from them yesterday," the colonel concluded.

"Yes, they are," General Carlton agreed. "You see, they were on their way to visit me when the incident occurred. I've been friends with Art and Gwen for a long time. In fact, I was the one that gave them your address, after we found out from the police report who the good Samaritans were."

"Well, I'm just glad we were able to help, ma'am," Dean offered.

"Colonel, can we drop the formality a little? I think two months of walking on eggshells has been enough for the both of us. Mind if I call you Deanna when we're in private conversation?" The general's expression softened considerably, erasing at least ten years of age from her face.

"No, ma'am, I don't mind a bit, but I'd prefer Dean."

"Well then, I'd prefer Mary to ma'am," the general said, smiling. "Now tell me why you didn't tell the police about identifying the flags as Algerian and recognizing the passenger as a mercenary."

"Actually, I didn't think they would be able to do anything about it even if they knew. You know how the first words out of the mouth of an embassy official caught in a situation like this are 'diplomatic immunity.' So I just kept it to myself, but I have to admit, it has piqued my interest." Debating whether or not she should inform General Carlton that she had done a mini-search of her own, she decided that the general would not likely be opposed to her unsolicited inquiries. "I ran Gentry through our computers this morning, and I'm positive that was him in the car. I'm also very curious as to why he is with the Algerians. Unfortunately, this is his first sighting in three months, but I did hot flag his file."

"Any reason in particular?" Mary asked, now also very interested.

"Sorry, I can't put my finger on it. It just raised the hairs on my neck, if you know what I mean." The general nodded in comprehension: intelligence gathering was often a "gut feeling" with seasoned veterans, and Dean was well seasoned. "It all happened so quickly, but I could almost swear the driver was intentionally trying to run your friends' car off the road."

"That's a very real possibility. You see Art is retired from the British MI 6 Section. He and Gwen have been enjoying a majority of their retirement traveling, mostly in the Caribbean. You said this Gentry fellow was in Nassau three months ago? Well, my gut tells me that's too much of a coincidence."

"If I may...Mary," Dean said, obviously still uncomfortable with the relaxed mode, "has your friend indicated noticing any-thing amiss in his travels?"

"Oh no. He hasn't. Gwen knows he's bothered about some-thing, but he hasn't said what yet. Just said that he needed to make some contacts here in the States, hence their visit with me."

"Does he know what your current assignment is?" Dean asked, surprised that the former agent hadn't confided in the Intelligence chief officer.

"Yes, he does, but he's still in his formulating stage. He'll come out with it when he's ready. Always been like that. Has to have all his ducks in a row before he pitches his theory," she said shaking her head. "I'm just afraid that after that near heart attack you and your friend saved him from, he's going to try to do something stupid to prove he's still fit enough to do his old job."

The general stood and walked over to the window, seeming to decide something in her head before she spoke again. "I would like you to do me a favor," she began. "I know you've been assigned as my aide, but I've seen your file and I know you're one hell of an intelligence operative." She hesitated. "I'd like you to investigate this situation further—in addition to your regular duties as my aide. I'll try to lighten the burden so you'll have more time to work on this." She turned and walked back over to Dean, tense lines showing in her face once more. "This is personal, Dean. I can't order you to investigate. There are no grounds—as yet. Think about it and let me know."

Dean read the plea in the tense face staring at her and immediately made up her mind. "I'd be happy to follow up on this, Mary. In fact, I was pretty interested in the case already."

The general smiled, relieved that she had read Dean correctly. "Good. Then the first order of business is for you to meet Art and Gwen again. I don't want him to know that you're on the case, but I thought that perhaps if you were able to sit with him in a relaxed atmosphere, he might let something slip." She smiled conspiratorially, then added, "How about dinner tomorrow at my house, 2000 hours? Bring Agent O'Malley with you, too. I understand from her file that she's quite adept at putting people at ease and getting them to relax. Perhaps the two of you can slip past his defenses."

Dean stood and agreed, thinking to herself, *Well Dean, you don't know what you're getting yourself into, but you do love a challenge.* "I'll have to check with Agent O'Malley, but I'm sure she'll be available." General Carlton handed Dean a set of directions to her house, then added that the dinner would be a typical English affair and to dress in something appropriate. *Great.* Dean thought as she left the general's office, *Guess we'll have to go shopping for "something appropriate" tonight. Oh, Katie will love that.*

By 1745, Dean was pulling into a parking space at the Fashion Centre at Pentagon City. She had called Katie earlier in the afternoon to see if she would be able to go to dinner at the general's house, and to let her know that they'd have to stop on the way home and do some shopping for something appropriate to wear. Katie, of course, was overjoyed at the prospect of spending some time shopping, though it wasn't one of Dean's favorite things to do.

"C'mon, Dean, lighten up. I'm sure we'll find something here that you'll like," Katie said as she bounced out of the car, ready to do some serious damage to her credit card.

"Yeah, yeah. I'm just not the fashion type. That's why I like the military so much. Not much of a decision to make getting dressed in the morning," the tall, dark woman responded.

"Well, it's about time we get you something sexy to wear." Katie said winking. "Too much green in that closet of yours. What's your favorite color anyway?"

"Black," came the unembellished reply.

"Black, huh? That figures." The young woman smiled as they entered the shopping center. "Well, let's see what we can find in black that will knock their socks off."

An hour before the shopping center closed, they finally had the outfit completed. Katie had spied a small boutique called "Silks by Sylvia" that had a dress that Dean actually approved of. It was form fitting, cut in a low, but not too low, "V" in the front and back, with a healthy slit up the right side. It even came with a short silk jacket for cool weather cover. The black silk was very nice to the touch. In fact, when Dean put it on, Katie had a hard time keeping her hands off the smooth fabric. That alone was reason enough for Dean to purchase the dress. She also bought shoes and a bag to match. Although Katie didn't need to purchase anything new, she decided "what the heck" and bought a dark emerald green, silk jumpsuit that had a black silk jacket to go over it. To complete the outfit, she decided on a pair of shoes that would give her an extra inch or two of height.

"See, Dean, that wasn't so bad, now was it?" Katie asked as they headed back out to the parking lot.

"Took way too long for my liking," the dark-haired woman responded.

"Yeah, but we got some really sexy outfits for tomorrow," the blonde countered happily.

"Yeah, tomorrow..." Dean repeated, wondering what the evening would uncover.

Tuesday was pretty much a carbon copy of Monday for Katie, more files to check and enter into the computer. The stack never seemed to diminish. Just about the time she'd get to the last of the files, in would come another batch. Dean, on the other hand, had spent several hours setting up a surveillance of the Algerian Embassy for a lead on Scott Gentry. With that accomplished, and the rest of her paperwork tidied up, she left a bit early so she could stop at a store she'd spotted the previous evening, before picking Katie up at her office. By the time they got home, they had a few minutes to relax before they were to leave for dinner. Dean figured the drive to Falls Church, where General Carlton lived, would take her about thirty minutes if she took I 95, then I 495. That gave them thirty minutes of free time that she already had plans for.

Dean was out of the shower first and was standing in her robe drying her hair. She had to wear it up every day to meet military standards, but tonight she had decided to wear it down. She really liked her hair long, so as soon as she was out of uniform, down it came. She had just set the hair dryer down when Katie came charging out of the bathroom, hurriedly scurrying around to get dressed.

"I can't believe we lost track of time like that." the blonde said as she began drying her hair.

"I didn't lose track of time, love, I just wasn't finished with you yet," Dean said with a twinkle and a half grin. "And I don't think you would have wanted me to stop in the middle, now would you?"

"Ahhh, no." Katie's reply included a rosy coloration to her cheeks. "That would not have been a good idea," she agreed as she softly placed a kiss on the lips closing in on hers. "But we'd better get a move on if we're going to get there on time."

"No problem, love." Dean slipped into the dress and put on the matching jacket. She added a single strand of pearls and diamond teardrop earrings to complete her outfit. Then she went over to her briefcase, pulled out the box she'd bought at the jewelry store, and handed it to Katie. "How about you wearing this tonight?"

The look of surprise on Katie's face as she took the box and opened it made Dean smile.

The heart shaped diamond pendant was simple and elegant at the same time. "I think it will look okay, don't you?" Dean asked quietly.

Katie was stunned, and her eyes sparkled with her tears of joy when she finally found her voice to answer. "Dean...it's beautiful! But when did you get this?" Katie turned and handed the necklace to Dean to place around her neck.

"This afternoon, before I picked you up. I saw it last night and thought it would look great on you." As she finished clasping the necklace on Katie, she looked into the mirror at their reflections and smiled. "Not a bad looking pair of women."

Katie looked into the mirror and smiled back. "Not bad, love. Not bad at all."

The ride to Falls Church actually took a few minutes less than Dean expected, so they managed to arrive right on time.

She parked the SUV in the driveway of the two-story English Tudor styled home. It sat on a lot that had to be at least five acres, and was recessed from the road to mask the traffic as well as to lend an air of country. The house itself was very large and well kept. The two women exited the SUV and walked up the path to the front door. Just as Dean reached to push the doorbell, the door opened and the general greeted them with a sincere smile. Mary was dressed in an elegant maroon pantsuit that contrasted completely with her military persona.

"Good evening, Dean, I saw the lights of your vehicle as you pulled in." She looked over at Katie and smiled warmly. "This must be Agent Katherine O'Malley. It's good to meet you." The general extended her hand to Katie in a welcoming gesture.

Katie smiled, taking the general's proffered hand saying, "Please call me Katie, and thank you for inviting me tonight, General Carlton."

"You're welcome, Katie, but you'll have to call me Mary tonight. My uniform is off for this evening."

Katie nodded her acceptance with a smile and Mary stepped back, gesturing them into her home. As they entered the foyer, Dean and Katie took in the simple grace of the furnishings and layout of the house. To the right was a formal living room done in soft earth tones, with large comfortable looking furniture placed on each side of a beautiful fieldstone fireplace where the other guests were already ensconced. To the left was the formal dining room, all set for the evening's dinner guests with the finest china and crystal Katie had ever set eyes on. Straight ahead, were the stairway to the second floor, and a hallway that led towards the back of the house. Behind them, Mary closed the front door, before leading them into the living room to be formally introduced to Arthur and Gwenevier Lyons.

Arthur and Gwen were occupying two of the chairs next to the fireplace when the three women entered the room. As the general led the way, Arthur stood to meet the two women who had come to his aid four nights before.

"Arthur, Gwen, I'd like to introduce you to the two women who assisted you last Friday." She introduced Dean, who smiled a bit self-consciously, then Katie, who gave them both a dazzling smile.

Arthur became a bit tongue tied—certainly owing much of that to the beauty of the two women—but soon recovered.

"Ahh...yes, yes. I must say...umm...quite good of you to come by." Then, turning to his wife said, "I say, Gwen, they really quite look like guardian angels, don't they?"

Gwen just tittered at her husband's obvious discomfort. "Oh, Art, you always did have a time trying to talk in the presence of beauty." This comment caused Dean and Katie to blush, and Mary, Art and Gwen to laugh quietly.

"Ah, yes. I dare say, I always have," Art said apologetically as he and Gwen shook hands with the two beautiful women.

Mary came to Art's rescue, asking if anyone would care for a cocktail. Dean and Art requested scotch, neat, while Katie and Gwen asked for white wine. Once the drinks were served, the fivesome sat down for some friendly conversation before dinner.

"So, Colonel..." Art began, "whom should I thank for putting you in the right place at the right time?"

"Please call me Dean, and you would have this young lady to thank," Dean said gesturing towards Katie. "I had just picked her up from the airport, when the incident occurred. I'm just glad that we were able to help, and that the both of you are okay."

"Oh, yes, quite all right, thanks to the two of you," Gwen interjected. "Art's just retired, and we've been doing a good deal of traveling. The doctors suggested that it would be a way for him to unwind after all his stressful years with MI 6."

"MI 6? Really?" Katie chimed in, looking for an opportunity to get Art talking. "What did you do, sir?"

"Oh, I say, please don't call me sir...makes me feel much older than I am," Art said with a wink and a self-conscious chuckle. "I work, or should say, worked, in the cipher section. You know—code work and all. Not quite what it was years ago...before computers and all...but still very challenging work and quite stressful."

"Have you ever been a field agent?" Dean posed the question nonchalantly as she sipped her scotch.

"Arthur? In the field? I should think not. I didn't want to see him out in the field," Gwen offered whimsically. "Not my Arthur. He's never been into action that I know of. Oh, except for that one time at the Embassy party. But he is the absolute best at cracking codes. Aren't you dear?"

"Now, now, Gwennie, I could have gone to field agent training," Arthur protested, "but we'd just had the twins and all..." His sentence was cut off by Gwen's next comment.

"Yes, dear, and I thank you every day for making that decision." Gwen patted Arthur's arm affectionately in an attempt to
smooth his ruffled feathers some.

Katie picked up on the slight tension and cut in smoothly,
asking the obvious, "What happened at the Embassy party?"
Which led into a lengthy description of an encounter with a double agent who was passing secret information during the party.
Gwen had uncovered the exchange through her ability to read
lips. Arthur saved the day by managing to capture the spy by
shooting him in the eye with a well-aimed champagne cork.
They all had a good laugh at the ending, where the blinded agent
stumbled into the arms of the security police. About the time
that the story was finished, Mary's cook entered the living room
to announce that dinner was ready.

The main meal passed without the two women obtaining
much more information from Arthur. He, on the other hand, had
learned about the events of the previous winter that had tran-
spired in the Catskills of New York, then played out its dramatic
conclusion at the UN in New York City.

"My, my. That would have been quite the disaster if old
Kasimov had pulled it off," Art offered at the conclusion of the
story. "Imagine the chaos that would have occurred across the
globe if all those heads of state had been murdered." They all
were nodding in agreement when the cook brought out the des-
sert—plum pudding.

"Now, Art, I know you love this, so I had Tessie here make
it special for you," Mary said, as the cook put the bowl in front
of Arthur.

"Isn't that nice, dear? I'll bet it's better than Ned's," Gwen
offered.

"Well, Ned's not the best cook, but we always manage to
talk about something interesting over his plum pudding. Why,
just the other day he was telling me that he's noticed an awful lot
of mercenary soldiers going in and out of Freeport Airport
lately." As soon as he said it, he realized that he had said too
much, and quickly changed the subject. "Well, what say we see
if Tessie receives the Arthur Lyons award for plum pudding,
shall we?"

Dean and Katie subtly raised an eyebrow at each other and
caught the eye of Mary who was smiling at them. *Yep, Mary, I
think he just slipped.* Dean's thoughts seemed to penetrate the
general's mind as she nodded back at the colonel.

After dinner, the conversation was mostly about Gwen and her job as a speech and hearing specialist. She had explained how that was where her ability to read lips originated. Art had become more cautious in his conversation and directed most of it in Gwen's direction. By 2300, Dean and Katie were back on the road for home after expressing their thanks for the wonderful dinner. In the car, the two agents began to plan their course of action.

"I'll get together a list of all known mercenaries we have on file," Dean began, "and start a check on who has been in or out of Freeport in the last six months."

"I think that is the most logical place to start," Katie agreed. "Then, I'll take the list and check it against any records the Freeport DEA division has, too."

By the time they arrived home, they had their campaign mapped out and had made plans to meet for lunch the next day at the Pentagon to update General Carlton on their findings.

Chapter
4

Both women spent Wednesday morning compiling their lists of known mercenaries from their respective data banks. They targeted the entire Caribbean during the previous eight months, and checked all of the customs offices. The next step was to cross-reference them with each other to see if there were any common denominators. Then they each checked to see if any of these persons were seen in any of the countries that were known enemies of the U.S. They also included enemies of Britain, since Arthur was a British citizen and his friend Ned was the chief of the MI 6 section located at the Nassau Embassy. By the time they were each finished with their lists, it was nearly 1100.

"Hey," Dean said without preamble as she heard Katie pick up her line at her temporary office, "are you interested in lunch?"

"Just about. I'm printing the last list now. Meet me in your lobby in fifteen minutes." Katie replaced the receiver with one hand while the other hand removed the last sheet from the printer.

At 1200, Dean was waiting outside the main entrance to the Pentagon when she spotted Katie coming up the walk. "Did you walk over or catch a cab?" Dean asked as Katie drew near.

"Walked of course. You try catching a cab at lunchtime. Besides, I need the exercise. I really hate sitting at a desk all day."

"Yeah, I think we should set up the exercise equipment tonight when we get home. I could certainly use a good workout myself." Dean held the door open for Katie to enter the main lobby. "Here, put on this Visitor ID, or you won't get past the MP's up ahead." Dressed in her uniform, Dean led the way past the security post, returning a salute as she passed. "Let's grab a sandwich and then go over our notes in my office before we meet with General Carlton." Looking at her watch, Dean informed the young agent that they had a 1430 appointment.

"Sounds good to me." Katie eagerly followed Dean through the wide corridors as they headed down to the cafeteria.

By 1215, they were in Dean's office comparing lists. Dean had a total of thirty-two mercenaries, while Katie had seventeen prospects. When they compared their two lists, they found fifteen names that appeared on both.

"Okay," Dean began, "let's take a look at the ones that weren't duplicated." Of those seventeen names, they deleted six when further investigation revealed their current whereabouts as various federal prisons. Another five were eliminated for one reason or another. The last six were added to the overlapping names—for a final count of twenty-one names to be considered potential threats. Dean added these to her "hot flag" notices on the computer system. With this done, the various intelligence communities would contact her with any sightings of these individuals. When they were finished, they had a few minutes to spare before their meeting with General Carlton.

Katie looked over at Dean who was rocking in her leather chair. "Any theories at this point?"

"Mmm. I'm not sure I want to venture any guesses. We have only three facts at this point in the game." She began ticking them off on her fingers. "One, Scott Gentry was in that limo, and he is on both of our lists. Two, in my opinion, the limo was definitely trying to run the Lyons' car off the road. And three, Art's friend Ned has noticed more mercenaries than usual, coming and going." She sighed before she continued. "Now, one reason people of all kinds go to the Bahamas, besides the weather and beaches, is for the gambling. Mercenaries are risk takers and, more likely than not, gamblers. It could be just as simple as that. Or, it could be that there's a lot more to it. It's much too early to tell."

"Maybe General Carlton picked up more information after we left," Katie offered.

"Maybe. But I wouldn't count on it. You saw how Arthur clammed up after his little slip." Dean checked her watch and stood. "Well, we'd better get going."

The two women walked the short distance to the general's office, entered, and were greeted by a waiting Sergeant Major Tibbits. "Afternoon, Colonel," he said as he smiled at Dean.

"Afternoon. Sergeant Major, this is Special Agent Katherine O'Malley," the colonel offered as the sergeant major rose to shake the hand that a smiling Katie extended.

"Glad to meet you, ma'am. The general is waiting for you." Tibbits opened the door to the general's office. "You can go right in."

Dean entered with strict military form, standing at attention until the general gave her the "at ease" command. General Carlton relaxed, smiling at the two women. "Have a seat, ladies." She motioned to the small meeting area to the right of her desk. Dean and Katie selected the leather couch, and the general sat in a chair opposite them. "What have you found out so far?" she inquired, getting straight to the point.

Dean took the lists they had worked on all morning and went through the process they used to gather the data, and their reasons for eliminating some of the mercenaries.

After Dean itemized the facts once more for the general, she concluded her comments with a statement that this was all the information they had at the moment. "Until we hear from our folks in the field, we won't know much more."

Katie's input included inconclusive information on where many of these individuals were located at present. "It appears that most of them are somewhere here in the U.S. They could also be in a country that doesn't require a passport, at least as far as our customs records show. A few are out of the country, mostly in various parts of Africa. I'm sure with all of the unrest on that continent, there are plenty of employers."

"You are undoubtedly right on that one," Mary agreed. "What's your plan from here?"

Dean addressed this portion of the meeting, indicating that she had "hot flagged" the persons on the list. "If you look at the backgrounds of these individuals, you'll see that most of them have had dealings with various terrorist groups in the world. At least, alleged dealings. None have been brought up on charges, because no one has had enough proof."

"Yes," Katie interjected, "and their backgrounds are varied.

However, we've noticed they're a bit heavy on the technology side, not that they can't handle themselves in other areas, too; but then, this is the age of computerized conflicts, as the Gulf War has shown us."

"What can I do to help out?" Mary asked the duo.

"Well, if you could have Katie loaned to us from the DEA, that would be a start. They have her just sorting files right now, and I could certainly use her expertise more than they currently are," Dean suggested hopefully. The tall woman noted the mild look of surprise on her partner's face, since they had not talked about this possibility prior to the meeting.

The general smiled at the request and thought a bit before she replied. "Katie, your director is Keith Evans?" Katie nodded in the affirmative. "Well, let me see what I can do. He owes me a favor or two. I'll let you know as soon as possible. Is there anything else?"

"Not at this time, unless of course you were able to get anything else from Mr. Lyons last night," Dean inquired.

"Not yet, but I have Gwen subtly working on it. She's going to use her lip reading skills the next time they go to the British Embassy." Mary stood, an indication that the meeting was over. "Well, if there's nothing else..."

"Only, I'd like to thank you for inviting me to dinner last night. Everything was exquisite," Katie said as she stood to leave.

"You're welcome, Katie," the general replied. "And I'm glad I had the opportunity to finally meet you. You and the colonel here made quite a team on that Kasimov assignment. I'll do my best to get you assigned to us, temporarily at least." The general walked to the door with Katie and Dean.

"Thank you, General Carlton. It would certainly make things easier," Katie replied as she exited the office.

"Colonel," the general called to Dean, "step back into my office for a minute."

"Yes, ma'am." Dean stepped back into the office, closing the door behind her.

"Did you ask Katie about coming to work on this over here before you asked me?" Mary queried. .

"No, ma'am. I just thought of it at that moment. I apologize if I put you on the spot," she hurriedly offered.

"Yes, you did. In the future I would like to be apprised of things in advance, but this shouldn't be a problem as long as you believe that Agent O'Malley will be comfortable in our atmosphere. We're not as relaxed as some of the civilian agencies."

"Yes, ma'am. I'll make sure she's fully aware of military protocols."

"Good. That's all then. I'll call you after I talk to Evans. And Dean," the general said with a smile, "she's a keeper."

Dean flashed a brilliant smile and said, "Yes, ma'am." before executing a military turn, leaving the office beaming.

The meeting with General Carlton only lasted a short fifteen minutes. Katie could hardly wait to get back to Dean's office so she could find out just what was so amusing to cause Dean to be smiling. As soon as the door closed behind her and they were in the privacy of Dean's office, Katie asked, "And what canary did you eat?" To which Dean just smiled even more broadly.

"Ah...well...the general thinks you're a 'keeper,' and I have to agree with her," Dean said proudly.

"A 'keeper', eh?" Katie smiled back at her lover, slowly walking to within a half inch of Dean, then in a very silky, seductive voice, said, "and what am I being 'kept' for?"

"Oh..." Dean replied in her lowest sultry voice, "as an agent, of course." Then she bent her head and quickly stole a kiss from the temporarily flustered young DEA agent. "And that reminds me, we'll need to go over military protocol if you're going to be working here. By the way, what I just did is definitely not military protocol and will be the last one you'll ever get in this building, or, while working anywhere around here on this case, or, when I'm in uniform." She looked into Katie's emerald eyes and sighed. "Will you be comfortable with that?" Katie nodded her agreement. "Good. I won't be, but that's the way it has to be."

"Dean, I promise I won't ever jeopardize your career..." Katie started.

"I know, love, but there's a lot of people around here who would love to see me get kicked out of the military, for any reason. Some of the 'good old boys' are still ticked off about my promotion to Lieutenant Colonel, and they wouldn't mind dragging Mary down with me, either. So we have to be really careful, especially here." Dean walked over to her leather chair and sat down, indicating that Katie should take the visitor's seat.

The next thirty minutes or so were spent on a discussion of military do's and don'ts, so Katie wouldn't get into any difficulties on the job.

"So, I don't have to salute anyone..."

"No, just make sure you show due respect. Imagine yourself as, let's see—you'd be a first lieutenant now if you were in the Army, so just about anyone you see, except for the enlisted soldiers, would be your superior officer, so treat them accordingly." Dean stopped then winked at her lover. "I'm sure you'll fit in very well. You just have a way about you that makes people fall all over themselves trying to help you."

"Yeah, right." The blonde laughed out loud, but was cut off from further comment by the ringing of the phone.

"Colonel Peterson," Dean said answering the phone. "Yes, ma'am. Yes. Fine, I'll take care if it right now." Replacing the phone she said, "General Carlton just got off the phone with your director. You've been temporarily assigned to the Pentagon, effective immediately. I will be your immediate supervisor, but you ultimately answer to General Carlton. I need to take you to the processing section to have your photo ID made now, but we need to stop by the general's office to pick up the paperwork." Dean hesitated before adding, "I know I didn't ask you if you wanted to be on loan here. You still have time to back out."

"Not on your life, Colonel," came the unwavering response.

The rest of the day was spent processing Katie as a civilian attached to the Pentagon. Katie never saw so many papers that had to be signed, and so many regulations that had to be covered. By the time they were finished, it was time for them to go home. On their way home, Katie just sighed and ruminated over all the paperwork that had to be done for a simple temporary transfer and photo ID. "Wow," Katie said jokingly, "I'd hate to see what I'd have to do if I wanted to come over permanently."

"Well, love," Dean shrugged, "it's like I said, the military way is much different than the civilian way."

Katie turned towards Dean and in a deep, husky voice said, "There's the right way, the wrong way, and the Army way." Then in her normal voice, she amended, "At least that's what my Uncle Sean used to say whenever I'd ask him why he did something a certain way."

"Your Uncle Sean wasn't far from the truth." Dean said laughing. "How about we get some Chinese take-out for dinner, then we can spend the evening putting the exercise room together?"

"Sounds like a good plan, ma'am, but is it a civilian plan or an Army plan?" Katie asked, laughing.

"It's MY plan," Dean answered with a growl and her best feral grin.

"Oooo, then it's got to be the only plan," Katie answered seriously, then leaned over to give her lover a quick kiss, but stopped short remembering her promise to Dean. "Umm, do I have to wait until we get home before I can kiss you?

"Yeah, we better wait." Dean smiled at her lover. "Never know who might be in the next vehicle, and I am still in uniform."

"Oh, I can already see this is going to be difficult." Katie grudgingly moved back over to her side of the SUV and crossed her arms in front of her chest.

The next morning the two women had just pulled out of their driveway when Dean's cell phone chirped. "Colonel Peterson," Dean said as she picked up the phone and listened. "Are you sure about that? Okay, give me the address. Get big blue out for us, okay? Then give us ten to change, and we'll be on our way." Dean checked her watch and added, "Our ETA will be 0730." Then she replaced her phone. "That was Sergeant Major Tibbits. Seems we have a hit on one of our mercenaries," Dean explained as she turned the SUV around and headed back to the house. "We'll need to change, then set up surveillance at a warehouse. Are you ready for some undercover work again?" Dean asked with a big grin.

"Aye, aye, Colonel." Katie replied with a small salute.

"Katie, it's 'Yes, ma'am' or 'Sir' in the Army. 'Aye, aye' is for the Navy," Dean corrected her while shaking her head.

"Oops. Guess I watched too many episodes of *JAG* while in El Paso," Katie said blushing.

"Well, don't try that around our folks, they'll tease the hell out of you."

"Got it. Now, what's big blue?"

"Big blue is my favorite surveillance vehicle for city work," Dean said as she pulled the SUV into her driveway. "You'll really like it. All the comforts of home and then some."

They parked the SUV in the drive and hurried into the house

to change. When they came out five minutes later, they were dressed in jeans, polo shirts, athletic shoes, and lightweight jackets. Dean had let her hair down, and Katie had on her favorite baseball cap, sporting the logo of the New York Liberty basketball team. They were back on the road in eight minutes flat from the time Dean hung up the cell phone.

"Phew." the blonde exclaimed as she hooked up her seat belt, "that was quick."

"Yeah, well, you learn to be quick after sixteen years in this business." Dean said as she smoothly entered the flow of vehicles commuting to D.C. on I 95.

During the thirty-minute drive, Dean explained that the mercenary, Jerry Stockton, was seen entering a warehouse in the southeast part of town near the Navy Yard. The informant said he was still in there, so they decided to mount a little surveillance to see what came out. As they slipped into Dean's parking place at the Pentagon, Dean said they would need to take their weapons case from the security locker in the back of the SUV. Sergeant Major Tibbits had arranged for the surveillance vehicle to be parked next to Dean's spot. "We'll be using this van," Dean explained as she opened the door of a rusty blue Chevy van that had the markings from the city water department barely scraped off. "We're going to be in a not too nice area today." Katie nodded as she walked to the back of the SUV, opening the door to retrieve the weapons case from its security locker.

"Looks a little ratty, don't you think?" Katie commented as she walked around the van to the passenger side.

"Yep. Just what we need for where we're going." The tall woman smiled as they got in and strapped on their seat belts. In no time, they were crossing the Rochambeau Bridge towards their target.

The back of the van was windowless. The only windows were in the cab, and the back of the van was obscured from view by sliding doors that would allow them to enter from the cab in the front. These doors locked from both sides to insure security while they were working. On the outside, the van looked like it was on its last legs, but on the inside, it was a surveillance dream. Air-conditioned for warm weather use, heated for cold weather, totally soundproofed against passersby and bullet proof, except for armor piercing shells. It had all the latest equipment including an updated Thermal Dynamic Scanning Converter that was even better than the one they had used in the

Catskills. This one was so small and compact, that the external scanner probe was located in the little yellow flashing caution light that one usually sees on top of most municipal maintenance vehicles. This housing allowed for a three hundred sixty degree rotation that could be adjusted without anyone noticing. The TDSC was mated with a directional sound unit that could pick up voices through the thickest brick buildings around D.C. It even had a small refrigerator stocked with water, soda, and a few snacks for lengthy operations. The only amenity it lacked was a bathroom, and the only real problem with the van was that it was cramped. There were two comfortable captains chairs in the back, but not much room to stretch out; for Dean that was one concession she made to have use of this van. It was even equipped with a special set of shocks, so any movement by the occupants in the van would not cause the van to rock, thereby alerting any onlookers that occupants were inside.

After a quick stop at a local convenience store to use the restroom and pick up a few extra goodies that were Dean's favorites, they pulled into a parking lot opposite the fenced entrance to an old warehouse. The neighborhood had several empty buildings and warehouses, but still had a few stores that seemed to be doing a brisk business, including a sandwich and coffee shop halfway down the street. The lot was next to a building that sold janitorial supplies, so their vehicle wasn't easily noticeable with all of the trucks and vans going in and out.

"Okay, time to get in the back and see what's out there," Dean said as she slid the door to the right and indicated that Katie should go back first. Dean followed, then slid the door shut and locked it.

This was Katie's first glimpse into the back of the van with all its state of the art equipment. Her immediate reaction was one of awe, but she soon got down to business as Dean gave her quick operating instructions for the various pieces of equipment. There were five 9" TV monitors lined up; when Dean turned them on, four of them showed ninety-degree views from each of the corners of the van. The fifth one was for the TDSC. A set of headphones rested on the short bench in front of each chair for the directional sound system. At the back end of the small space, there was a computer system that included a laser printer and a CD tower. Katie looked around and asked where the taping equipment was. Dean pointed to the computer system and told her that they were no longer using tapes, but CD's, and were able to satellite link anywhere in the world.

"Satellite?" she asked curiously. "Where's the dish to up-link?"

Dean unlocked and slid the door back and pointed to an object on the dashboard, then closed and locked the door again.

"You mean to tell me that that piece of souvenir trash is a satellite dish?" Katie asked in amazement.

"Pretty neat, eh? It looks like any of those 'tip 'em upside down to make it snow' pieces of junk that you've gotten from your dear old Auntie Maude, doesn't it." The little snow globe on the dash board was a bit larger than most, but looked just as tacky and had a fountain in it with a gold paper label on the base that said "Good Luck Fountain, Kansas City, Missouri" on it. "The bowl of the fountain actually moves to track the satellites," Dean informed the young agent. "It's the very latest in micro technology and works like a charm." Katie just shook her head in wonder. "Remind me to take you to the research and develop-ment lab for our Intelligence Section. Some of the stuff they're playing with there will really knock your socks off."

Once Katie was comfortable with operating each piece of equipment, they settled down for what was going to be a long, probably uneventful surveillance. The day, evening, and night passed without a sound coming from the warehouse. Not even one vehicle pulled in during the entire time. Finally, at 2300, Dean decided it was time to pack it in for the night. Before they left, they decided to make an up close and personal visit to the warehouse. Changing into night gear, the two women added their shoulder harnesses for their new H & K Mark 23's, checked the ammo clips and returned the weapons to safety. Checking the four monitors, they noted that no one was in sight, so they each grabbed a set of night vision goggles and com units, then left the van.

Once outside the van, they donned their night vision gog-gles. Dean motioned for Katie to circle the building to the right, while she circled to the left, both looking for promising points of entry. In a short span of only three minutes, Dean's earpiece came alive with Katie's voice.

"Got it." Katie whispered into her com unit. "There's a window open in the back, and several 50 gallon drums that we can use for a boost up."

"Be right there, I just want to bypass the alarm system first," Dean answered, before swiftly running to the back to meet up with Katie.

The window was big enough for them to slip through with ease. Dean silently boosted herself up on the drum and peeked through the window, checking the interior for any signs of life.

"Looks good," she whispered to Katie as she reached her right hand down to give Katie a hand up. Dean was the first through the window, silently dropping to the floor with Katie following just as quietly. The warehouse was full of crates and boxes that, according to their labels, contained a variety of food: cereals to rice to canned fruits and vegetables, and then some. As they walked past the stacks waiting for shipping, they noted that they were all headed for the Caribbean port of Freeport, Grand Bahamas, with a final destination of the island's Little Dixie grocery chain.

"That's interesting," Katie whispered as they continued down the aisles.

"Yeah," Dean commented, "I would have thought that the Little Dixie shipping point would be from Miami and not D.C. Seems awfully expensive to be shipping from this far up the coast. Let's see if we can find the office. You take this aisle, I'll head down that one."

Katie nodded as they parted, going down separate aisles and heading towards the front of the warehouse. Dean's choice of aisles led her to the office first, and she whispered into her com unit for Katie to swing her way. While waiting for Katie to catch up, Dean checked the handle on the office door. Finding it locked, she pulled out her set of picks and set to work on the lock. As Katie rounded the corner, Dean was just standing up and opening the door to the office.

"Nice work, Colonel," the blonde remarked as Dean held the door open for her. "Let's see if they lock their file cabinets, too." Katie pulled on the top drawer, and it slid out easily. Running her hands through the files and doing a quick check of the labels, she found nothing unusual in the folders. Shipping orders, customs forms, invoices, etc., everything looked quite normal and respectable as she checked each drawer.

While Katie checked the file cabinets, Dean set to work checking the rest of the office. Desks were neat and orderly. Just a little too neat and too orderly for Dean's suspicious mind. The whole office reminded her of a military materials manage-ment office, rather than a civilian shipping and receiving ware-house. Checking the ashtrays, she noted that even the cigarette butts were "field dressed" in military fashion where the filters were separated from the remaining tobacco. Things just weren't adding up. *Hmm, if this is a legitimate warehouse, why wasn't anyone working today? Granted the crates of food aren't perishable items, but there should have been some activity.* "Things don't add up here," Dean commented as she walked toward the office door. "Check out the computer, I'm going to have a closer look at some of those crates."

Dean exited the small office and started to walk down the aisle toward the back of the building to the last stack of crates. On a tool bench by the loading dock, she found a box knife, pry bar, and clear tape applicator, then began an "eenie, meenie, minee, mo" chant to herself as she selected the first crate. It was labeled powdered milk, and when she carefully opened it, that's exactly what she found. She resealed the crate, and went to her next selection. This one was labeled coffee, and again, she found just that. Resealing that case, Dean decided to advance a few rows and select another crate of cases. This time she settled on ones labeled canned vegetables. *Hmmm, nothing here but mixed vegetables...how about ketchup...*again and again, finding just what the label indicated. Dean continued her careful search and found just about anything you would find in a grocery store, and nothing more. "Everything looks legit, but I've just got this gut feeling," Dean mumbled as she returned to the small office.

"Any luck with the computer?" Dean peered over Katie's shoulder and watched her scroll through the contents.

"Nope. Just lots of order forms for all sorts of grocery items. Also shipping invoices and customs forms to match. The company's name is Island Commodities, Incorporated. I'm downloading their personnel files now. Maybe we can get a clue from their workers," Katie answered as she entered a few more keystrokes. "Now, this could be interesting," she paused as she down paged through several forms. "Seems like every shipment has the same customs officer's signature. A coincidence?"

"Hmmm, a little too coincidental if you ask me," Dean replied.

"Yep. I concur with that," the blonde acknowledged as she looked up into Dean's vivid blue eyes.

"What's the officer's name?"

Looking back down at the monitor screen, Katie responded, "Ernest P. Comstock." Raising her head up once more she asked,

"Did you have any luck with the search?"

"Nah. Everything seems kosher." Dean shook her head in frustration. "All right, let's put things back the way we found them and get back to the office. We can run a check on Mr. Comstock there, and make arrangements to have the warehouse put under long term surveillance."

It took them a few minutes to shut down the computer and check to be sure they left everything the way it was, before leaving the building through the loading dock's side door. Dean rearmed the security system, and they returned to the van, making sure that they weren't seen leaving the warehouse grounds. When they arrived back at the office, it was 0230. They filed the surveillance request, set the wheels in motion to do a full background check on Ernest P. Comstock and Island Commodities, Inc., and e-mailed a report to General Carlton regarding their findings. Dean also left a note for Sergeant Major Tibbits to call them on her cell number if anything came up before 1300. With those items out of the way, they finally left for home.

Chapter
5

Dean woke first, opening her eyes to see her lover's blonde head resting on her chest. Katie was in the exact same position as when she fell asleep, five hours earlier. *Guess we were a bit tired last night, eh, love?* The dark-haired woman began to stroke Katie's short hair with her left hand and tightened her grip around the blonde's waist with her right hand. This action brought a slight moan from the blonde's lips as Katie tightened her grip around her lover's waist. One green eye slowly opened as Katie mumbled, "Tell me it's not time to get up yet, plee-asse?"

"Sorry, love, duty calls. Besides, it's almost 0930, and we need to get in our exercise session that we missed last night." Dean said this with a smile, then placed a soft gentle kiss on Katie's forehead. "Wouldn't do for us to get out of shape, now would it?"

"Mmmppff. I suppose not. But one day couldn't hurt, could it?" Both green eyes now pleaded with the sapphire blues looking softly down at her.

"No, one day wouldn't hurt, but we had that one day yesterday, remember?" One sapphire blue eye winked at the still pleading blonde, then Dean reached down with her left hand and started to tickle the sleepy blonde awake.

"Eeeeaaa! No fair." Katie tried to roll away from the taller woman, but was held in place by the strong arm that was around her waist. "Okay, okay...Uncle." she pleaded with her tormentor. Dean immediately stopped her barrage of tickling, and captured her victim's lips with a slow passionate kiss while her left hand trailed lightly up the taut abdomen and came to rest between her breasts. The kiss and touch evoked a sensual moan from the young woman who immediately responded to them with more kisses, each becoming longer and deeper until Dean realized that the young woman had maneuvered her to the point of no return...the fire was lit.

Dean was blow-drying her long dark hair when Katie came into the master bathroom carrying a steaming cup of mint tea. "Now that's how I like to exercise in the morning," she said, as she placed the tea on the counter and stole a quick kiss from the still flushed woman. "Cold shower didn't help, huh?" Katie winked as she took the dryer from her lover's hands and continued the drying process.

"That," Dean said to Katie's reflection in the mirror, "was a very well planned diversion, my clever young friend. But it still won't get you off the hook from exercising twice as hard tomorrow. Paybacks, as they say, are hell."

"Pish, posh." Katie exclaimed waving back at Dean's reflection. "It was well worth it."

Dean turned on her stool and placed her arms around Katie's waist, looking slightly upward into the smiling eyes. "Yes, love, it was." Then she pulled Katie down into a scorching kiss that nearly seared the young woman's lips on contact, and caused her knees to buckle as she neatly swooned into Dean's lap.

"Umm, Dean, we really shouldn't..." Katie began as she opened her eyes to see Dean's sapphires twinkling back at her and a dazzling smile on her lover's face.

"Nope, we shouldn't." Dean responded and quickly stood up, unceremoniously dumping the young woman on the carpet.

"Wha..." Katie choked out as she looked up at the chuckling woman.

"Didn't your mother ever teach you not to play with fire?" Dean laughed as the blonde lay back on the carpet, enjoying the joke herself. Once they both regained control of their laughter, Dean reached down and helped Katie back up to her feet.

"Are we going to be in or out today?" Katie asked as she reviewed the clothing options in her closet.

"Dress casual today, a slacks outfit is good," Dean responded, as she emerged from the walk-in closet in the slacks version of her officer's uniform. "I'll take a casual change with me, just in case."

Katie opted for her normal DEA field attire, which included cordovan loafers, tan Dockers, a blue button down shirt, and a navy blazer. She decided to wear her shoulder holster with her H & K Mark 23 nestled safely under her left arm. Katie really liked the feel of her new handgun better than the old Glock, but she still felt she needed a bit more time at the range with it before she could feel truly comfortable. Within fifteen minutes, the two women were pulling out of the drive heading north on I 95. They arrived at Dean's office at 1230 and immediately went to work reviewing the information gathered on Island Commodities and Ernest Comstock.

Island Commodities, Inc. was a subsidiary of the Beir and Beir Corporation out of the Cayman Islands. They looked squeaky clean on paper as far as the results of their normal inquiries indicated. However, B & B Corp, was a subsidiary of another holding company, which was part of another, and another, and so on, until they could barely remember how many companies removed Island Commodities was.

"Wow," Katie exclaimed as she shuffled through the print-outs, "there are more layers to this than a dozen flaky croissants stacked on top of each other."

"You got that right." Dean agreed as she leaned back in her leather chair. "Now I definitely know there's more to this than meets the eye. We'll just have to dig deeper to get to the good stuff."

"Hey, how about looking at the personnel files I down-loaded last night?" Katie smiled as she picked up the disc and put it into the computer. A few keystrokes later she let out a throaty "ah ha." and hit the print sequence.

"What's so interesting?" Dean inquired.

"Well, I found a familiar name in the personnel files. Looks like Enrico Gaiyoz is working at the warehouse as a loading dock hand." Katie turned in her seat to face Dean. "Enrico and I had a run-in or two a couple of years back. I didn't realize he was out on probation already," the blonde said thoughtfully. "We should be able to use this to our advantage. He's a real worm, kinda slimy and slick, but he'll give with the slightest pressure. Can't endure pain, real or imagined."

"Well, let's go dig up this lowlife shall we? Where does he live?" Dean asked as she stood and stretched. Katie looked at the address on the personnel form, then up at Dean.

"Over by the train yards near the Washington Navy Yard."

"Okay. I'll just change into something more intimidating, and then we'll go find us some fish bait." Dean grabbed her gym bag and pulled out her black jeans, white T-shirt, and boots. "Back in a flash," she said, grinning at Katie.

When Dean returned, she looked every bit as menacing as she intended. She had let her hair down and pulled it into a ponytail, and put on a black baseball cap. Pulling her clip holstered weapon out of her desk drawer, Dean slipped it into the small of her back. Her final addition was a black leather jacket she removed from the small coat closet in her office. "Okay. I'm ready if you are," she said, smiling at Katie as she hung up her uniform in the closet, "Let's find that worm, shall we?"

Katie looked her over carefully and whistled, "Whoowee! I wouldn't want to run into you in a dark alley, that's no lie. One look at you, and he'll be singing for sure." Then the two women left the office and walked out to the SUV. Katie noticed how several of the officers they passed in the halls, and the MP's at the security station, smiled at Dean as she passed through the halls and out of the building. "Hey Dean, what do you think they're thinking when they see you in a get up like this?"

"Who?" Dean asked in all sincerity.

"All those people in there. They practically broke their necks to watch you walk down the hall, that's who."

"Hell, they're probably just jealous they aren't coming along." Dean answered as they got into the SUV and headed out to find Gaiyoz.

At 1553 they pulled up in front of Enrico's shabby apartment building. "This is the place," Katie said as she put the file back into her briefcase. "Wonder if the worm is home."

"Only one way to find out...knock on his door." Dean scanned the area using her vehicle's mirrors, and then looked out the window at the opposite side of the street.

The narrow street was littered with food wrappers from a variety of fast food specialty restaurants, as well as discarded bottles—glass and plastic. There weren't too many people on the street since the day was windy and overcast, but there were five young toughs sitting on the apartment steps.

"What floor?" Dean glanced over at Katie who was doing her own scan of the neighborhood.

"Third. 3D. How would you like to do this?" The blonde finished her recon of the neighborhood and turned toward Dean.

"Right up the steps, and straight in. Don't want to give those punks a chance to warn him. Ready?" Dean watched Katie nod in agreement, then reached for the door handle. "Let's go."

As the women exited the SUV, Dean hit the door locks before shutting her door. They casually crossed the street, keeping a close eye on the young thugs. As they stepped up on the curb, the tallest in the group stood up and attempted to block the stairway, staring at the women as they approached, while his stepmates started making low whistles and clucking noises.

"Afternoon, boys," Dean said in a low growl. "Mind stepping aside?" She sneered at the punk standing in the stairway. Although he was standing on the first step, they met eye to eye.

"Well, I don' know," he answered in a heavy Hispanic accent. "You gotta pay to get in this place, see?"

"Oh yeah?" Dean snarled. "And why's that?" she added with her feral smile.

"'Cause we just don' let any gringo bitch into our building," he spat out. "Let alone a big bitch like you with a little *puta* like her." His statement led to hoots, whistles, and sexist remarks in Spanish by his friends.

With lightning speed, Dean reached out and grabbed the punk's crotch, squeezing his genitals in her left hand, while whipping out her H & K with her right hand. She placed the muzzle at his temple as he tried to reach down and extricate himself from her grip. Katie reacted in kind, taking her weapon out and warning the rest of the group to stay where they were.

"Oh, Pancho..." Dean said contemptuously, "you should know I speak the language, and your boys shouldn't say such vulgar things. Now, I suggest you apologize for them." Dean continued squeezing even harder, causing sweat to pop out on the punk's forehead as he nodded.

"Hokay. I'm sorry," he squealed, as one of his friends on

Dean's left jumped to make a move on her. Without even blink-
ing, Dean threw the thug she was holding into his friend, causing
the two of them to tumble over the concrete rail and into some
trashcans. As those two fell to the cement, two others that were
sitting on the right of Dean, made a move toward Katie, who
spun efficiently and kicked one of them over the other railing,
and flipped the second one over her head, sending him flying
onto the sidewalk. A fifth young ruffian started to run up the
stairway, but was stopped short, as Dean picked up an empty
Corona bottle, throwing it neatly to peg him on the back of the
head. He fell forward, causing him to smack his forehead on the
doorknob. He then slid limply down the door and came to rest
on the top step. Dean and Katie moved quickly to begin their
run up to the third floor, in search of Enrico's apartment.

"Damn. Too much noise," Dean murmured as she took the
stairs two at a time. As they rounded the final flight of stairs,
she caught sight of a man exiting the fire escape window at the
end of the hall. She turned, shouting over her shoulder to Katie,
"He's going out the window at the back, I'll follow this way. Go
back down and cut him off!"

Katie holstered her weapon while reversing her direction,
heading back to the front door. When she got there, the five
guys that were previously out front had disappeared. *Thank the
gods for small favors,* she mused, as she vaulted over the concrete railing and ran to the alley on the right. The alley was an
obstacle course of crates and garbage cans that slowed her
progress, but she managed to turn the corner just as Enrico
jumped from the fire escape ladder, closely pursued by Dean.
Removing her H & K from its holster once more, she leveled it at
him and shouted, "Freeze!" Caught between the two women,
Enrico came to a halt, raising his hands in defeat.

"Hey, lady...I din' do nutting. Why you chasin' me?"
Enrico complained.

"Just put your hands up on your head and spread your legs,
Enrico. You know the drill," Katie ordered as she approached
carefully.

Dean reached him from behind and patted him down. "He's
clean," she said as she encouraged him forward with a vigorous
push.

"Hey, I know you. You the fed put me in prison. What you
want wit' me now?" Enrico stammered as Katie holstered her
gun.

"Yeah, Enrico. I guess I just missed you." Katie patted his shoulder roughly as she smiled at him.

"Hey, take it easy, I bruce easy," the wormy man answered as he rubbed his shoulder.

Dean came up behind him and snarled in his ear. "Naw, you don't have to worry about her, she won't hurt you. But then, I might." He turned to see Dean raise an eyebrow and give him a menacing smile.

"Now, Enrico. I just want to ask you a few questions, okay?" Katie began, as she walked around him slowly. He followed her every move, and when she came around in front of him, he blinked hard and swallowed.

"I'm not messin' wit' drugs no more. I got a good job. I'm clean," he said nervously.

"Yeah, yeah. Sure you are. That's why you like jumping out fire escapes." Katie reached out and put her hands on his shoulders. "But you're not hangin' with the right people, Enrico." Katie slid her hands down and smoothed the lapels to his cheap jacket. "I just want to know some things about your new friends."

"What new friends?" he asked, starting to shake a bit.

"Oh, you know, the ones you work with." Katie smiled sweetly at him as she removed her hands from his jacket.

"I don' know nuttin' 'bout dem guys. I just load the crates. I don' even know where they gets shipped to," he pleaded innocently, as he looked back and forth between the two women.

Now it was Dean's turn. She came around in front of him and got right in his face, her large strong hands grabbing the lapels that Katie had just smoothed down. "I don't think I believe you, Enrico. Now, tell the lady what she wants to know, or I'll break both your legs. Got it?"

The petrified man began to shake even more, and sweat began to pour off of his brow. "I'm tellin' the truth. I just load boxes all night. You gotta believe me." he answered, as he trembled violently. As Katie came back in front of the scared punk, she gently put a hand on Dean's arm. "Who's da Amazon?" he asked Katie while Dean slowly released his lapels. The comment put a big smile on Dean's face as she stepped back, circling back around to stand behind him.

Katie saw Dean's smile and almost broke into laughter herself before she continued. "She's a very good friend of mine, Enrico. She's not in the DEA like I am, so I guess you could call her your worst nightmare. Do you understand what that means?" He nodded vigorously. "So, how about you tell me about your new job while we take you for a nice ride around town, okay?" Again he nodded vigorously, and the two women led him to the SUV. No one was in sight as they locked him in the back seat, but Dean noted a few curtains pulled aside as they drove off.

They headed out to Anacostia Park and found an empty picnic table where they grilled him for two hours. By the time they were through, they had determined that the "boss" was one of the mercenaries on their list, and that Enrico had seen them adding items to some of the crates, but he couldn't tell what the items were. He had assumed they were smuggling drugs. The shipping containers were loaded onto eighteen-wheelers once a week. That was when he was called in to work, to load the shipping containers. He had no idea where they were going. At the end of the two hours, Dean made a discreet phone call to an old police friend of hers, and they dropped Enrico off at his place. After that they went back to the office to run a check on the boss, one Roger Golding. It turned out Golding had been a cellmate of Gentry's in Leavenworth. He was incarcerated for downloading the computer programs used for "smart" weapons. Although he wasn't caught selling the programs—he claimed he was downloading them to work on improving them—he was still convicted of tampering with military weapons systems.

"Hmmm. What's a computer geek got to do with Gentry?" Katie questioned, as they printed out his file to add to Gentry's.

"Gentry's a bit of a geek too, but he's more diversified," Dean answered as she rocked in her leather chair. "Now that we have Enrico in protective custody, so to speak, Golding is going to need another loading dock worker for this next shipment. Wonder if he's liberated enough to hire a woman?" Dean mused softly as a plan began to formulate in her head.

It took the entire day on Saturday to work out the logistics for the plan, but they finally had everything in place. It was now 1715 hours on Sunday, and they were just waiting for Golding to call Enrico in to work.

"So, tell me again how you're going to pass as his cousin?" Katie asked, smiling at Dean.

"I'm going to answer his phone speaking in Spanish. When

they ask for Enrico, we'll buzz Floyd to pick up and put Enrico on. He'll explain he's gotta go back to Mexico on family business, but his cousin can fill in for him while he's out. He'll explain that although his cousin is a woman, she can more than carry the load, and doesn't understand much English, so he'll be protected." Dean finished the explanation for the fifth time now. "Also, I can look the part, and I do speak fluent Spanish. I just need to be there long enough to figure out what's what. Besides, you and Lieutenant Jarvis will be in the van for back up."

"Yeah, you're right. I'm just wanting to get in on the action, but I guess it's your turn to go undercover, and mine to be on the outside watching." The sadness in Katie's voice was easy to pick up. "I don't know how you were able to do that on the Kasimov case. It would have driven me nuts."

"Well, don't worry, it did drive me nuts to have to sit and stare at the monitor while you and Lin went out on your little escapade. I just about lost it when the power cut out." The tall woman shook her head and shivered, playing the scenario back in her mind.

Katie, seeing the discomfort her lover was feeling, reached out and placed her hand on Dean's arm, giving her a gentle squeeze. "It all came out fine, Dean. This will, too."

Dean nodded her head, hoping that this case wouldn't be a repeat of that one. Her mind rolled back the tape of her actions as she entered the lodge, hearing the automatic gunfire from the basement, then her race to get to Katie in time. Only to get there seconds too late. She relived the agony of holding an unconscious, bloody Katie in her arms. The memories were so vivid, she felt the tears well up once more, and the pain felt very real again. The only thing that kept her from breaking into tears, was the shrill sound of the telephone ringing.

"Okay. This may be it. Get ready to get Floyd on the line." Dean reached for the phone, answering in a deep throaty voice. "*¿Bueno? Sí. Un momento, por favor.*" As she spoke, she motioned for Katie to hit the direct dial to Floyd, who answered on the first ring. Dean hit the transfer switch that added the caller to Floyd's line, where he handed Enrico the phone. The conversation was already choreographed for Enrico, so when he picked up the line, everyone held their breath, hoping that he would follow his directions.

"Yeah?" Enrico answered.

"Time to go to work, Rico. Dump the broad and be there at

midnight," the caller ordered.

"Man, I gotta problem. And that's no broad, it's my cousin from Juarez," Enrico answered.

"What do you mean, you got a problem," the caller questioned. "You know our shipping timeline is thin. What's this about, Rico?"

"Maria came to get me, my papa was shot by *ladrones*. I gotta go to Juarez today, man. It's a matter of family honor." Enrico sounded very convincing.

"Yeah, well, what about honoring our agreement? Who's gonna do your job?" the caller asked angrily.

"No problem, man. That's why Maria's here. She can do my job."

"A woman? Whadya nuts?" The voice on the other end of the line was getting very angry now.

"No, no, man—I mean, yeah, she's a woman, but she's big and strong and stupid. She can do the job, man." This Enrico said with a pleading voice. "Probably stronger than me. And she don' speak much English, just yes and no... Point her to the job, and she'll do it, man, I promise."

"Well, I don't have much choice now, do I?"

"Hey, man, I'm sorry. But she'll work good for you. Maybe you even like to spend some time wit' her, she's a real looker, too." This said a bit lecherously. "C'mon, Roger, gimme a break. I gotta go avenge my papa."

The comment about Dean's looks was not planned, and Katie gave her partner a wink at which Dean scowled.

"All right, but make sure she gets to the warehouse by midnight." Roger replied, adding, "What's she look like?"

"Oh, man. You won' believe it. She's a big one, six foot at least. Dark hair, blue eyes." He ended the description with a whistle.

"Never seen a Mexican with blue eyes. You sure about this, Enrico?"

"Yeah, man. Her papa was a gringo my *tia* slept wit' one night before he took off."

"All right, but if you're not back by next week, she may have to work twice for you."

"No problem, man. You can get her at my number. Just tell her the day and time," Enrico said.

"All right," Roger agreed before hanging up.

Dean picked up the line and told Enrico he did a good job,

but next time he should stick to the lines he was given. Floyd got on the line and promised to take good care of Enrico before he hung up.

"Well, looks like it's a go." Dean smiled at Katie. "We better get Lieutenant Jarvis notified."

"Yeah. We've got about five hours before we have to be in place. Do you think we could run back to the house?" Katie asked hopefully.

"That's what I was thinking. I've got to pick up some equipment and get dressed accordingly. We should have enough time," the tall woman considered as they stood.

Chapter
6

"Hey Dean, are you ready yet?" Katie called from the kitchen as she cleaned up the dishes from the cats' evening snack and Sugar's medicine. All three felines were winding around Katie's legs purring up a storm. "Yeah, guys, I miss you too." She reached down to give each one a little extra attention. Spice, being the most vocal of the threesome, made sure she got her rubs in first. The three cats were actually Katie's charges, but Dean had become very fond of them over the past several months, even taking them in while Katie was on assignment in El Paso. "How do you guys like living in the new house?" she asked, as they all gave her their complete attention.

"YEOW." cried Spice, followed by loud purring from Butter, and a barely audible squeak from Sugar.

"Me, too," she confided, as she stood up to find out what was keeping Dean. They still had plenty of time to get set up, it was only 2005 hours, but Dean wanted to make sure everything in the van was up and running before she entered the warehouse.

"Well, what do you think?" Dean asked, as she silently entered the kitchen.

"Jeez, Dean." Katie jumped at the sound of her lover's voice. "I'm never gonna get used to your sneaking up on me."

As Katie faced her lover, her breath caught at the sight. Standing in the doorway, Dean was dressed in black jeans, boots,

and a turquoise form fitting T-shirt. She had a silver concho belt
and petite turquoise dangling earrings, a black bandana around
her neck, and a little blush to highlight her cheekbones. She had
added rich red lipstick to complete the south-of-the-border look.
Once Golding got past Dean's obvious beauty, he would be hard
pressed not to notice the graceful strength of her well-muscled
body beneath the skin tight T-shirt.

"Wow!" was all that came out of Katie's mouth, followed by
another "wow" as she walked up and put her arms around Dean's
neck.

Dean began reciting: "Not too much? Should I take the lipstick off? I really hate lipstick."

"Umm, yeah, you could probably ditch the lipstick." Katie
smiled as she reached up for a quick kiss. "That way, I won't
have to worry about lipstick stains on my body or clothing when
I meet Lieutenant Jarvis tonight."

"Down girl, we've got work to do," the tall woman admonished, but then gladly swept her up into a loving embrace, planting another kiss on the young woman's lips. "Okay, let's get this
lipstick off us and head out."

"Are you going to carry any weapons in with you?" Katie
asked as they headed up I 95 to meet with Lieutenant Jarvis.

"Just my boot knives. I have one in each boot. I don't think
I'll have to worry about weapons with you two out there loaded
to the teeth," the dark woman replied with a grin. "Oh, and I've
got one of those knockout pens in my back pocket. Just for back
up." She laughed as Katie told her that she really doubted she
would need to use it, because they'd all fall over once they got a
good look at her.

"Is that all?" Katie grinned. "No special earrings?"

"Nope. They haven't made them in turquoise yet." Dean
laughed as she pulled into the parking lot for the Pentagon.
"There's the van." She lifted her chin in the direction of the
waiting van and headed in that direction, pulling up next to it.

As they arrived, a tall dark-haired man in his late twenties
stepped out and waved. He was about the same height as Dean,
maybe an inch taller, with a short brush cut, clean shaven, and
astounding green eyes. He was wearing black jeans and a black
long sleeved T-shirt that did very little to hide the fact that he

could probably be the next Mr. Universe. He walked across to the SUV with a grace that defied his bulk and reached up to salute Dean.

"Evening, Colonel." The lieutenant saluted—even though the gesture wasn't necessary—and grinned, showing perfect white teeth in the parking lot lighting.

"Evening, Bill," Dean returned, smiling warmly back at him. "This is Special Agent Katie O'Malley. Katie, First Lieutenant William Jarvis. One of my best men." The pride in Dean's voice was obvious.

"Nice to meet you, Lieutenant," Katie replied and returned the smile in earnest.

"Just Bill will do on this op." He took her weapons case from her hand and walked over to the van with it. "I know we talked on the phone yesterday, but you sure aren't what I pictured in my mind."

"Oh? How's that?" Katie asked curiously.

"Well, I figured you'd be as tall as the colonel here, and at least as mean looking." This he said with a chuckle that got a raised eyebrow and crooked smile from the aforementioned colonel.

Katie chuckled too before replying. "Well, Bill, sometimes small packages can be very deceiving."

"She's got that right." Dean cut in. "On my last case, she dumped me on my butt and had my throat blocked before I knew what hit me."

"Whoa! You're telling me that this little wisp of woman got the best of you?" Bill scoffed, disbelieving.

"Yep. So you'd better watch your step, big boy." Dean responded with a nod and a grin before adding, "Besides, she's not your type anyway."

"Ohhh, meaning she's your type?" Bill grinned at his commander.

"Yeah, so make sure you keep her safe, got it?"

"Yes, ma'am." the young lieutenant beamed.

This conversation left Katie a bit confused, but obviously Dean's admission to the young lieutenant was okay, or she wouldn't have done it. Just to be sure, Katie pulled Dean aside as Bill got into the van with the weapons case.

"Dean? Something you want to tell me here?" the blonde questioned.

"Oh. I forgot to tell you. Bill's one of us. He's a really

good guy, and we watch out for each other. His partner is a civilian computer consultant that works for the Pentagon. They're two of the nicest guys around. We manage to get out once in a while when I'm in-between assignments." Dean looked apologetically at Katie. "Sorry, I should have warned you."

"Hey, no problem here, just nice to know I don't have to watch my p's and q's." Katie gave Dean's arm a squeeze as they both got into the van.

They pulled into the same convenience store they went to the previous time they had the van out. Katie jumped out to get a few "extras" for the night ahead, while Dean and Bill stayed in the van.

"I gather you forgot to tell her about me," Bill stated as they watched Katie enter the convenience store.

"Yeah, but she's caught up now," Dean said quietly. "Just make sure she stays safe, okay? I almost lost her last time. I don't want that to happen again."

"No problem, Colonel. We'll make sure we keep each other safe and you too, in the process," the big man replied seriously.

"Thanks, Lieutenant. I knew I could count on you."

They sat there in silence as they waited for Katie to return with a sack full of goodies to keep her hunger at bay for the entire night and then some. When she put the sack down, Dean immediately pounced on the package of Ho Ho's she spied sitting on the very top, daring the young woman to try to take them away.

When they arrived at the warehouse, it was only 2245 hours, and the place was still deserted. They pulled into the same parking lot and turned on the equipment to make sure everything was operational. They did a quick scan with the TDSC unit for any possible warm bodies lurking inside. The place was still empty.

"Hey, how are we going to pick you out from everyone else? You don't have that necklace on," Katie inquired a bit apprehensively. Dean smiled and pointed to a gem in her concho belt, indicating that she would show up on the screen as a nice blue dot. Much relieved, Katie nodded her approval, then they finished going over the emergency signals.

"Right, Colonel." Bill repeated. "You say '*gringo ladrones*' and we'll come in like gang busters."

With that, they pulled out in the van and went ten blocks away from the warehouse to drop Dean off.

"Are you sure you want us to leave you here?" Katie asked

for what seemed to be the millionth time.

"Yeah, I'm sure. Now get the van back before they start coming in," Dean ordered. "I'll be fine, trust me."

With that, Katie and Bill closed the van door and headed back to set up their surveillance before the warehouse workers started to arrive. Dean watched them leave before beginning a slow walk towards the warehouse, conscious of all the night sounds and shadows that lay in her path.

Despite the slow pace Dean set, it still only took her twenty minutes to make it back to the warehouse. When she arrived, it was nearly 2345, and she found that some of the dockworkers were beginning to arrive. She walked in the front entrance, casually looking around until she recognized Golding from the picture in his file. Rather than go directly up to him, she began asking each man she saw if he was "*Señor* Golding." A few of the men hooted out catcalls, which she ignored, while some tried to see how far this beauty would let them go. Dean took care of that easily. The first one who tried to touch her found his hand grasped in a vise like grip that quickly told him the lady wasn't here to play. Finally, one of the men she asked pointed Golding out to her. She thanked him with a simple *gracias* then walked over to the boss. Golding had been watching her approach from the time she hit the front door to see how she carried herself, and to give himself time to let his instincts come into play. By the time she walked up to him, he had decided that she certainly looked like she could handle herself well enough to do the job.

"*Señor* Golding. *Soy Maria. Estoy aquí en vez de Enrique.*"

"So you're Enrico's cousin?" Golding looked at the tall woman nodding.

"*Sí,*" was her simple response.

"Do you speak English? *Habla ingles*?" he asked, knowing that Enrico said she didn't.

"No good," Dean stammered out.

"Can you lift heavy boxes?" he asked, pointing at the boxes and making a lifting motion.

At first Dean made a face as if not understanding him, then when he made the lifting motion, she began nodding and repeating the lifting motion saying, "*Ah, sí, puedo hacer el trabajo,*" and smiled at him.

"Okay," he nodded back, "follow me." He made a motion with his hands indicating what he wanted her to do.

Dean obediently followed Golding to the back of the warehouse, where he went up to the foreman and explained in a low voice that the woman was replacing Enrico for the night. He told the guy that she couldn't speak English, but seemed to catch on to hand signals pretty well. He also warned the man that he shouldn't try anything stupid with her, just get the shipment out on time. He walked over to Dean and pointed at the man and said, "Burt." Then he pointed at her and looked at Burt and said, "Maria," as he left to return to the office at the front of the warehouse.

"So, cutie pie—you're here to load boxes are you?" He looked around at the other dock workers and grunted. "Well let's see how strong you are, eh boys?" Dean had anticipated that there would be some macho maneuvering, so she just looked at the man with a questioning look.

The foreman was of medium size and seemed to be solidly built. He made his right bicep bulge and pointed at her. Dean looked back thinking, *Okay, let's just get this bullshit out of the way, shall we?* She walked over to Burt, nodding her head and smiling, and touched his muscle saying, "*Sí, fuerte.*" She quickly bent her knees, reached over to his safety back belt tucking her right hand under it to secure her grip, then reached up with her left hand, grabbing a handful of shirt to pull the man forward onto her shoulders. When she felt him settle, she stood, lifting the man easily off the loading dock floor.

"What the...?" he shouted as she lifted him up. Dean walked over to shipping container that was being loaded and deposited him fairly gently on top of the first box, all to the cheers of the other dock workers. A very embarrassed Burt scrambled off the box and nodded, saying, "Yeah, yeah, *fuerte.*"

Once the cheering stopped, Burt led Dean to the work table to give her a safety back belt and a pair of leather gloves. Then he took her over to the stack of boxes that were being transferred from the forklift to the shipping container, miming what her job was.

Dean nodded, put the safety equipment on, and began moving boxes, all the while tuning in to the conversations around her and stealing looks around the warehouse for anything that looked different from the time she was here last.

Katie and Bill were settled comfortably in the van, keeping a careful eye on the blue dot that danced back and forth on the screen and tuning in to the conversations in and around the warehouse. For some reason they kept picking up static from the office area.

"Why can't we tune in the office better? I didn't think there were any limitations to this equipment other than the shielding we encountered in the Catskills?" Katie asked Bill as she kept trying to home in on the signal.

"They've got an electrical blanket over the office throwing up interference to keep out unwanted listeners," Bill said simply. "We can filter the interference out at the lab, but that won't help us here. We've just got to keep taping and pull out the information later."

"But what if Dean gets into the office and then uses the emergency signal. We'll never know." Katie was obviously worried about a worst-case scenario after her escapade in the Catskills.

"The colonel is very flexible. She'll adapt if we aren't johnny on the spot," Bill said, smiling at Katie. "She's got great instincts, Katie. She'll be all right. She'll warn us first chance she gets."

Outwardly, Katie appeared to be placated by Bill's rhetoric, but inside she still worried over the possibility.

Sensing her discomfort, Bill decided to try another tack. "So how'd you take the colonel down?"

"Excuse me?" Katie asked, misunderstanding and blushing a bit.

"Sorry," Bill said chuckling. "I just wanted to know how you were able to knock her on her butt."

"Ohh." Realizing her mistake, Katie blushed deeper, then went into the story of how they'd met on the mountain that fateful night. Bill was obviously surprised at the level of skill the young woman had in hand-to-hand combat, and quickly asked if she'd mind showing him some moves. He told her that he and the colonel worked out in the officers' gym whenever they had the chance, and he was hoping some day to be able to do exactly what Katie had done. Only so far, it was his butt on the mat. As they amiably shared stories about Dean, they continued listening in and watching Dean's blue dot.

Dean worked for a solid two hours moving boxes without a rest stop, mentally tallying each box and the cargo it was supposed to hold. The two other guys at her workstation started out trying to out-do her, but soon gave up and took a break. *Wusses,* Dean mused to herself. *Bet they haven't worked a full eight-hour shift since they started here.* Not wanting to put herself in an awkward position with her fellow workers, Dean did slow down, but refused to take a break until she definitely needed one. At the three-hour mark, Dean stopped, stretched and began looking around the warehouse. Finally, one of the guys she was working with, a short squat man named Fred, came over as she continued to look around.

"You lookin' for somethin', honey?" Fred asked in a fairly pleasant manner.

Dean just looked at him, then continued her visual search. Fred tried again thinking that maybe she needed the john. He tapped her on the shoulder and asked, "Bathroom?" to which Dean nodded vigorously, stating, "*Sí, sí, baño.*"

"Follow me." Fred waved his hand for her to follow as he led her down the main aisle towards the front of the building. He stopped a short distance from the main office and pointed her in the direction of the bathroom.

"*Gracias,*" Dean said to Fred as she walked into the small bathroom. She really did not need to use the facilities, and once inside, she was glad she didn't have to. *Why is it that these kinds of places never keep their restrooms clean? And their choice of wallpaper always includes nudes.* Dean reviewed the wallpaper nudes to pass the time. *Ooo, that one's cute. Kinda looks like Katie, but with long hair.* She dallied a little longer before flushing the toilet. As she exited, she noted that no one was in sight, so she purposely turned the wrong way and began walking through the maze of crates in a haphazard fashion back towards the loading dock. Halfway back, she silently turned a corner and found two men standing by an open crate. They had effectively removed the center boxes of CheerieFlakes cereal, creating a cavity within.

"Okay, now slip it in carefully. Roger will have a fit if this unit gets busted," one man said as he helped the other lift the bubble wrapped item.

"What is it this time?" the second man asked as he carefully slipped the bundle into the cavity.

"Some kinda radar thingy—it's one of the last pieces he needs. I just know Rog will have our heads if it gets busted, so be careful will ya." As the man turned to get better leverage on the package, he noticed Dean at the corner. Hurrying to slip the package into place, he turned and yelled to her.

He quickly walked towards Dean pointing at her. "Hey, you." Dean just played innocent, pointing at herself. "Yeah, you." he shouted as he came face to face with her. "Where'd you come from?"

"*¿Yo?*" Dean said, still maintaining the innocent look.

"Yo, you. What's your name?"

Dean just cocked her head at the man with a questioning look, making him even angrier. He grabbed her arm roughly and led her towards the office. She put up a mild protest along the way repeating, "*¿Qué hice?*" and, in a broken accent, "No bad." When they arrived at the office, the man roughly pulled her in, startling Roger on the phone.

"What's this?" Roger asked, quickly putting the phone down. "What's she done?"

"Ed and I were putting the package away when I turned and saw this broad watching us," he said tersely. "You want me to take care of her?"

"Let's see what she knows first," Roger said. "Call Jose, have him get over here quick. Put her in the bathroom until he gets here."

Out in the van, Katie and Bill stopped talking as they noted Dean's blue dot moving towards the office area.

"Looks like she's on the move," Bill stated evenly.

"Yeah, nice touch, looking for the bathroom." Katie smirked. "I'd like to have seen how she got that message across."

They noted the area where she stood for a couple of minutes, then identified the sound of a toilet flushing. "Okay, she's moving again," Bill commented.

"Yeah, but she's not going back the same way she came. She must have found an opportunity to do some snooping." Katie observed the blue dot zigzagging on the screen.

They watched as her dot stopped near two additional ethe-

real bodies on the monitor and tuned in the conversation. "Uh
oh," Katie said quietly. "Looks like she's in a bit of trouble.
Should we go in now?"

"No, she hasn't given the signal. Let's just keep an eye on
her for now," Bill said, the tension becoming visible in the posture of both watchers.

Ten minutes later, Jose showed up at the warehouse, and
they brought "Maria" back into the office. Roger told Jose the
questions to ask and then evaluated the responses, along with the
dark woman's posture as she was questioned. After about fifteen
minutes of this drill, he seemed satisfied that the woman was
telling the truth, and was just disoriented after leaving the john.
He told Jose to take her back to the loading dock and to keep an
eye on her, just in case.

The next five hours went smoothly and by the end of the
shift, all the shipping containers were loaded, locked and waiting
on the flat bed trucks for their next destination. At 0800 Monday morning, the workers lined up at the warehouse office and
waited to receive their pay for the night's work. As Dean moved
along the line, she caught snatches of comments from the workers that there was only one more shipment, and then they'd have
to look for other work. When her turn came to receive her pay,
Roger told Jose to tell her that she would need to be back in one
week if Enrico wasn't back from Mexico. Dean nodded her head
in affirmation as she counted her cash smiling. *Well, you're one
cheap bastard.* Dean thought, as she counted out one hundred
bucks for eight hours of back-breaking work. *Not exactly what
I'd call prime wages, Roger, but then you paid everyone else four
hundred. Trying to get away cheap with the immigrant help, eh?
Well, we'll just take care of that next time.*

Dean smiled at Jose, telling him to tell *Señor* Goldman that
she'd be happy to work for him next week for such fine wages.
She left the building whistling a snappy Latin tune. It took her
fifteen minutes to backtrack through the alleys to the parking lot
where the van was located and stealthy enter. Inside the van,
Lieutenant Jarvis and Katie were glued to the monitors watching
the stationary blue dot on the screen.

"Wonder why she's just standing there?" Bill fine-tuned the
audio. "I can't hear anything in that area at all. Can you?"

Katie shook her head and responded, "Nope," as she continued to stare at the screen.

Dean put her head between those of the two watchers and asked, "Whatcha lookin' at?" smiling as they came unglued at her presence in the van.

"What the fu...?" Bill began. "Jeeezz..." Katie exclaimed at the same time. "How'd you...but, you're still..." they both finished together.

"Nah, that's not me." Dean continued smiling at the two flustered agents. "That's just the scanning chip from my belt." She pointed at the obvious hole in her concho belt. "Just thought it would work as a temporary tracking device since we didn't bring any with us. I slipped it into the container carrying the extra package in the CheerieFlakes cereal crate as a last minute idea. It's in the packing slip casing on the outside. What do you think?" Dean leaned on the back wall of the van, unable to stretch to her full height in the cramped space.

Bill was the first to reply. "Guess it should work, as long as we have access to a TDSC unit to track it."

Katie just nodded, since the technical capabilities of the Intelligence Section were outside her realm of expertise.

"Yeah. I'll call Tibbits now to put the satellite unit section on alert to track this shipment before it starts moving." Dean checked the GPS coordinates before she called in her request. After a short chat with the sergeant major, Dean hung up and with a dazzling smile asked, "Anyone up for breakfast?"

Chapter
7

After dropping off Lieutenant Jarvis, Dean and Katie went back to the house for a quick nap before returning to the Pentagon at 1800. As they opened the door to the house, they were greeted by three very annoyed felines. Katie quickly fed her brood, medicated Sugar, and followed Dean to the bedroom. Dean was just coming out of the shower, still dripping from the quick wash.

"Mmmm, you look good in that outfit, too," Katie purred as she reached for a towel to help dry her partner off. "Too bad I'm so wiped, or I might try to take advantage of your vulnerable situation here," she said as her towel-covered hands slowly caressed Dean's breasts.

"Who, me? Vulnerable?" Dean's eyes twinkled as she made a lightning-quick move, pulling Katie into a tight embrace. The tall woman leaned down, placed her lips on the young blonde's, and administered a soft, passionate kiss. "Still too tired?"

"Mmm, actually, yeah. I'm afraid real life is interfering with my romantic life," the blonde answered softly. "Rain check?"

"Rain check," Dean affirmed as she deftly picked the young woman up and carried her to the bed, gently putting her down. She then removed Katie's clothes and slipped her under the covers before returning to the bathroom to finish drying off. By the time she returned to bed, Katie was already asleep, so she quietly settled in next to her lover and entered Morpheus' realm.

"Well, it's been moving since 0900," Lieutenant Jarvis commented, as he entered Dean's office. "Looks like it's headed north. Maybe they're going to ship it out of New Jersey?"

"At least we'll be able to track it." Katie looked over at Dean. "Thanks to the colonel's quick thinking."

"Hmm?" Dean mumbled as she looked up from the current manual she was reading.

"The package is on the move. Looks like it will be going out of a port somewhere north of here," Lieutenant Jarvis reiterated. "What's got you so distracted?"

"I'm trying to figure out what that package was. The guy said it was some kind of radar 'thingy', and I'm just trying to see if I can pinpoint it." She sighed as she put the manual down and stood to stretch. "I'm not making much headway, though. Any ideas?"

Bill picked up the manual Dean had just set down and began scanning. "Phew. This is some pretty technical stuff here. What would a bunch of military misfits want with a radar set up?"

"Maybe they want to be able to set it up for defense of their headquarters, wherever that might be?" Katie offered. "You know, like a warning system if anyone tried to enter a specific area."

"Yeah, or maybe they have their own airfield, and they need it for air traffic control," Bill chimed in.

"Or, maybe they just want to beat the speed traps," Dean sighed. "There are just so many uses for radar these days. Unless we know what kind of set-up they're working on, it's just a crap shoot." Dean went back to her chair and sat down, beginning her rocking motion. "Wish I could have gotten a better look at the package they were loading."

The sound of the telephone ringing broke the silence in Dean's office. She reached over to pick up the offending instrument. "Colonel Peterson," she stated into the receiver.

"Yes. Really? That's interesting. Well, keep tracking it, okay? And thanks." Dean looked at her two partners, brows knit together, and stated, "The package is now headed west by train. That's certainly not the direction I was expecting."

"West? Wonder what's going on here. Maybe a circuitous

route to make sure the shipment isn't compromised?" Katie offered, considering the final destination site that they had anticipated.

"Could be. Why else go in the opposite direction of where its final destination is supposed to be?" Bill supposed agreeably.

"Well, the Satellite Surveillance Section is still tracking it. They'll let us know of any changes." Dean looked at her watch. "I don't know about you two, but I'm ready for a change of scenery. Anyone interested in a workout in the officers' gym?"

It took the trio about fifteen more minutes of filing research and shutting down the computer before heading to the gym. Thanks to Dean's advice, Dean and Katie kept a set of workout clothes in her office closet on the off chance they would get to use the facilities in the Pentagon. Going to the gym was an even better idea. Entering the women's locker room, Dean led Katie to the attendant's desk to get a locker assignment for her. The women's locker room was larger than she'd expected, brightly lit, and smelled better than any locker room she had ever been in.

"So what kind of facilities do they have here?" Katie asked the attendant.

"Just about anything you'd need to keep in shape, except a pool," the attendant replied. "We've got all the high tech stuff, as well as the good old free weights, an indoor running track, and a couple of small gyms for hand-to-hand work, aerobic and step routines."

"Hey, not bad." Katie accepted her locker assignment slip and signed it, returning the attendant's copy and keeping hers. The attendant handed her a towel and asked her to review the rules on the reverse side of her assignment slip. "Will do." Dean read her locker number from the slip and led Katie to where it was located. It was only two aisles from Dean's.

"So, what do you want to do first?" Katie asked as she rounded the corner into Dean's aisle.

"Well, I'm feeling a little stiff right now, so a little warm up on the free weights and a short jog, then maybe a workout with Bill on the mats," Dean replied easily.

"Sounds good to me. Bill asked me if I'd show him a few moves, so that'll work out just fine."

The women went to the weight room first, hitting the circuit

along with several other men and women. The weight stations
were actually located in the middle of the oval indoor running
track. Whether the designers had intended the effect or not, the
breeze caused by the runners and joggers kept the weight lifters
cooled. After completing their strength training, they joined the
others on the modest track and worked on the aerobic portion of
their program, with a warm up walk before breaking into a run.

Calculating they had hit their target heart range for twenty
minutes, they slowed to a walk once more to cool down before
proceeding to the gym, where they had promised to meet Bill.
For the next forty-five minutes, they took turns working on
defense and attack tactics.

No matter who came at her, every round that Katie was in
was won by her; and she graciously critiqued them regarding
their techniques after each bout. Finally, Dean and Bill decided
to team up on the young woman for one final round. Katie had
anticipated this approach much earlier, so when they both
attacked, she was ready for them. Utilizing a combination of
techniques from aikido, judo, Tang Soo Do, kung fu, and karate,
Katie prevailed again, landing both would-be attackers on the
mats several times. Bouncing on the balls of her feet, Katie
waited for them to rise and come at her again, but Bill and Dean
finally remained down.

After catching her breath, Dean rolled her head over to look
at Bill and said, "Well...that was fun." earning a hearty chuckle
from him.

Katie, the typical gracious winner, reached down to help
them both up before taking a winner's lap around the small gym,
making   cheering   crowd   noises   as   she   jogged.
"Yea...cheers...Atta girl...roar..." Having maxed their endur-
ance levels for the night, the trio headed to the locker room for
well-deserved showers.

"Well at least we won't have to work out when we get
home," Katie commented as the two women exited the officers'
locker room. "In fact, we could probably skip tomorrow, too,
after the workout we had tonight." She added this afterthought
hopefully.

"Don't count on it, Katie. That run up the stairs after
Enrico made me realize how much I've gotten out of shape. And

our little exercise tonight reinforced that." the older woman said with conviction as she met Katie's best puppy dog look. "And that little pout won't help either."

"So you're saying that if you had beat me tonight, you wouldn't consider yourself out of shape?" the blonde teased her older partner, giving her a gentle elbow in the ribs.

"Oh, no, I'm saying I'm out of shape. If I was in better condition, I'd have whupped your butt." Dean replied with a feral grin. "Just give me a week, and we'll go through that little exercise again."

"Oooo. Do I sense a little challenge here?" the blonde responded jovially. "What say we make this a bit more interesting then."

"What do you have in mind?"

"How about the loser has to give the winner a massage every night for a week?" Katie smiled, raising and lowering her eyebrows in true Groucho Marx fashion.

"A week?" Dean laughed. "Guess you're not very confident. How about a month?"

"You're on." Katie quipped as she entered Dean's office. "You know what they say, 'The bigger they are, the harder they fall.' But don't worry, I'll let you down gently."

"We'll see," Dean answered with a grin of her own, knowing that even if she lost, she'd still win, since she enjoyed giving Katie a massage as much as receiving one. "But right now, let's see where our package is at the moment." Dean lifted the phone and called down to the Satellite Surveillance Section. She found that the package was just about to Chicago, and they would know in a few hours where the next stop would be. Dean thanked them and said she'd contact them at 0200 for an update. After checking the latest information on the other prime mercenary targets, they decided to call it a night, and headed home.

At 0145, Dean rolled over and turned on the lamp on her bedside table. She punched in the number for the Surveillance Section and waited for someone to pick up. After six rings, the phone was finally answered. "This is Colonel Peterson. What's the location of my package now?" Dean waited until the staff sergeant found her information and returned to the phone. "It's where?" Dean's voice boomed through the quiet bedroom, rousing the sleepy blonde who was still semi-wrapped around her waist. "How the hell did it get there so fast? Yeah, uh huh. Well, can you pinpoint it exactly? Then do it and get back to me immediately." Dean gave the staff sergeant her phone number then hung up the phone. A heavy-lidded Katie opened one eye and peered at her frustrated partner.

"So, where's it at?" Katie was now sitting up on the bedside next to her partner.

"Would you believe Las Vegas?" Dean replied, shaking her head. "Seems it took a plane there. A commercial plane. Not FedEx, or Airborne, or any of the normal shipping airlines, but a goddamned commercial jetliner."

"The whole shipment?" Katie asked inquisitively as she began to knead at the knots she knew would be developing in her partner's shoulders.

"I doubt it. There were too many shipping canisters for that," the tall woman said, still shaking her head in wonder. "It must have been removed from the shipping container for some reason or another. Maybe they've got to add it to another part or something. Who knows?"

Dean threw the covers off and slid out of bed, grabbing her robe and putting it on as she stood. Once out of bed, she began to stalk around the room waiting for the phone to ring. It only took three minutes for the return call, but in that time, you could almost see a path in the carpet from her constant pacing. Grabbing the phone she muttered, "Peterson." She listened intently to the caller. "Yeah, got it. Look, this is a priority. Keep an eye on that blip and let me know immediately if it moves again." She paused as the caller asked for clarification. "No, just if it leaves Vegas." Hanging up the phone she looked at Katie and said, "Seems like it's somewhere on the Strip. That's as close as they could get right now. They have to wait for the next satellite to get into the right orbit before they can delineate the location any further."

"Any way a ground team could pinpoint it better?" Katie asked.

"That's a great idea, Katie. It'll still be like finding a needle in a haystack, but at least we could get a better bearing on what's going on with it." Dean smiled at her partner and sat back down on the bed next to Katie. "We've got a team of new Intelligence recruits going through training out in New Mexico. We could get a team up to Vegas by daylight. With the new hand

held TDSC units, they could use this as a practical exercise."
Dean reached for the phone and made a quick call to General
Carlton, explaining the situation and the recommendation. The
general concurred that this could be a valuable training exercise
for the recruits, and the addition of a seasoned field instructor
was also a plus. They agreed that the only information they
needed at this point was the location and condition of the package. General Carlton said she would issue the orders immediately. "Now we just have to wait and see what the team finds
out." Dean sighed as she stood to take off her robe, then slipped
back under the covers.

"How long before we get a response?" Katie asked, yawn-
ing.

"Probably within six to eight hours, depending on how long
it will take them to track it without being noticed."

"Well, then, we'd better get back to sleep," the young
woman suggested. "Not much we can do for now."

"Oh, I wouldn't be too sure about that," Dean stated as she
turned off the light and slipped her hand out toward her lover's
body, finding her objective with exquisite precision.

"Mmmm." A soft moan escaped from Katie as she relaxed
into Dean's ministrations. "You can always find something cre-
ative to do, can't you?"

"You've got that right," Dean mumbled as she burrowed
under the covers towards her ultimate target.

Chapter
8

At 0500 a young second lieutenant was leaning on an empty stool at the bar. It was located next to a very busy crap table in the Imperial Palace Hotel and Casino on the Vegas Strip. He was keeping an eye on a short, bulky man who was rolling the dice.

"Major Fellows, I've located the target, but you won't believe where I found it," the young lieutenant informed his superior on his miniature communications unit. The major's voice came through loud and clear into the lieutenant's earpiece, requesting the location.

"Would you believe—the crap table in the back of the Imperial Palace Casino?" The lieutenant listened, and then replied, "Yes, sir. I'm sure. Yes, sir. I'll maintain contact." With that, the young man sat down on the stool and took on the appearance of just another tourist who was watching a hot craps game in progress, as he waited for the rest of the team to show up.

When the major and the rest of the team arrived, Lieutenant Petri nonchalantly walked over to him and identified the short, burly man. They confirmed that the man was indeed carrying the TDSC/ID stone. As the rest of the team deployed to various areas surrounding the craps table, Major Fellows exited the casino to report and get orders on how to proceed. The current package was obviously not what they were supposed to find, and he needed to know what steps he and his team were to take next. After an interval of only one minute, his call was transferred directly to Colonel Peterson.

"Colonel Peterson," Dean said, answering the phone while checking her watch. She noted it was 0930 in D.C., and then mentally calculated the time difference for Vegas.

"Colonel, this is Major Vince Fellows. I'm the officer in charge of the Intelligence unit in Vegas. General Carlton's office put me through to your line to get orders on what to do next." The major paused, waiting for Dean to reply.

"Is the package still in the crate?" Dean asked.

"No, Colonel. That's the problem. The TDSC/ID stone is now in the possession of a man at one of the craps tables at the Imperial Palace Casino," he informed her.

"Say again, Major," Dean ordered.

"The TDSC/ID stone is not, I repeat, not in the package. It is in the possession of a man playing craps." The major waited for Colonel Peterson's reply.

"Damn it!" The colonel swore into the phone. "How in Hades did he get it?"

"We do not have that answer, Colonel. That's why I'm calling." The major requested his orders once more. "What do you want us to do now that we've located it?"

"See if you can find out how he got it. I need to know if it was found by the owners of the package, or what the circumstances were." Dean thought a moment longer before adding, "But do it in a way that won't draw suspicion."

"Yes, ma'am," the major acknowledged. "We have a female trainee with us. We'll see if she can get the information."

"Good thought, Major. Let me know as soon as you can," Dean ordered, then gave Fellows her office extension. She turned to inform Katie and Lieutenant Jarvis of the situation.

Major Fellows returned to the casino and pulled Lieutenant Tina Wilson aside, giving her instructions on what information was needed. They discussed possible ploys and decided that since she was familiar with the gambling game, she would join the table if a space became available next to the target. If not, they would wait it out until he left the table and proceed with a second option.

After forty-five minutes, a space did open next to the man who now carried the ID chip, and Lieutenant Wilson quickly replaced the man who vacated it. She threw a one hundred dollar bill down on the table and waited for her chips. The game was currently in progress with a shooter two spaces to the right of her target. It was very lively at the table, and there was quite a bit of betting going on between rolls. She smiled at her mark as she picked up her chips, and asked him how the table was running.

"Oh, baby. It's been great to me. I started with just five hundred, and I'm up by two thousand now." He offered his comments eagerly after appraising the beautiful young woman, then reached for his drink resting on the beverage rail below the table's main railing.

Yeah, bud. Keep the booze flowing, and you'll be losing that edge quickly, the young lieutenant thought to herself, as she placed her bets on the six, eight, and field. The game continued, and before the shooter crapped out, Lieutenant Wilson was up by forty-two dollars. The next shooter didn't last long at all, crapping out on the third roll. It was now her target's turn. Before he chose his dice, he reached into his shirt pocket and pulled out a gemstone that she recognized as the TDSC/ID stone. He rubbed it in his hands first, then replaced it in his pocket before selecting his dice.

On his first throw, he rolled a seven, earning him twenty-five dollars on his pass line bet. The next throw was an eleven, earning him the same winnings.

Lieutenant Wilson smiled at the man and asked, "You're pretty lucky. Was that your good luck charm you were holding before?"

"Yeah, baby—been givin' me good dice all night." the man responded as he threw the dice the third time, rolling an eight. "Ohhh baby, I love them eights." the man cried out as the table became lively with betting.

"I've never seen a stone like that before. Have you had it long?" she asked, smiling warmly at him.

"Nah, just got it today, or actually, more like yesterday. But as soon as I got it, I knew it would bring me luck." He reached in his pocket, pulled out the stone, and gave it a kiss. After returning the stone to his pocket, he picked up the dice and threw.

"Nine." the stick man called out as his table crew paid out the winners.

The guy pulled the stone out again and went through his ritual before returning it to his pocket. Then he place a hundred dollar bet on the hard eight, picked up the dice and threw again.

"Hard eigh,." shouted the stick man as the crowd around the table hooted and cheered.

"See what I mean, baby?" The stubby man smiled and laughed as they paid him his nine to one odds on the "hard way" bet and his pass line winnings. "I've been hot all night."

Lieutenant Wilson flinched internally at the chauvinistic "baby" comments, but oozed charm as the man reached down for his drink once more. *Maybe if he has enough to drink we'll be able to liberate the stone from him.* She caught Major Fellows slipping into the next opening at the table. Just then, the cocktail waitress came by asking for orders. The target placed his order for another bourbon on the rocks, and turned to ask the young lieutenant what she wanted. *Well, I might as well play along*, she thought then said, "Make mine scotch," and then, "Thanks," to the man at her side. "My name's Veronica, by the way," she added with an inviting smile.

"Bart," the man replied, smiling eagerly at the young woman. "Maybe when I'm finished here, we could go someplace nice and quiet. Just the two of us," he added before taking out the stone once more and giving it a very sensual kiss, watching for her reaction.

"Maybe," she replied, while thinking, *Yeah, the two of us, and my entire team.* As she reached down and placed her bet, he slid his hand down and over her buttocks. It took every bit of her self control to keep from hauling off and flattening the guy right there. *Prick! Why do some men have to be such jerks?* The major, catching the motion, gave the young lieutenant a cautionary look, and she smiled in response.

Play at the table lasted nearly two more hours before Bart was sufficiently inebriated to be led away by Tina, with her team close behind. It was now 0900 Las Vegas time, and she knew the information about the stone had to be relayed back to D.C. as soon as possible. She led him into one of the empty side lounges and had to put up with his pawing until she could get him situated in the booth. She knew she'd have to work fast before the burly man passed out from the fifteen plus bourbons he had consumed since she came on the scene. So far she'd found out he worked for the railroad at Grand Central Station loading freight trains. He'd taken a train to Chicago to meet his brother, and then the two of them flew to Vegas for their annual boys'-weekend-out.

"So, Bart. You said you just got that stone today?" she prompted, smiling at him.

"Uh, yeah, um, at the train station," he said in a very slurred voice.

"Train station? In Chicago or New York?" she reached out and slid her hands up and down his chest.

"Umm...nuh uh, in the city. Grand Central fucking Station." he smiled as she continued her massage of his chest. "Ya wanna fuck now?" he suggested with a wobble of his head and a barely discernable wink.

"In a little bit." She involuntarily paused, not wanting to consider the prospect of having to go to his room with him. "Did someone give it to you?"

Bart just raised his drunken head, eyebrows furrowed in question. "Who d'ya say gived it ta me? You gived it to me?" He paused, trying to blink himself awake. "C'mon...let's go fuck." His head wobbled back and rested on the booth. Heavy breathing indicated he'd soon be out cold.

"C'mon, Bart, I just wanna get one of those lucky stones, too," Tina suggested.

"Nope. Nope. Can't," Bart said, starting to go under.

"Why not?" she crooned in his ear once more.

"'Cause it was just layin' there. No more, just it, layin'..." Then he was out for the count, and she gently laid him down on the booth bench.

Lieutenant Wilson signaled the team to enter the lounge while she removed the stone from his pocket. As Major Fellows entered, she handed him the stone and informed him how Bart came to be the owner of it. "At least it looks like it was just found at Grand Central Station," she recapped. "So whatever was being tracked, it must have just come loose from the source."

"Looks that way," Fellows replied. "Good work, Lieutenant." The major sent one of the recruits to find a security guard and bring him back to the lounge. When the guard arrived, the major told him the man on the lounge bench was a big winner at the craps table, and had also had a bit much to drink. He suggested that the hotel find a room for the man to sleep it off before he was rolled for his winnings right there in the lounge. The security guard called in to his supervisor, who immediately sent several men to the lounge to pick him up and settle him in a complimentary room for the day.

"That was a pretty nice thing you did for that guy," Lieutenant Wilson commented as the team left the hotel.

"Yeah, well, I didn't want to see the poor slob get taken

advantage of just because he'd passed out." The major shrugged
his shoulders while memories of his dad replayed in his mind.
He could remember many occasions when his dad came home
empty-handed on payday, having slept it off in some gutter
behind the local tavern. "Right now, let's get this information
back to D.C." As soon as they entered the van, the major relayed
the information to Dean's office number. It was now 0930 in Las
Vegas.

Dean had been pacing her office or rocking in her leather
chair since the earlier phone call from Major Fellows. When the
phone finally rang at 1230, Dean picked it up on the first ring.
"Yes," she answered simply, "what have you got?"

After a short conversation, Dean hung up the phone, satisfied that the errant stone wasn't a plant, but just an accident.
"Well, at least we know we aren't compromised. The damned
thing must have shaken itself loose and fallen through the slats
in the crate. Evidently, the guy found the stone at Grand Central
Station in New York, where he works loading shipments. He
found it lying on the side of the track."

"But now we don't know where the shipment went," Katie
commented.

"No, but we'll get another crack at it next week. Our final
chance, so we'll have to do it right," Dean answered. "Bill,
make sure we have several tracking devices available in the van
for the next trip to the warehouse."

"But, what if they check the crates before shipping?" Bill
asked.

"We'll just have to plant them after the shipping containers
are loaded, after the workers leave," the colonel responded with
a wry smile.

Roger Golding sat comfortably in his Falls Church home
sipping a glass of Glenlivet on the rocks and listening intently to
the caller on his phone. As he swirled the amber liquid, he nodded occasionally to comments made on the other end of the line.

When it was his turn to speak, he assured the caller that all
was well on his end, and the final pieces for the radar array

would be coming in the next shipment that was scheduled to go out on Sunday.

"Yes, Scott. The warehouse is receiving goods daily. By this Friday, all of our orders will have arrived, and we can conceal the final pieces for the radar array." He smiled as the liquid loosened the tight muscles in his neck. "It's too bad you had to leave the country so fast." Roger flashed back to the near miss in driving the Lyons' car off the road permanently. *Too bad that SUV had to intervene, or we could have put an end to that little British pest.*

"Yeah, well there's nothing we can do about that now," came the reply from the other end of the line. "Look, Rog, these final parts are crucial. We can't let anything happen to this last shipment. It took me an entire year to assemble all the parts for the Ares array without anyone noticing, and to replace these by our deadline now would be nearly impossible." Scott Gentry's voice registered a very serious tone. "As it is, it's going to take most of the remaining time to assemble the final product at the base."

"Yeah, the Combined Forces exercises are due to start November 12th. Are you sure you'll have enough time to put it all together?" Roger inquired. "Saddam won't pay off the balance unless we get the job done."

"I'm sure. Besides, our plan won't be put into motion until the final week of the exercises. You just make sure I get the rest of those parts on time. It takes a good deal of time to get them transported secretly to the base once they arrive in Freeport," he answered brusquely.

"Isn't there a better way of sneaking on that old base without being seen?" Roger questioned.

"No. This way is foolproof," Scott responded. "The chances of anyone finding our secret entrance are one in a million."

"Yeah, but that scientist stumbled onto it. What if someone else does?" the man countered.

"Then he'll be taken care of in the same way." Scott said laughing, "Nitrogen narcosis is very painful and can happen to the most seasoned diver."

"Especially when his tank is doctored with a little supplement of nitrogen gas," Roger agreed, joining in the laughter.

Chapter
9

"That should do it." Dean looked up at her two partners as she folded the map detailing the location of the three surveillance teams watching the warehouse. "Now we need to just sit tight and see what turns up."

"Colonel, now that we've found Golding's home, shouldn't we set up a surveillance unit there, too?" Lieutenant Jarvis suggested.

"It wouldn't hurt. I doubt if he'd be stupid enough to have any of his contraband hidden at his home." Dean thought about the suggestion a bit more. "But, maybe we'll get lucky and intercept some information. Go ahead and do it."

"Yes, ma'am. Right on it," the young lieutenant responded, stood, and left the office to set up the unit.

"Are we still going to go in and take another look around tonight?" Katie asked as she checked the computer for updates on their list of mercenaries.

"Yeah. I'd like to get in and do a more thorough search before the warehouse fills again," Dean commented. "At least we can skip the crate searches since they make the additions the night they load."

Katie looked up from the computer shaking her head. "You know, it's really weird how we haven't been able to find hide nor hair of any of the guys on our list since the night of the Lyons'

accident. Except for Roger Golding, every report has been negative since then. Like they all went to ground."

"I know what you mean. Maybe Gentry was afraid he was
recognized and sent them under. At least we found Golding.
He's got to be a key player if he's in charge of the smuggling
effort. They probably had to leave him here to finish the job."

Katie nodded her head in agreement, then asked, "Is Bill
going with us tonight?"

"Yes. I thought it would be a good idea to have the three of
us there. We can cover more ground that way, and besides, Bill's
really turning into an excellent field officer. He's bright, obser-
vant, and can think on his feet extremely well, plus, he's as loyal
as they come," Dean answered with an air of pride.

"Yeah, I like him too," the agent replied, winking and smiling as the color rose in her partner's cheeks. "He's kinda like
the brother I never had."

"Or the little brother I once did," Dean answered wistfully,
as she turned to stare out her window.

Katie sensed the emotion running through her lover and
reached out, giving Dean's arm a gentle squeeze, remembering
the tale of Dean's brother's tragic death. "Are you okay?" she
asked, as she felt the tension in Dean's arm.

"Yeah." Dean sniffed, then turned back to Katie and gave
her a crooked smile. "I'm okay." Sighing, she added, "How
about we take a break for lunch?"

"Food. All right. I thought you'd forgotten about lunch,"
Katie replied enthusiastically, as she quickly stood, heading for
the door. She was just about to turn the knob when Dean's intercom came to life, stopping her in her tracks. She turned to watch
as Dean responded, flipping the talk button. "Colonel Peterson,"
Dean drawled. On the other end was Sergeant Major Tibbits
relaying the general's order for their presence in her office,
immediately.

"I wonder why?" Katie inquired.

"Generals don't have to give you a reason, Katie, but I'd
imagine it's about Art and Gwen." She smiled at the young
woman as Katie held the door open for her, and they headed
down the hall to the general's office.

As they entered, Sergeant Major Tibbits greeted them with a
smile. He stood and saluted, then opened the door for them.
"The general is expecting you."

"Thank you, Sergeant Major," Dean said warmly as she

entered the office first and proceeded to where the general was sitting on the couch.

"At ease, Colonel," General Carlton ordered before Dean could go through the normal report protocol. "Have a seat." She indicated the chairs across from her. As Dean and Katie sat, General Carlton began speaking.

"How is the investigation going?" She eyed Dean, then Katie. Dean spoke first, bringing the general up to date on the current situation—including the elusive TDSC tracking stone that found its way to Las Vegas, and the training team's success-ful retrieval.

"Thanks for allowing us to use the training team. They did a commendable job," Dean reported.

"Yes, they did. It turned out to be a good practical exercise for them, too. Major Fellows is a very competent training officer," Mary commented before continuing. "So where do we stand now?"

"We're waiting for another call from Golding to call 'Maria' to work," Katie offered. "And we have three teams on ware-house surveillance right now, tracking the incoming shipments."

"What ever became of the first mercenary spotted at the warehouse?" The general paused, recollecting the man's name before speaking again. "I believe his name was Stockton?"

"Yes, ma'am, Jerry Stockton. Now that's a real mystery. Our source stayed at the warehouse until we were set up. He didn't see him leave the warehouse, but when we got there, we couldn't detect anyone in the place," Dean recounted. "We assumed that he must have exited another way or was missed by the street source, perhaps when he went to call it in to us. Any-way, when Katie and I entered the building, there was no one in sight."

The general nodded before asking her next question. "And Mr. Gaiyoz is behaving?"

"A model citizen," Katie replied confidently. "He's very interested in helping us—now, and Floyd is keeping a tight rein on him until this is all over."

"Have you had any break in determining what type of radar these mercenaries are going to deploy?" came the general's next question.

"No, ma'am. Not yet," Dean informed Mary. "We're hop-ing to find out more tonight. Lieutenant Jarvis, Katie, and I, are going to do a more thorough job of checking out the warehouse."

"Good, but be careful. We don't want them to get wind of the fact that we're watching them," the general cautioned. "Now, Gwen has been doing her covert thing with Art, and his meetings with his old MI 6 pals. Unfortunately, most of the meetings were just with Art, while Gwen was occupied with their spouses, but she did come up with some small tidbits of information." Mary completed this comment by waggling her hand in a "so-so" motion. "It seems MI 6 in Freeport has been watching the comings and goings of several mercenaries that match the folks on our list. Unfortunately, being an island, there are miles of shoreline that are not patrolled as diligently as the airport or the cruise ship ports. There's no telling how many individuals are involved at this point, but the main island that seems to be involved is Grand Bahama. It's one of the largest, yet has a very small population, and if these men are working off of boats in the area..." She let the sentence trail off with a shrug of the shoulders. "Gwen also was able to find out that MI 6 is concerned that this may have something to do with the joint exercises that are planned for this month."

"Excuse me, General, but are you talking about the war games scheduled with Canada, Britain, Australia, New Zealand, and the U.S.?" Dean asked.

"Exactly." The general's voice became more serious. "As you know, we've been planning these exercises for nearly three years, and they will be taking place in both the Atlantic and the Pacific, to test our combined forces' readiness to respond to a threat. It's been a massive undertaking that none of the participating countries wants to see canceled or postponed."

"Yes, the intel projections estimate that our forces—including all the reserves—would be able to respond fully within forty-eight hours of call-up," Dean added for Katie's benefit.

"Wow," Katie uttered, "that's quite an ambitious undertaking. I can see why MI 6 is concerned."

"I've been having daily sessions with the Joint Chiefs for weeks now, and I can tell you nothing has ever been mentioned about any possible threats," Mary added. Katie then asked why MI 6 didn't inform the Canadians and U.S. about the situation with the mercenaries. "From what Gwen gathered, they have nothing concrete to go on, so they're just watching the situation. They don't want to jeopardize the exercises. If these mercenaries are deemed a threat, they feel they are no match for our combined forces. Besides, these men are on Bahamian soil. It's also a natural tourist spot, and it could all be just coincidence."

"I'm not buying that coincidence theory," Dean said with a shake of her head.

"Neither am I, Colonel, but that's the official line right now." The general stood and walked over towards her desk, stopping in front of it and reaching for a sheet of paper. "I did a little checking on your accrued vacation time, Colonel, and yours too, Agent O'Malley. And I was wondering if you two would like to take a little vacation in the Bahamas?" Mary asked the question as she replaced the sheet of paper on her desktop, then turned around, leaning back against the front of her desk. "The official line prevents me from cutting you orders to go there since we can't prove it's a clear and present danger. Plus, it's foreign soil. However, I'm sure I could secure the assistance of the local authorities to allow you some latitude in a discreet investigation. So once again, I'm asking you to volunteer to do this, and you do have the option to say no." The general finished speaking as she returned to her seat on the couch. "If you need time to discuss this, it's not a problem, as long as I have an answer before you leave today."

Dean looked over at Katie, each reading the thoughts of the other. Dean nodded, and turned towards the general. "I don't think you'll need to wait that long, Mary. Our answer is yes. As a matter of fact, we had been hoping to meet some friends of ours at their timeshare in Freeport for the middle two weeks of November, until this case came up that is. I believe that we should stay with that plan and appear to be just the typical vacationers on holiday," Dean answered.

General Carlton considered this for a moment then decided, "I'm not sure I would want you to involve anyone in a possibly dangerous situation. Especially civilians."

"Not a problem, General," added Katie. "The friends we're talking about provided invaluable help with the case in the Catskills. I'm sure we can count on their discretion and maybe even minimal assistance, since they know the island well."

"Would these friends happen to be Tracy Kidd and Colleen Shore?" the general inquired, then added, "I went over your report on the Kasimov case when I first came on board. Very impressive assistance by those two."

"Yes, ma'am," Dean acknowledged. "And perhaps you remember Tracy from Ft. Leonard Wood?"

"As a matter of fact, I do." Mary nodded with a wry look of

amusement remembering the then-young Lieutenant Kidd. "If
they agree to act only as island guides, and to stay out of harm's
way, it might prove to be an adequate cover. In addition, Art and
Gwen are returning to Freeport tomorrow morning. They'll be
staying with their friend Ned, from MI 6." She stopped and
thought a bit longer. "I think it's time I have a conversation with
Art tonight. I'm going to inform him about what you have
uncovered to date. I'm sure once he realizes that we believe in
his suspicions, he'll be only too happy to help put you in touch
with his friends, should the need arise."

The general had Tibbits bring up lunch for them, so they
could continue their conversation without the interruption of the
loud growling coming from Katie's stomach. While they ate, the
three women planned for contingencies, and Dean drew up a list
of items that would be helpful for the investigation. Dean and
Katie finally left the general's office after everything was
checked and rechecked, requisitions made for necessary equipment, and provisions put in place for that equipment to pass customs. By the time they were finished, it was nearly 1700, and
they still needed to meet with Jarvis regarding the plans for that
evening's operation.

The beat-up looking blue van was parked in its safe spot
across from the warehouse by 2300. After checking in with the
other two surveillance teams, Dean did a scan of the building for
signs of human inhabitants. Finding none, they checked their
gear one more time before embarking on their tour of the facility. Dean was in the lead, heading for the alarm system while
Bill and Katie covered her actions. It took Dean less time to dis-
arm the security system the second time around. Once that hur-
dle was cleared, they moved to the back of the warehouse to the
loading dock.

"I got a good look at the personnel door on the loading dock
last week," Dean commented as she jumped up on the loading
platform. "Just give me a sec," she said as she pulled out her
lock picks. It took her a mere twenty seconds before the trio was
able to enter through the personnel entrance. Once inside, they
spread out to cover their assigned areas, according to the plan.
Katie had the back of the warehouse, Bill the front, and Dean
had the office. There weren't as many crates and boxes this time

around, so Bill and Katie were able to keep each other within visual range while they looked for anything unusual. To Katie, it seemed like the same type of sundry orders that were in the warehouse before: lots of cases of canned goods, cereals, coffee, pasta, laundry supplies. Nothing seemed unusual or out of the ordinary. After opening several crates and boxes, Katie and Bill decided to take a closer look at the structure of the warehouse.

Dean had to use her picks to get into the office again. Once inside, she began a systematic search of the desks, bookcases, trashcans, and finally the file cabinets. Though the latter were also locked, they were no match for Dean's picking skills. Everything was in order. Again, too much order for a typical warehouse. *Hmm, there has to be more here than meets the eye.* Dean retraced her steps around the office, only this time doing a careful visual of the office layout. *Something's just not right here.* Dean surveyed the office once more, then stepped outside, visually inspecting the office from that perspective. *Aha! Gotcha!* She mentally clapped her shoulder and quickly reentered the office, stepping to the back wall. As Katie and Bill entered the office, Dean was shining her high intensity flashlight on each piece of furniture located on the back wall and the floor surrounding each, and then she retraced her steps, tapping on the wall as she went.

"Find something interesting?" Katie surmised as she watched her partner.

"Yeah, just haven't found the key yet." Dean shrugged as she came to the end of the back wall once more. "It's probably right under my nose, only I don't recognize it."

"Ahh. Like that time in Mexico when you sat on that old sofa in the hanger and thought it was just lumpy?" Bill offered with a smile.

"Yeah, sorta like that," Dean replied with a frown.

Katie scrunched her eyebrows and looked from Bill to Dean and back. "So what was it?"

Bill laughed and said, "The biggest *Crotalas adamanteus* you ever saw."

"The biggest what?" Katie asked, shaking her head in total confusion. "Mind translating that?"

"A diamondback rattlesnake," Bill informed her, still chuckling. "If it hadn't been for the seat cushion, and Dean's quick reflexes, that damned snake would have done some serious damage to our colonel here."

Katie's eyebrows shot up as she looked over at a blushing Dean and started to chuckle. "Oh...my...God. What did you do?" she asked Dean as another wave of chuckles hit.

"As soon as I felt it move beneath me, I got up and grabbed the first thing I laid my hands on and threw that at it as it poked its head out," Dean answered modestly.

"Oh, yeah!" Bill interjected. "I've never seen such fluid movement in my life. I was just standing there and the next thing I knew, the colonel was standing next to me throwing Garcia's lunch plate at the rattler like a Frisbee. She threw it with such force that it took the head clean off. Damned thing had fourteen rings on its rattler and was over eight feet long when we laid it out."

"Made a nice meal though," Dean added casually.

"You ate it?" the young blonde groaned.

"You bet," Bill answered her with a smile on his face. "Best roasted rattler I ever had."

"If you two are finished chatting now, I could use your help," Dean admonished them as she pointed to the bookcase on the back wall. "If you look closely at the floor here, you can notice a slightly worn arc. I've tried pushing the bookcase, but it won't budge. There's got to be a trigger mechanism that will release it." Dean was explaining as she carefully moved each item on the bookshelf looking for the release as Katie and Bill joined in the search.

"Secret moving bookcases. Just like something you'd see in an old 'B' movie," Katie was mumbling to herself as she reached up and looked at a light switch next to the bookcase. "Naw...that would be too obvious," she said as she flicked the switch and watched the bookcase slide open, to the astonishment of Dean and Bill. "Well, I guess if it had been a snake, it would have bit ya," Katie said with a grin as she swung both arms in the direction of the opening, inviting Dean and Bill to enter the dark interior. "After you."

They cautiously peeked into the dark space, examining it with their flashlights before they went any further. The area directly behind the bookcase was a small landing before a series of stairs descended into darkness. Dean searched the wall inside the opening and found a double switch. "Bet this one closes this thing," she conjectured as she flipped the switch farthest from the opening, "and this one is for the lights." As she finished speaking, a series of small wattage light bulbs came to life, illuminating the passageway. It appeared to be at least six feet across and seven feet high. The walls were poured concrete with a light fixture every twenty feet or so. It was dry in the passageway, but cool, and the air smelled slightly damp. "Okay, let's see where this goes, shall we? Better close the bookcase behind us, just in case." And before the other two could answer, she was silently and cautiously moving down the stairs.

Imitating their leader, Katie and Bill followed closely after Dean. When they got to the bottom of the stairs, the passageway turned right and went for quite a distance before turning to the left, continuing for five to six hundred feet. At the end of the passageway they came upon a large steel door that reminded Dean of the doors on Naval ships, only larger. The door almost filled the entire width and height of the passageway itself and had a keypad-locking device on it.

"Damn. Now what?" Bill asked as he noted the keypad lock.

Katie reached into her belt pack and pulled out a palm sized device. "No problem," she answered as she stepped up to the door. Dean had already pulled out her pick set, selected the Phillips head screwdriver she always kept there, and began unscrewing the panel on the keypad, exposing the wires.

Katie reached up and selected the red and green wires and attached them via alligator clips to her instrument, then punched in a few keystrokes. "This'll take just a few minutes," she said as she checked her watch, then noted the numbers that began appearing on the keypad digital display. "Seven... four...nine...one." When the four numbers were on the display, it began a series of blinks in red then switched to a solid green. "Looks like it's done," Katie commented as she unhooked the wires, allowing Dean to replace the panel on the keypad. Before Dean opened the door, she pointed to the switch on the wall by Bill and told him to douse the lights. Once the lights were off, they waited until their eyes had enough time to adjust to the darkness before slowly opening the door and cautiously stepping through. What they found on the other side was the tunnel for the utilities servicing the Navy Yard. One corridor led directly to the Navy Yard, while the other apparently led to an outlet near the Potomac.

"Well surprise, surprise," Dean commented as she recognized their location. "Looks like our boys have a direct link to the Navy. Maybe that's where they got their radar equipment.

Nice little delivery system they've got here."

"I haven't heard any scuttlebutt about missing radar equipment from my Navy buddies," Bill said as he closed the door behind them. "But that doesn't mean there's nothing missing."

"Is there any way we can have them check for missing or stolen equipment?" Katie inquired as the trio walked slowly towards the Naval Yard.

"We'll have to get the general to request a quiet audit of all the services," Dean answered. "I'll bet Golding and Gentry have buddies in all the branches. It would be too risky to steal from just one place or one branch. Easier to hide what you're taking if it's only a piece here and a piece there."

"As long as the pieces are interchangeable," added Bill.

"Mmm, makes sense," Katie said thoughtfully. "But won't it take a long time to find out what's missing, and from where?"

"Yep, and that's probably what Gentry's counting on," the colonel posited. "Let's see where this tunnel comes out. Maybe we can put a discreet surveillance on it, and see what turns up."

At the end, the tunnel made an upward turn, where the various conduits snaked their way into the Yard's main power plant. "End of the road," Dean confirmed as she climbed back down the vertical ladder. "Okay, let's get back to the warehouse."

It took them fifteen minutes to get back to the van, after insuring that they had left the warehouse exactly as they had found it, and enabling the security system. Dean turned the driving over to Bill while she called General Carlton regarding their findings. It was 0237 hours on 2 November when she dialed the general's home number.

"General, this is Colonel Peterson." Dean spoke quietly into the phone. "We've just finished our exploration, and I felt there were some developments that you needed to know about immediately." Dean went on to explain about the hidden passageway and its link to the Navy Yard. She included their suspicions that Gentry was stealing parts from various branches of the services and from several different posts, to avoid detection. "I don't know if it is possible, ma'am, but I would recommend that a general audit be ordered of all branches, if you feel that you would be able to request one."

"I agree that an audit is in order, but," the general cautioned, "it might be difficult to set one in motion quickly enough to provide us with usable data." *And I'll have to call in a few markers just to get that initiated, since the information gathered to date is not from an official investigation.* "I will see what I can do about making the investigation official at my meeting with the Joint Chiefs later this morning, and I would like to meet with you after that."

"Yes, ma'am," Dean replied, knowing that the general's administrative skill was going to be taxed to the limit in this phase of the operation.

"I should be back in my office by 1400. I'll have Tibbits contact you when I'm available to meet. Good work, Dean," the general commended before disconnecting.

"Okay, troops, let's call it a night," Dean ordered, as she sat back in the seat and relaxed for the drive back.

Chapter
10

Sergeant Major Tibbits stood as Colonel Peterson opened the door to the general's anteroom. "She's not in a very good mood, Colonel," Tibbits commented as he stepped over to open the door to the general's office. "I don't think her meeting went well this morning," he reflected as he turned the doorknob, pulling the door open and allowing Dean a view of a very red-faced general pacing her office.

"Thanks, Tibbits." Dean slipped past him, coming to attention just inside the general's office. "Lieutenant Colonel..." she was stopped in mid-report as the general turned and said, "Sit," a bit harshly. Dean immediately sat in the nearest chair, waiting patiently as the general continued to pace, and wondered where this hostility was coming from. After a few more trips up and back, the general seemed to make up her mind, and joined Dean in the informal sitting area.

"Sorry," she began, "but I'm a bit out of sorts right now. I just got back from my meeting with the Joint Chiefs, and it's a wonder I can sit at all after the butt chewing I just got from the man himself." Dean waited patiently for the general to continue. "I was able to get the audit in motion, but only after I promised to cease further investigation until after Operation Teamwork is over. They don't want any bad press to hit prior to the war games."

"But, General, aren't they concerned that this may have

something to do with the joint exercises?" Dean asked in amazement.

"Yes, and no. They feel that there may be a tenuous link, but they're not willing to admit that a bunch of washed up mercenaries could do anything to jeopardize an operation of this magnitude. Plus, the other countries have not mentioned any mercenary involvement in their intelligence reports, so they aren't too concerned."

"Unbelievable," Dean commented as she shook her head. "General, I can feel it in my gut. I can't explain how, but I know they're planning something to disrupt these exercises. Maybe even cause damage to the units participating. Something. And I know we won't like it when we find out what it is." Dean paused before continuing. "Damn it, General. Some portions of these exercises are live fire."

"I know, Colonel, but my hands are tied. They won't let me take the investigation to official status."

"Here we go again," Dean said with a tinge of bitterness in her voice. "Only this time, it's the military leaders instead of the political leaders."

"Colonel, I promised I would cease my investigation until after the exercises...but I can't give you orders concerning what to do or not do on your vacation." The general finished with a softer edge to her voice as she made eye contact with Dean.

"Understood, General. The 'toys' I've checked out to take on vacation with me, are they still available?" Dean asked with a raised eyebrow and a slow smile appearing on her lips.

"Well, if you don't find the time to turn them in before you leave...I guess you can turn them in when you get back," Mary stated, now obviously in a better mood. "But make sure you take the satellite phone with you. Never know when I might need to contact you," she added, now grinning fully.

"Yes, ma'am," Dean replied. "I'll be ready whenever duty calls, ma'am."

The general smiled at her aide's obvious enthusiasm. "When were you scheduled to start your vacation?"

"Next Friday, 10 November."

"Well, if you clear your desk earlier, you have my permission to start sooner if you wish," General Carlton added as she rose from her seat on the couch. "And I'm sure Director Evans will approve Agent O'Malley's leaving early, too. Especially since my request for her services, has been deemed unnecessary at this time." This she said with a wink.

"Yes, ma'am. I'm sure Agent O'Malley will look forward to a little extra vacation time," Dean speculated as she rose to leave. "Thank you, ma'am. I'll be sure to send you a postcard. By the way, I'll be moonlighting Sunday night. I'll just try to tie up any loose ends. Is that all right with you, ma'am?"

The general thought for a moment, and nodded her head. "I'm sure if you've finished up any reports before you leave tomorrow, you could start your vacation Saturday." With that, Dean left the general's office in at least a little better frame of mind, but fully aware that she wouldn't have the three team back-up she had planned on for her second visit to the warehouse as Maria.

Looks like it's just going to be Katie and me. Good thing I've already checked out the portable TDSC unit and the audio surveillance equipment. I'd hate to go in totally naked, Dean thought as she walked briskly down the hall to her office.

"So, that's the plan...for now anyway. Any questions?" Dean queried the two individuals opposite her in her small office.

Bill and Katie exchanged looks and both began to speak at once. "That's it?"

"Yup. Looks like you and I are on vacation as soon as I clear up some paperwork on my desk," Dean recapped.

"Colonel, I have thirty days on the books. Mind if I put in for it starting tomorrow?" Bill asked hopefully.

"I can't ask you to do that, Lieutenant. After all, we may actually be on a wild goose chase, and I couldn't ask you to give up your time. Besides, if anything happened to you, I don't think I could face Dirk," Dean replied honestly.

"Well, if it is a wild goose chase, what better place to spend it than the Bahamas? And you don't really think it's a wild goose chase anyway," Lieutenant Jarvis responded. "And if you're worried about it being dangerous, that's all the more reason you need additional back-up." He smiled at her before he continued. "Besides, Dirk would never forgive me if I stayed behind and let something happen to you or Katie."

Dean swiveled her chair to face the window, silently thankful for the loyalty of her young officer. "If you get your paperwork in to me within the hour, I'll sign it and send it forward to the general. But it will be up to her to make the final decision." She swiveled back around to face him. "Until then, Lieutenant, I believe you have several boxes here to pack into my SUV before 1800 hours."

Lieutenant Jarvis quickly stood, assumed attention, and replied formally, "Yes, ma'am. Thank you, ma'am," and exited the office with his arms full of surveillance equipment. On his trip back from the parking area, he decided he would stop at his cubicle, fill out the required request-for-leave forms, and submit them to the colonel. He also decided he would put in a call to Dirk, apprising him of the situation.

Watching the young lieutenant leave, Katie smiled and returned her gaze to her lover. "I do believe that young man would follow you to Hades if you asked him to."

"Don't forget 'and back,'" the colonel added, watching the door of her office. "He's one of the best officers I've ever had under my command. I trust him implicitly, and I'll do everything in my power to make sure we all come back." Dean turned to face Katie and peered seriously into her emerald eyes. "You don't have to go on this assignment, Katie. I have no supervisory control over you once this day is over."

"Ah, ah, ah. You can't get rid of me that easily. After all, I'll be on vacation too, and I think a trip to the islands is in order. Besides, three heads are better than one." Katie stopped and cocked her head to the side. "Do you suppose Tracy and Colleen will have room for a third person?"

"Hmm, I don't know. Guess I'd better give Trace a call and see what she thinks," Dean responded as she reached for her phone and punched in Tracy's work number. After a short wait she heard Linna answer on the other end. "Linna, it's Dean. Is Tracy in?" Once Tracy got on the line, she quickly summarized the situation and broached the question of Lieutenant Jarvis. Tracy assured her that the additional guest wouldn't be a problem.

"So, it looks like we may be having a little 'extra fun' on this trip?" Tracy questioned. "Hope you'll be able to use a couple of extra hands."

"You know, Trace, I can't ask you to help, but I did mention to General Carlton that we were going with you and Colleen, and she seemed to approve. Of course, she couldn't say anything in the affirmative at the time, but now with the unofficial status this operation has taken, I'm sure she'll feel better that we're not going it alone."

"Great," Tracy replied. "You know, since we've been going down there every year for the past few years, Col and I have made friends with a lot of locals. Some may even be helpful."

"Yeah. Well, we'll be contacting Art Lyons once we're there, and he'll have some contacts for us, too. Hopefully, we won't need a small army, and we'll be able to get this done ourselves. We'll just have to wait and see what happens once we're there. I'll call you again as soon as we have our arrival information. And Trace...thanks."

"No problem, Dean. Hey, after last winter...this'll be a cakewalk. Talk to you soon."

Hanging up, Dean looked up at Katie. "Well, looks like it's a fivesome. Now we just need to get lucky at the warehouse Sunday night."

The rest of the afternoon and all day Friday were spent clearing paperwork, reviewing what was known about the case to date, checking the list of equipment they had packed in the SUV, and what they would be taking from their private arsenals. General Carlton signed Lieutenant Jarvis' leave forms, gave Dean Art's phone number in the Bahamas, and finally, requested that she be kept up to date on their "vacation." At 1830 on Friday, they left the Pentagon to begin their vacations.

Chapter 11

"Hey, this is pretty good barbecue," Bill commented as he licked the sauce that had oozed onto his fingers, being very careful not to drop any on himself, or the new rug under the dining table that Dean and Katie had just purchased two weeks prior.

"Not as good as some of the places in Kansas City, but for an east coast barbecue, it's not bad," Katie said before she took another huge bite out of her sandwich.

Dean watched the two of them inhale their food with abandon, as she took another forkful of coleslaw chewing it slowly while she mentally prepared for the night's masquerade, her mind racing around several thoughts. *Hope we can find out some solid information tonight. Like what Gentry is up to in the first place. I hate going into a situation without enough pertinent facts. Damn, I wish we knew what kind of radar array Gentry was installing. Maybe tonight we can find out...maybe. I sure hate the thought of having to use Tracy or Colleen on this case. I'll be busy enough watching Katie's back. Good thing Bill's coming along. Maybe we won't have to use Tracy and Colleen at all. Maybe...* Dean was totally lost in her whirling thoughts until she felt a gentle nudge on her shoulder. Looking in the direction from whence the force came, she found emerald eyes searching hers.

"Uhh, umm. Sorry, just lost in thought," Dean answered the unspoken question. "Trying to get a handle on all this." She shrugged as Katie placed strong hands on her shoulders and began a gentle massage of the tight muscles she felt. "Umm, I'll give you twenty-four hours to stop that," Dean sighed as she relaxed into the massage.

"Well, love, if we had twenty-four hours, I'd be glad to oblige. Unfortunately, you'll have to get changed in about thirty minutes," her young lover informed her softly.

"Oh, in that case then, I'll give you thirty minutes to stop that." Dean turned to look at Katie, allowing a thin crooked smile to appear on her lips. "What's Bill doing?"

"He's cleaning up the kitchen, and then he's going to give Dirk a call. How about we go to the bedroom, and I'll give you a proper thirty minute massage?" Katie raised one eyebrow and gently blew a kiss into her lover's ear.

"Oooo, blow in my ear, and I'll follow you anywhere," Dean responded in a seductive voice.

"And back," came the blonde's sultry reply as they both stood and moved toward the bedroom.

Dean pulled the SUV into the convenience store parking lot and slipped into the slot next to the beat-up looking blue van. The driver's side door of the van opened, allowing Sergeant Major Tibbits to exit and wave at Dean and her crew. Putting the SUV into park and turning off the ignition, Dean opened her door and walked around to meet Tibbits who was swallowing hard at Dean's appearance. She was attired as she had been the previous Sunday, and the image she projected was one of subtle strength and palpable sexuality.

"Are you sure the general isn't going to get into trouble over this?" Dean asked, pinning Tibbits with her ice blue stare.

"You can ask her yourself," Tibbits replied as he backed away from the intense gaze. Dean swung around as she caught the movement of someone standing behind her, and came face-to-face with General Carlton.

"General." Dean nearly shouted at seeing her commander, and automatically came to attention. *Now how did she slip up behind me without my sensing her? Hmm, maybe my skills are losing their edge, or, maybe she's a lot better than I gave her credit for.*

"At ease, Colonel," the general said softly. "We don't want

to attract the attention of anyone around here now do we?"

"No, ma'am," Dean responded in a softer voice. "But..."

"Look, just consider this as a little unofficial help. I requested the van as a kind of 'shakedown cruise' to check out the new equipment that was installed a couple of weeks ago. I haven't had time to see it in operation, so I had Tibbits here pick it up so we could take it on a test run of sorts." She looked up at Dean and smiled. "You don't mind if I test it out on you, do you? You know, General's privilege and all. Besides, I wouldn't want Tibbits here to get into trouble for unauthorized use."

"No, ma'am. I just wouldn't want you to get in trouble for it, either," Dean answered honestly.

"Well, just let me worry about that. You worry about whatever it is you need to worry about tonight." She smiled as Bill and Katie joined them. "You two don't mind if I join you, do you?"

"Umm, no ma'am," Katie said smiling. *Now where in Hades are we all going to fit?* Katie thought as she recalled the cramped quarters inside the van. "Glad to have the extra company."

"Yes, ma'am, glad to have the extra company," Lieutenant Jarvis echoed.

Dean gave in and nodded, motioning for the general and Tibbits to enter the van. As the general passed Dean, she looked at her and winked saying, "Nice outfit, Colonel," bringing an immediate flush to Dean's neck and face.

"Thank you, ma'am," Dean replied, catching Katie's desperate attempt to refrain from laughing out loud, and silently sending a message to the young blonde that she'd better not. As Katie passed her lover on her way to the van, her twinkling eyes sent back a reply that she'd behave.

They dropped Dean off in the same place they had the previous week so she could begin her slow walk to work. By the time the colonel made it to the warehouse, the van was set up in its surveillance position with all systems operational. "Okay team, here we go," Dean remarked to no one as she walked into the warehouse parking lot.

Katie and Bill were in the chairs in front of the monitors, while the general and sergeant major opted to stay in the background to observe the workings of the new equipment and the skills of the threesome on this case. Katie was giving General Carlton and Sergeant Major Tibbits, a blow-by-blow account of where Dean was, and what to expect during the course of the next eight hours or so.

Burt smiled at Dean as "Maria" entered through the loading dock door. Dean returned the smile saying, "*Hola, Señor* Burt. *¿Qué usted quisiera que hiciera esta noche?*" Burt just looked at her with a blank expression, totally unsure of what she was asking. *Okay Burt, let's try it again.* "*¿Usted quisiera que trabajara aqui?*" Again, Burt had a blank expression on his face, so she added a few hand signals indicating lifting boxes and added, "*¿Trabajara aqui?*"

Burt at last caught on, and replied in the affirmative. "Ahh, *sí, sí.*" Burt nodded his head and led her over to the workbench to give her a back belt and work gloves. "You're one pretty lady," he said, smiling at her and nodding.

Dean just smiled back and said, "*Gracias,*" as she accepted the safety equipment before returning to the same station as the week before.

The night progressed pretty much as it had previously. As the forklifts brought new crates over to be transferred to the shipping containers, Dean took careful note of any that might have been opened and resealed. So far, the only boxes she noted that might have been opened were a few that were marked with a slight fold in the packing tape indicating that these were the ones examined by Bill and Katie a few nights ago. *Well, nothing looks out of place, yet. Maybe I'll get a chance to wander into the warehouse again. I wonder if the old bathroom trick would work twice? Hmm, no, better try something else.* Dean thought about several other options as she watched as much of the warehouse floor as she could without arousing suspicion. After about two hours of loading, the crew took a short break. One of the younger guys came up to her and asked if she wanted a soda. At first, following a failure to be understood, the young man almost gave up but instead tried one more time. He reached over and tapped her shoulder, motioning with his head and hands for her to follow him. *Okay,* Dean thought, *why not? If I remember correctly the Coke machine is up front. Maybe I can catch a glimpse as we walk up.*

"That's it, just follow me." The young man smiled at her as he led her to the Coke machine. "My name is Pete." He was a nice looking kid, about twenty-four or twenty-five years old. He was a little shorter than Dean, with blazing red hair that was definitely not from a bottle, and had a mass of freckles on his youthful face. His body build suggested he spent a lot of time lifting weights.

Dean wondered what a seemingly nice, clean-cut kid was doing in a place like this. *He sure doesn't look like the rest of these jerks. Wonder why he's working here?* Almost as though the young man could read her thoughts he started talking to her in a nervous tone of voice.

"Boy. I don't know what I'm going to do for a job after tonight. Burt said this was the last of the shipments, and that he wouldn't be needing any of us back after tonight." He looked up at Dean and smiled. "Too bad you don't speak English. You look like a nice person, not like some of these other jerks around here." His voice was quiet and almost conspiratorial.

Okay, Dean, careful here, he could be a plant trying to check me out after last time, she thought to herself as she gave the young man a blank look. When they got to the Coke machine, she reached in her pocket to find some change. Pete placed a hand on her arm and shook his head saying, "No, no. My treat." Then he put the coins in the machine and motioned to her to select her choice. *Well if he is a plant, at least he's got some manners.* Dean smiled at him, then punched the button for a can of grape juice, picking it out of the drop slot while he put more coins in, selecting orange juice for himself. Taking his can out of the drop slot, he reached up and tapped her can in a salute, before opening it and downing at least half of it. Dean opened hers with a nod and a "*Gracias*" before drinking half of her can, too. While they drank the rest of their juice more slowly, the young man continued to prattle on about the weather, lifting weights and his family, conscious the whole time that the woman sitting next to him probably didn't understand a word he said. He even took out his wallet to show her the pictures of his young wife and twin boys, who were miniature versions of their dad, minus the body building physique.

"Well, well," Bill said smiling, "looks like the colonel found a friend." They were all watching the blue dot move from the back of the warehouse to the front, and listened to the chatter as the young man attempted to make conversation with Dean. "Wouldn't he be surprised to find out she understands every word he's saying?"

"Do you suppose he's a plant?" Katie asked as everyone in the van listened to the conversation on the external speakers.

"He could be, but I'm sure the colonel has thought of that already," General Carlton cut in.

"Yeah, you're probably right," the young agent agreed. "But he really seems out of place here."

"Maybe he really is trying to support his family with this job," Tibbits offered. "It would make sense that they'd have to hire a few guys off the union rolls to keep suspicions down."

"Do you have their personnel files downloaded on this computer?" the general asked Katie.

"Yes, ma'am. Good idea." Katie swiveled around to face the computer and started entering codes on the keyboard. In a short span of time she was scrolling through the personnel files. "Let's see, there are two 'Peter's' listed in the files." She pulled up the first one scanning the personal information. "Nope, not this guy. He's originally from Brooklyn, and I'd lay odds he hasn't lost that accent yet." Looking at the next file she smiled. "Yep, this sounds more like our guy here. Name's Peter O'Brien. Lives in, oh get this, married student housing at Georgetown University. Hmm, he's twenty-seven, a student obviously, and is claiming three dependents on his W-4." Katie exited the personnel files and changed programs. "Okay, let's see what else we can find out about him." As she pulled up his file from student records at Georgetown, she whistled slowly. "Take a look at this. This guy carried a 4.0 in medical school, is currently a surgical resident at the hospital, has a wife and two kids, and seems to be working part time wherever he can. Wow! Look at those MCAT scores." She looked up at the three faces reading over her shoulder. "I don't think he's a plant." Three wide-eyed faces nodded back at her.

"Well, I guess we better be getting back to the dock." As he spoke, Pete motioned to Dean to follow him. As they walked back, Pete kept up his non-stop talk on all sorts of subjects, explaining that it was nice to have someone to talk to, even if she couldn't understand him. At that comment, Dean couldn't help herself and allowed the slightest smile to appear on her lips. About halfway back, Dean caught a glimpse of movement off to her right and recognized the same two guys from the previous Sunday working with an open crate. The contents of this crate were boxes of tin foil. *Wonder what they're smuggling this time. Must be something they want hidden in all that metal, safe from detection by any x-ray scanning devices. There must be at least ten crates of tin foil. Guess I'll have to tag each one with a scan chip. Getting away with planting a chip on one box could be tough, especially after last week. Getting away with ten chips...now that will test my skills.* Dean came out of her thoughts in time to see Golding watching her with a vigilant look. She turned to Pete and in a casual voice said, "*Gracias, Pete, para la bebida. Usted es un hombre muy bueno.*"

"Yeah, whatever you said," Pete replied laughing.

Dean joined in the laughter then said in halting English, "Thank you."

"You're welcome. Uh, I mean, *gracias*," he said back to her.

"No, no. *De nada*." Dean tried explaining. "*Gracias*." She pointed to her chest. "*De nada*." She pointed to his chest.

"Oh I get it, yeah, 'thank you' is *gracias* and 'you're welcome' is *de nada*." He started nodding his head in approval. "I'm not really a dope, I just never paid attention to foreign languages. I'm more of a math and science man. Plus, I took Russian, which doesn't resemble anything you're saying." He began chuckling again.

"*Si*." Dean said clapping him on the back. They continued to the loading dock smiling and laughing. During the rest of the night, Dean taught him several more words for simple things and short phrases. He was a very quick learner, and Dean was quite impressed, wondering even more what he was doing in a place like this. Their banter back and forth was just the distraction she needed to place the ten chips on the tin foil crates. When they returned to the dock, the others were paying her quite a bit of attention, but when she began her language lessons with Pete, they soon lost interest in anything that might be remotely educational. The rest of the night went quickly, and by the time the last shipping container was loaded, Pete was asking "Maria" if she would like to go for some breakfast after work, when Burt came up.

"That's it, guys. Last container truck is loaded. Time to

line up for your pay," Burt bellowed as he led the workers to the office area. Dean was last in line and was musing, W*ell, let's see if I get a raise this week,* when it was her turn to be paid. As she counted her cash on the way out, Burt came up to her and tapped her on the shoulder.

"Boss wants to see you," he said, motioning for her to follow him back to the office. Pete was waiting for her at the back door, and he heard Burt come up to her. When he made a move to go with them, Burt turned and told him to go home, in no uncertain terms. Dean turned and looked at Pete who was in the process of telling Burt he'd wait outside for her, when she caught his eye and shook her head, motioning for him to leave. Confused, the young man shrugged and stepped out the back door.

Chapter
12

"Wonder what this is about?" Bill asked as they watched Dean's blue dot return towards the office.

"Better fine tune that audio. We don't want to lose a word of this conversation," the general cautioned as she started to become concerned.

"Yes, ma'am." The young lieutenant reacted immediately, reaching for the audio dial.

As Burt led her to the office, Dean could feel her neck hairs start to bristle. *I don't think I'm gonna like this,* she said to herself and mentally began preparing for the worst by counting the guys left in the warehouse. *If they're just looking for a fun time...well...ten's a bit much, but somehow I don't think that's what's on their mind.* She began running through her options. *If they get me in that office, I won't be able to call for back up. Okay, time to improvise.* She stopped just outside the office door, refusing to enter.

"Inside." Burt shouted, pushing her towards the door. Dean shook her head and refused to move, causing Burt to shove her harder. "I said inside, bitch."

Dean turned and said "No. *Aquí.*" To which he shoved harder, while two other guys came up behind her to help, but stopped as Roger Golding came out of the office smiling evilly.

"Good evening, Colonel Peterson," he said as he walked around her. "You don't remember me, do you?"

Dean just continued to stare straight ahead and said, "*No comprende señor.*"

"Oh, drop the act, Colonel. I finally remembered who you were when I heard you laughing with that young dockhand. I did a little checking of my own tonight, and what did I find? Surprise, surprise, that young lieutenant I remembered is now a lieutenant colonel." He came back around to face her. "No, you wouldn't remember me, but I certainly remember you." He pulled back his fist then hit her square in the gut, causing her to bend over, but going with the blow that she had anticipated. As she stood, two of the guys behind her grabbed her to keep her from returning the action in kind. "I was on a supervised squad assigned to clean the recovery room after they patched you up. Must not have been a successful trip, eh, Colonel? That was just before they shipped me off to Leavenworth to do my time. But I remember your laugh. I heard you with that Patient Admin Officer as I cleaned the floor in the hall outside your room. Never liked intelligence officers. One of them put me in Leavenworth." He reached in his pocket, pulling out a handful of scanning chips. "Now, it's my turn to laugh. Look what my boys found on my special crates before the trucks left." Dean quickly counted them and mentally had the last laugh, noting that there were only seven in his hand.

"Hmm, wonder where those came from?" Dean asked, smiling at him. *Okay guys, any time now. I know I didn't say the* gringo ladrones *bit, but you should have caught on by now.*

"So, Scott had reason to worry about his shipment after all," Golding continued as he tossed the chips in his hand. "Well, too bad you won't be able to track it." Roger returned the smile as he dropped the chips to the floor and then made a show of crushing them with the heel of his foot.

Just about this time, Dean caught a movement in her peripheral vision. *'Bout time guys.*

She was just about to tell Golding what he could do with those crushed chips, when Pete came rushing out of the shadows and charged the guys holding her. *Damn it, Pete. You should have gone home.* His unexpected charge toppled both of the goons holding Dean, along with Dean and himself. Unfortunately, Pete hadn't had the presence of mind to check out how many other guys were still in the warehouse. Dean quickly regained her feet and managed to pull out her boot knives in the process. One knife immediately went flying into the shoulder of Burt, who was attempting to slam the butt of his pistol into Pete's head. The knife lodged deeply, causing him to drop his weapon, as well as giving Pete time to get back on his feet. Golding recovered from the attack quickly, pulling out his Glock, aiming it at Dean. He got off a round but missed her, as she dove for Burt's dropped weapon. His missed shot hit one of the guys behind her, as he was attempting to stand. The bullet sent him back to the concrete floor on a permanent basis. As three of the other guys came out of Golding's office with weapons drawn, Dean shot on instinct and managed to hit all three with disabling shots.

*Four down, one wounded, five to go...*Dean counted, as she spared a glance over at Pete who seemed to be holding his own with one of the other guys he'd knocked down. *Okay, make that five down, one wounded, four to go.* As she turned to focus her attention back on a wounded Burt and Golding, she noticed two thugs moving around to her left and behind the two forklifts that were parked there. The rest of the warehouse was nearly empty, and she and Pete had no place to hide. Burt, Golding, and another mercenary had retreated to the office to stay out of her line of fire as they began attempting to hit Dean and Pete with a fusillade from their weapons.

Damn, no place to hide except behind the bodies for now. She quickly told Pete to hide behind the big brute he had just subdued. He was totally surprised to hear her command in perfect English, but quickly did as she had instructed. Surveying their situation, she noticed a small trash dumpster by the bathroom to the right of the office, and estimated the distance to be under thirty feet. *Damn, where are those guys? Okay, we'll do this the hard way.*

"Stay where you are, Pete!" Dean shouted as she moved from her prone position and returned fire with two shots towards the office and two towards the forklifts. She raised herself into a sprinter's position and took off for the dumpster. Four weapons began sending shots in her direction as she ran toward her goal. Only one bullet came close to its mark, grazing her thigh as she dove behind the dumpster. As soon as she rolled up to her feet, she checked her clip to see how many rounds she had left. *Okay, one in the chamber and three in the clip, plus I still have my other boot knife. Gotta make them count.* She got behind the dumpster and began pushing it towards Pete, who was barely able to hide behind the guy he knocked out. The harder she pushed, the faster it began to roll. "Get ready," she shouted over the din of weapons firing in her direction. When she was within five feet of Pete, he leapt up and made it to the safety of the dumpster without a scratch.

"*Gracias*," he said as he reached her side. They began slowing the dumpster so they could reverse its direction.

"Give it up, Colonel. You'll never make it to the door. We've called for back up and they'll be waiting for you," Golding shouted from the office.

"Well, I wouldn't be too sure of that, Roger. What makes you think I didn't come with back up myself?" she shouted back.

"You do have back up, don't you, Maria?" Pete whispered.

"It's Dean, and yes, I do. I'm just not sure why they're not here yet," Dean answered, but stopped talking when she heard the sound of the forklifts' engines starting. "Uh oh. We're in trouble. Get ready to push this sucker towards the loading dock with everything you've got."

One forklift came directly at the dumpster while the second one swung around to cut them off from the side. Dean chanced a peek over the top of the dumpster and realized she didn't have a clear shot at either driver. "Now!" she shouted and began to push with all her might, but the forklifts were faster than she had hoped, and the one coming straight for them had lowered its tines. As soon as it made contact, it began to lift the dumpster up and away, exposing them to the drivers. When the dumpster was lifted and they were left without cover, Dean moved and stood in front of Pete, raising her hands. Both forklift operators now had them in their gun sights.

"Drop the gun," the man behind the second forklift shouted.

Dean did as she was told. "Let Pete go. He doesn't know anything. He just thought he was helping a woman in trouble," Dean asked quietly.

"Afraid we can't do that. Especially after he clobbered Freddie." The two men extended their weapons and aimed. Two shots rang out, and the two operators fell forward at their controls, blood spilling from the bullet holes in their heads. Pete wobbled a bit before he realized he was okay, then sat down on the concrete floor putting his head in his hands.

"Cutting it a little close?" Dean called out to the two figures coming around the forklifts. "What took you guys so long?"

"We figured he was going to take you into the office, so we decided the best approach—rather than slugging it out with his thugs at the front door—was to come in his back door, through the tunnel. He'd never expect that," Katie said, smiling as she walked over to where Pete was sitting. "Hi, Pete. My name is Katie O'Malley, and this is Lieutenant Bill Jarvis," she said extending a hand to him. "Thanks for trying to help out tonight. We didn't expect that move," Katie said shaking his hand.

"No problem." The young man stood, somewhat in shock at nearly being killed. He accepted Bill's hand too and shook it, still in a trance-like state. Finally, he shook the cobwebs away and asked, "Now, mind telling me what's going on here?"

"Well, we'll have to let the general decide that," Dean said as she picked up the gun she had dropped. "Where are Golding and Burt?" she asked Katie.

"Tibbits has them and another guy covered." She jerked her thumb over her shoulder. "The general should be here any minute with the van."

Dean nodded as she began walking back towards the office, noticing her injury for the first time. Pete noticed it too, and moved closer to take a look.

"Looks like it just grazed you," he said, looking up into her eyes with concern. "But we'd better take a closer look just to be safe."

"Yeah, well, I can tell you it ain't all that bad, and I refuse to go to a doctor to take care of it," Dean replied curtly.

"Colonel, you should probably know that Pete here is completing his residency at George Washington University Hospital. I think he can take a look to keep you from going to a doctor." Lieutenant Jarvis looked over at a completely baffled Pete and smiled. "I'm sure there's a first aid kit around here somewhere, and if not, there's one in the van we can use when the general gets here."

This recitation elicited a surprised look on both Dean and Pete's faces, stopping them in their tracks. Pete was the first to speak. "Just who are you guys?"

"Later, Pete," Dean said smiling at him. "I knew you didn't fit in here. I'm just surprised to hear how much you didn't fit in." At that moment, they heard the van pull up to the loading dock.

Pete turned and looked at his placid companions. "What if

their back up is out there? They might shoot at your general."
Alarm was clearly showing on his face.

"Nah." Dean told him as she began walking toward the
office once more. "He was just bluffing."

"How'd you know?" he asked, confused once more.

"If he'd had back up outside, they would have come running
at the first gunshot," the tall woman answered him politely.
"Now, how about you take a look at this scrape so I can get back
to work, okay?"

"Okay," Pete answered as he entered the office, where he
quickly scanned it for a first aid kit. He was a bit nervous about
the three mercenaries, but relaxed when he saw them cuffed and
under the watchful eye of another man he surmised was Tibbits.

Before Dean entered the office, she looked over at Bill and
Katie speaking softly and motioning with her head towards the
prone bodies on the warehouse floor. "Take a look at those other
guys. I think a couple of them might need Pete's help too, and
they'll need to be cuffed. Though one or two of them might be
beyond anyone's help."

It didn't take long for Pete to care for Dean's flesh wound
and Burt's shoulder. He said the latter would take a bit more
medical treatment than he was able to perform with a first aid
kit, considering that the point of the slim blade entered his
shoulder from the front and only striking the scapula stopped it
from penetrating his shoulder completely. After immobilizing
the shoulder and bandaging around the still embedded knife, he
instructed Burt not to move his arm. Then he went out to check
the guys in the warehouse, leading Burt and the other mercenary
out into the warehouse with him. General Carlton entered the
office, nodding to him as he exited with his two charges.

"Sorry it took so long, Dean. I had to get in a commander's
face before he would let them into the power station and down
the tunnel," the general explained. "We could have tried the outlet to the Potomac, but we didn't want to take the time to find
it."

"Just a little close for comfort, General, but everything
worked out okay. Any chance he was able to get in touch with
Gentry?" Dean asked.

"Not possible. We clipped the phone lines as soon as we

heard you in trouble," General Carlton informed her.

Dean nodded as she walked over to where Golding was now sitting alone. "Okay, Roger, now it's time to play show and tell. How about you tell us everything from the top?"

"Damn. That guy is good at keeping his mouth shut," Lieutenant Jarvis marveled as they watched the D.C. police take custody of the six mercenaries. The morgue vehicle had already taken the four dead bodies out. "It's a good thing Floyd will keep these guys on ice for us, and take care of the cover story."

"Yeah," Dean agreed, "when we get to the bottom of this, they'll be facing much more serious charges." She smiled at the young lieutenant. "At least we can still track the cargo. Golding only found seven chips. That means there are three of them still active."

"Hey, that Pete sure was a surprise," Katie interjected. "Imagine in this day and age, someone willing to come to the aid of a stranger in trouble. Of course, a beautiful stranger makes it a bit easier," she added with a wink at her lover.

"Cut that out. He's a happily married man," Dean countered with a raised eyebrow and smile of her own. "How long has he been in with the general?"

"Too long, if you ask me," Lieutenant Jarvis replied. "I wonder what kind of a line she's giving him." As they looked over at the warehouse office door, they saw Pete and the general emerge, chatting amiably.

"Well, whatever it was, he swallowed it hook, line, and sinker." Katie added, smiling and nodding her head. They continued to watch as General Carlton walked to the loading dock door with the young man and shook his hand before he exited the door. "Hmm, nice touch. Okay, any bets on the line she fed him?" Two heads shook in a negative response.

As General Carlton approached, Dean and Bill unconsciously assumed a stance of attention. "At ease," she commanded softly. "There are still a few policemen around, and I wouldn't want them to be curious about the cover story your friend Floyd is concocting."

"Yes, ma'am," came the twin responses, as each adopted a more relaxed posture.

"So what's the next step in the agenda for your vacation

plans?" she asked as they all walked back toward the van where
Tibbits was waiting, making sure none of the police officers
decided to check it out.

"Well, we leave for Freeport on Saturday morning, so that
gives us the rest of the week to track the cargo and figure out a
way to send our equipment through customs," Dean replied as
she opened the door for the general. Mary, Dean and Katie sat in
the back, while Tibbits and Bill took the front seats.

"Where to, General?" Tibbits inquired as he started up the
van.

"Take a long route back to the convenience store. And
watch for any tails," the general commanded.

Once they were situated and on the way, Dean turned on the
TDSC unit and the computer and initiated the commands to link
the TDSC unit to the satellite. This took a matter of minutes, but
soon the small screen was tracking a convoy of trucks unloading
at a dock in Baltimore where the shipment was being placed on
board a container ship.

"Looks like they're taking a direct route to the island. That
ship is flying a Bahamian flag," Dean noted as she pointed to the
described item on the computer screen. "They must be on a tight
schedule to be shipping directly there."

Katie considered this then added, "If they leave port on high
tide tonight, they should arrive in Freeport by Thursday night or
Friday morning, if they don't have any interim stops for additional cargo. We can check the ship's itinerary on the computer."
She noted the ship's signage and jotted it down. "General, is
there any chance you can keep the van checked out until we
leave?"

"That's doable. I'll just let them know I'm going to run
some scenarios with a new training team." General Carlton nodded. "The team that helped out in Las Vegas is due in D.C.
today. It'll be a good cover, plus," she added, looking over at
Dean, "it will allow you to keep the satellite link active."

"General, it's a shame you never got a chance at field work.
You're a natural," Dean commented as she continued her obser-
vation of the container ship, memorizing her details for later rec-
ognition. "Now we've just got to come up with a way to get our
equipment past customs."

"That's been covered, too," Mary revealed. "I pinned Art
down before he and Gwen left for the Bahamas and told them
everything we had to date. He was actually relieved to hear that

his suspicions were confirmed. We discussed you and Katie going there to do a bit more investigation and the equipment I wanted to send along. He contacted his friend in the British Embassy here, and they will pick it up on Thursday morning and ship it through their diplomatic channels."

"Great." Katie was relieved that they wouldn't have to try to sneak the stuff in or, worse yet, try to do without it. "Will we pick the equipment up from the British Embassy contacts?"

"No, Ned will. You'll have to pick it up from him," Mary answered. "Art has arranged to introduce you to Ned soon after you arrive. You'll be able to get the equipment then."

"Thanks, Mary," Dean continued. "I know the customs people are pretty relaxed there, but I sure wouldn't want to be the one visitor who gets their luggage checked, and have to explain hundreds of thousands of dollars of high tech military surveillance equipment."

Tibbits pulled into the convenience store, parking next to Dean's SUV. Mary suggested she return to the Pentagon parking facility for her car and then follow Tibbits out to Dean's house to drop off the van. She also suggested they meet there on Tuesday evening to discuss their investigation plans further. With that settled, Dean, Katie and Bill exited the van and got into Dean's SUV for the trip to Occoquan where Dirk was patiently waiting for them to arrive.

When Dirk and Bill left at 1300, Dean headed for the shower while Katie pulled KP duty cleaning up the dishes from the brunch Dirk whipped up. After the chore was done, she paused for some quality time with her feline charges.

"Hey guys," Katie cooed softly as she sat on teh floor and was immediately surrounded by her brood. "Guess you guys missed us last night, huh?"

"MEOW." cried Spice while Sugar and Butter were satisfied with a spot on Katie's lap and began purring loudly.

"Well, we're gonna have to go away for a bit," Katie continued as she stroked each cat in succession. "But don't worry, we won't leave you here alone. Mary–that's General Carlton to you guys–will be taking care of you for a while." Katie changed position on the floor so she could lean against the sofa while she kept up the conversation with the cats as she told them all about the general's house.

Dean finished her shower, dressed, and then went looking for Katie who was supposed to be following her to the shower as soon as the dishes were done. When she entered the living room, Dean found her partner sound asleep on the floor, head propped up on the sofa cushion, and three cats softly purring as they sprawled across her lap. Dean just took in the picture and smiled.

"I guess Floyd can just wait a couple of hours for us to meet with him," she whispered to no one in particular as she bent down and began carefully removing the cats. Next, she gently lifted Katie to place her on the sofa and cover her with an afghan. She tip-toed out to the kitchen to call Floyd about the change in plan. When she returned to the living room, she sat in her leather recliner intent on firming up the course of action for Floyd and his three charges. *Oh yeah. Enrico is going to love spending time with Roger and Burt,* she thought, chuckling softly as she slipped the recliner back all the way.

At 1800, Dean awoke with a start and looked around the room. She had a dream that she was having a heart attack and the pressure in her chest woke her. The dream was so real that she woke up gasping for air. When she looked down at her chest, she immediately realized the cause of her chest pain. Butter, in all her twenty pound glory, was lying in a tight ball directly in the middle of her chest.

"Guess it's a good thing you decided to perch yourself here, or I'd probably be sawing logs," Dean whispered to the cat as she stroked her fur. Checking her watch, she realized that they were already two hours late for their meeting with Floyd. "Best wake up your mom now, or we'll be even later for our meeting."

It took another forty-five minutes to get her groggy partner up and showered before they finally left to meet Floyd. When Dean called to alert him as to the reason they were late, he just laughed and told her not to worry. Unfortunately, it made for another late night since they didn't get back to the house until 2330, but Dean was satisfied that the cover story on Roger and Burt's whereabouts would hold until they could figure out just what was going on in the Bahamas.

Chapter
13

1700 Hours, 7 November

"Wow," Katie commented as she rolled over in bed and stretched. "I feel like I could stay in bed for forty-eight hours." It had been a short nap, since they only crawled into bed five hours previously. "I think we really need a vacation."

"When this is over, love, I promise we'll go somewhere that no one will be able to find us." Dean, already dressed in jeans and an Army sweatshirt, strolled over to the bed and sat beside her young lover. She reached out and stroked Katie's hair, brushing a few errant strands from her eyes. Bending down, she gave Katie a soft kiss before helping her sit up. "I know a nice resort down in Aruba where we can just lie on the beach and watch the waves come in."

"Mmmm, sounds nice. Should be good and warm there too, now that winter is nearly here again." Katie reached over to pick up Dean's hand, placing a kiss on the palm. "Of course, I don't have to worry about being warm with you next to me. You're my own personal heater no matter where we are." She snuggled closer as Dean put her arms around her in a gentle hug. "Yeah, we could be in an igloo in Alaska, and you'd still be able to keep me warm."

"What can I say? I've just always been a hot number," Dean teased with a wry smile that earned her a playful slap on the stomach. "Better get showered and dressed, love. They'll be here pretty soon. I'll whip something up in the kitchen while you get ready."

"Oh? I hope it'll be edible." Katie's comment was greeted with a raised eyebrow as Dean headed off toward the kitchen.

Katie couldn't believe the aromas coming from the kitchen as she entered. "Mmmm, that smells wonderful. What is it?"

"Just a little something I picked up in Italy. I've adjusted the ingredients a bit more to my liking, but it's simple, quick, and a substantial meal. I call it 'Pasta Fagioli a la Dean.'"

"Sounds interesting, and you made enough to last a week. So, what's in it?" Katie picked up a spoon and tasted the food, smiling as she recognized Dean's penchant for hot peppers.

"Just onions, garlic, Italian spices, tomatoes, beans, tubetti pasta, some olive oil and..."

"Hot peppers!" Katie finished as she fanned her mouth. "What's in the oven?"

"Bruschetta. I conned Gino out of his recipe before we left the Catskills."

"Oooo, I loved Gino's bruschetta." Katie eagerly opened the oven to see if they were done.

"Give them another minute, and they'll be ready. How about opening a bottle of Montepulciano to go with the meal?" Dean suggested.

Katie walked over to the wine rack and selected the bottle as the front door chimed. Setting the bottle down, she walked to the foyer and peeked out the side window. Outside, General Carlton, Bill, Dirk, and three other persons were patiently waiting. Katie opened the door and invited them all in. The guests immediately began sniffing the air. As Bill and Dirk made their way to the kitchen, General Carlton introduced Major Fellows, and Lieutenants Wilson and Petri from the training unit.

"Nice to meet you." Katie extended her hand to each as they were introduced. "We were just getting ready to have a bite to eat. Dean made enough for an army, no pun intended, so why don't you join us?"

"Thank you, Katie," General Carlton said as they followed the young woman to the kitchen. "We'd appreciate that."

As the group sat around the large kitchen table enjoying the meal, they discussed the current location of the shipment. The *Island Queen* was stopping in Miami Thursday night to pick up more cargo before heading the short distance from there to Freeport. The loading would take place all day Friday, and the crew would have shore leave Friday night. A few crew members always remained on board for ship security. The ship was then scheduled to leave Miami on Saturday at 1500 hours, with an anticipated docking in Freeport at 2300 hours.

"That seems like a long time for such a short distance," commented Lieutenant Wilson. "Do they have to wait at sea for an unloading berth at the container port?"

The group considered the plausible explanation before Dean picked up the conversation. "We'll be landing in Freeport on Saturday at 1230. Tracy and Colleen are meeting us at the airport. We should be able to watch the arrival and unloading from the boat Tracy has chartered. My concern is that I'm not comfortable with the placement of those three TDSC chips. If they come loose during the unloading, we might lose precious time trying to track the package." Dean looked around the table before continuing. "I want Katie, Bill, and I to board the *Island Queen* on Friday night when the majority of the crew will be on shore. We need to find the crate with the package and insert another TDSC chip inside it." She looked at General Carlton, before turning her attention to Major Fellows. "Major, how would you and your team like to be a diversion while we do our dirty work?"

"I think that could be arranged. It will be a weekend, and we'll technically be off-duty, so a trip to Miami might be nice." The major looked around the table to see his two lieutenants beaming back at him. "I need to get some flight time in, so I'll check on scheduling a plane for the trip." General Carlton nodded her approval, and the group began planning the diversion.

By 0130 hours, everyone had left Dean's house for his or her own home. Katie was just finishing the clean up in the kitchen when Dean returned from setting the security alarms.

"All locked up for the night," Dean commented as she slipped behind Katie and enveloped her in a hug. "What's your opinion of tonight's plan?"

"I think it will work fine, but we'll need to find that crate fast. I'm not sure how long the ruse will withstand close scrutiny." Dean gently turned Katie around in her arms to look at her. "I know the general believes in the integrity of the Bahamian crew members, but a lot will depend on how convincing Lieutenant Wilson's act is. She definitely has the looks for the part."

"I don't think we'll have to worry too much about her acting abilities." Dean grinned at her lover like the Cheshire cat. "She did a lot of theater work in college, and has been acting in summer stock since she was eight."

"Really?" Emerald eyes searched the sapphire blues peering at her. "And you know this because..." Letting the sentence fade, she cocked an eyebrow at her lover.

"Because, I checked her file after the Las Vegas assignment. Major Fellows' report on the action was very detailed and quite approving of her undercover skills. I thought it would be good information to have for future reference." Dean returned the raised eyebrow look to her lover.

"So, you checked her out, eh?"

"Yes, as well as everyone else in the training group. Why? Does she bother you?"

"Nope, just as long as she doesn't make a play for you." Katie smiled as she tipped her head back in time to receive a very passionate kiss from Dean.

"Does that set your mind at ease?" Dean asked as her lips barely left Katie's.

"I don't know. Let's try that again."

Dean obliged her lover as she placed another scorching kiss on her lips, while reaching down and lifting Katie off the floor and into her arms. She opened one eye during the kiss to make the walk to the bedroom in safety. Stepping up close to the bed, she gently laid Katie down before stretching out alongside.

"Mmm, that was nice," Katie murmured as she stroked Dean's cheek with her left hand.

"If you think that was nice, just wait." Dean reached over and slowly began unbuttoning Katie's blouse, kissing each inch of bare skin that appeared. As articles of clothing littered the bed and surrounding floor, desires were awakened, sending messages of passion and pleasure that were received and answered throughout the night.

Wednesday and Thursday were spent in preparation for the execution of the plan. Fellows, Petri, and Wilson went through the attempted rape scene several times until even Katie was convinced by the action. Dean, Katie and Bill made a few practice dives near the Navy Yard and even simulated the grueling ship boarding via a rope and grappling hook. Petri would lower this rope, while Wilson and Fellows kept the security crew occupied elsewhere. In case he couldn't accomplish this, Bill would be carrying a small air powered gun that would be used to send a line and hook over the rail from the water. After practicing his technique, he was confident that he would be able to hit his target on Friday night. They would each carry a prototype weapon that combined the effects of a stun gun and knockout gas, and several TDSC chips. No one wanted any of the crew to get hurt during the episode, but they had to be prepared for a worst case scenario.

By Friday morning, everyone was satisfied with their role and ready to put the plan into action. The last things Dean and Katie had to do were to transport the cats to General Carlton's for the duration and finish packing for their vacation. General Carlton had already sent the equipment to Freeport via the British Embassy, and Art had called to thank her for the "presents" she'd sent, thus reporting their safe arrival.

Before splitting up, the entire team was flying to Miami with Major Fellows in the Lear jet he had chartered. At 1600 hours they would be landing at Miami International. Dean, Katie and Bill would be staying the night at the Airport Hilton so they could catch the 11:00 a.m. flight to Freeport. Fellows and his team would spend the rest of the weekend at South Beach before returning to D.C. Sergeant Major Tibbits had arranged for two plain vans to be picked up at the Hertz lot, and the rendezvous near the shipping piers was set for 2100 hours.

Chapter 14

2145 Hours, 10 November

The dark van came screeching around the corner of the warehouse, skidding to a stop in front of the *Island Queen* boarding ramp. The back door of the van slammed open and a disheveled woman staggered out, fell, got to her feet and began running up the ramp screaming for help. She was followed almost immediately by a tall, older man who scrambled out of the driver's door of the van, and a younger man from the back of the van. The younger man, slowed in his pursuit by his need to pull his jeans on, yelled after the woman.

"Hey, bitch! Get the fuck back here now, or you're really gonna be sorry!" He was screaming at the woman who was now halfway up the gangway, waving her arms as two crew members from the *Island Queen* ran toward the ramp.

The older man was gaining on the woman who was almost at the end of the ramp. "Damn it, Connie! Get the fuck back here!" Fellows was yelling, as Petri finally caught up.

Once Tina hit the deck of the *Island Queen*, she started running toward the bow of the ship with two crewmen and Fellows close behind. Petri yelled that he would cut her off on the other side, then turned to move around the pilothouse and headed toward the stern. As he came to the opposite side of the ship, Petri checked for any other crewmen before he slipped the rope ladder out from under his jacket, attached the hook and dropped the line over the side. As soon as he'd checked the security of the hook, he ran toward the bow where two crewmen were in the process of restraining Fellows. As he approached, two more crewmen grabbed Petri and "act two" of the diversion began.

Dean, Katie, and Bill were steadily swimming toward the *Island Queen's* stern when they heard the screech of the tires and the shouting begin.

"Okay, let's put a little more effort into this," Dean ordered softly, directing her two partners to increase the pull of their strokes.

As they reached the area designated for boarding, Dean looked up in time to see a nylon rope ladder uncoil towards her. She reached up and grabbed the end of the rope to stop its swing. They each took off their fins and tied them to the bottom of the ladder.

"Let's move." Dean reached up for the first loop in the rope and began the laborious process of climbing. The rope ladder was very narrow, and foot placement took time, but the trio managed to slip over the rail in under three minutes. "Okay, remember the container we're looking for is bright blue and numbered with a large 53F on its door. It should be midship and on the bottom row. Move out."

They each took a different row of containers to search. Dean found the container in the second aisle she checked. Taking out her dive knife, she tapped the container with the hilt once, then followed it with two more taps before replacing the knife. By the time she had the lock picked open, Katie and Bill were at her side. Opening the container door, Dean told them to look for the crates of tin foil. After carefully opening and resealing three of the crates, Bill found the one with the package in it. They removed the package from its cavity with great caution and placed it on the floor of the container. It was sheathed in a waterproof bag, similar to the type one would use on a canoe trip to keep the gear dry.

"Can we take it out without anyone knowing?" Katie asked, as Dean extracted some TDSC chips from her belt.

"We'll have to insert the chips." Dean meticulously removed the waterproof carrier and found the package encased in ordinary bubble wrap. "Whatever this is, it's pretty lightweight."

Carefully opening the protective cushioning, the trio was surprised to see two dozen computer motherboards, each wrapped in a foam envelope.

"I wonder what these are for?" Bill commented as Katie noted the identification numbers on one of the boards. "At least the TDSC chips won't look out of place with this stuff."

Within ten minutes, they were back in the water swimming toward the next pier and their waiting van. The nylon ladder was safely stowed in Bill's mesh bag, leaving no trace of their intrusion on the *Island Queen* to be discovered.

"Hey that was a good idea to have the MP's show up." Bill was toweling off his hair as he came through the connecting door between their hotel rooms.

"Yeah. Having the MP's show up and arrest Fellows and Petri on that AWOL charge was very convincing," Dean added. "They cut it kind of close though. We barely were over the side, when the crew resumed their security patrol."

"Good thing you remembered which container had the crate with the package." Katie looked over at Dean and gave her a broad smile. "At least now we'll be certain of tracking those boards."

"Yeah, but we won't be able to do any tracking if we don't get some sleep so we can get to our plane on time. Lights out," Dean ordered, causing Bill to dutifully return to his room and switch off his lights. Katie crawled under the covers, while Dean got up and doused their lights, too. Soon, the sounds of slumber were emanating from three very tired people.

Chapter
15

"There they are." Colleen shouted as she saw Dean and Katie come through the Customs gate. "Welcome to Freeport. Your carriage awaits." Colleen waved her hand towards the street, indicating the snappy Toyota Pathfinder that Tracy had rented. The four women exchanged hugs as a rather shy Bill stood by quietly.

"Oh, hey guys, this is Bill Jarvis." Katie swatted the quiet man on his abdomen with a gentle slap. "He's a little shy at first, but he'll get over it fast." After introductions were made, the group gathered up their luggage and headed for the SUV.

"I think we're in for some good weather," Colleen commented as she pulled out chanting: "To the left, to the left."

Tracy noted the expressions of confusion on the faces of their three passengers. "For the first couple of days we repeat that mantra to remind ourselves to drive on the left," Tracy explained, chuckling. "After a while it gets pretty easy, and you only have to be real cautious at intersections."

"Guess I'll leave the driving to you, then," Katie said laughing. "I'd probably have a wreck."

"Nah," Dean said patting her lover's thigh. "You just have to learn to concentrate."

It was a short ten-minute drive to the resort where Tracy and Colleen owned a timeshare. Colleen drove like a veteran down the back road, as the four women and the lone man chatted about their respective flights in.

"Did you guys see that hydrofoil when you flew in?" Katie asked, wide-eyed.

"Yeah. Pretty cool, eh?" Tracy answered, turning in her seat to face her guests. "There's daily service from Freeport to West Palm Beach on that. Takes about two hours."

"It must really be cruising," Dean commented, "but I prefer the thirty minute flight myself."

After slowing to make a partial turn around a small traffic circle, Colleen sped up again, heading down a divided road that was lined with palm trees and ran parallel to the ocean. There was absolutely no traffic on this stretch of road, and soon they were turning in to the resort that was located at the very end of it. There were two buildings three stories high, with one side of the apartments facing the ocean, and the other side facing the pool and intercoastal waterway. This year, they were assigned a ground floor apartment on the end of the first building. Across the road was a path leading to the private cove that the resort owned.

"Wow! This is really nice." Katie beamed as she got out of the car, taking in the sun, palm trees, and ocean. "Is this the only resort in this area?"

"Yep. Most of this end has private housing developments. There's one apartment complex down the road, and that one restaurant we passed. Otherwise, it's pretty quiet and secluded here," Tracy explained to the trio. "Hope you weren't looking for a lot of action. If you are though, it's only seven miles that-a-way." She pointed back down the road they came in on. "We'll take you on the grand tour later, but right now, let's get you into something more appropriate for the island...like bikinis."

Dean looked over at her old friend and shook her head. "You lecherous old woman you."

Tracy just grinned, nodding her head shamelessly in the affirmative and causing them all to break out in laughter. They gathered up the luggage one more time, and took it into the condo before taking a quick tour of the resort property. The back side of the complex was lush and green, with a pool begging for customers. The waterway behind the resort was clear and blue, and a variety of tropical fish could be seen swimming along the concrete sides of the man-made waterway. "No Swimming"

signs were posted at various points, and a huge cabin cruiser
came quickly into view to reinforce the "no swimming in the
waterway" rules. The land on the opposite side of the waterway
was barren of buildings, except for a marina located about five
hundred yards further down on the left. The main entrance to the
Grand Lucayan Waterway was off to the right. That part cut
straight through the island, so boats wouldn't have to go all the
way around to get to the other side. Dean surveyed the land,
marveling at the engineering that it had taken to build the connecting waterways.

"I can see why you like it here," Dean said approvingly.
"So where are the other guests?"

"Most of them like to go where the action is. Very few hang
out here. The place isn't full this week, or next for that matter,
so it will be fairly quiet," Colleen explained. "Except for the
kids. There's a family with four kids that is usually here the
same time we are. They're getting older now, and a bit quieter
too, but they're still kids doing kid things."

They continued the walking tour around the complex, past
the tennis courts, then across the road to the cove. There were a
few downed trees still lying about, remnants of the hurricane
that had barely touched the island, but they were in the pine for-
est and not obstructing the beach or the cove.

"The beach actually has more sand than last year. The
direction of the hurricane helped bring it in." Tracy kept up her
tour guide's recitation as the group walked to the very opening
of the Grand Lucayan Waterway. "This is the beginning of the
cut-through for boats getting to the other side. I have a map
back at the condo that gives you a better picture of all the inter-
connecting waterways. Being so close to the inlet will be an
advantage for tonight."

"Speaking of tonight, what kind of boat did you manage to
line up for us?" Dean was hoping that it would be more than a
three man Zodiac.

"Gee, funny you should mention that. Here comes the *Lady
Luck* now." Tracy pointed out at a white speck that was heading
toward the inlet. "I hope you won't be too disappointed. It's the
best I could do with such short notice."

Dean, Katie, and Bill kept their eyes pinned on the white
yacht that was quickly approaching. As it came closer, their
jaws dropped lower and lower.

"You have got to be kidding," Bill croaked, as the yacht

entered the waterway. "That baby has to be at least 50 feet long."

"65 feet to be exact." Tracy was really enjoying the expressions on her friends' faces. "It'll sleep eight and has room for a crew of two. Has a top speed of 25 knots, and is loaded with all the techno toys, too."

"Umm, Trace, did I remember to tell you this was an unofficial op? I don't think we can afford that beauty." Dean's expression was one of a deer caught in headlights. She was absolutely frozen to the spot, drinking in the lines of the graceful yacht before her.

"Yep, you certainly did, but don't worry, this one you can afford because we have use of it for free." Tracy waved at the captain as the boat slowed considerably. "The owner is even throwing in his crew for as long as we want. He'll be away for a month."

"So, who is our mysterious benefactor?" Katie asked, still in awe.

"I told you we had made a lot of friends down here. Nick Davos is a retired oilman from Texas. He was also a Navy Seal during Vietnam so we can count on the discretion of him and his crew—Tom and Tiny. They're also ex-Seals. That's Tom at the controls." She waved once more as the yacht prepared for its turn into the waterway behind the resort. "Let's head back, and we'll introduce you."

With the introductions over, the group returned to the condo to unpack before meeting Arthur and Ned to claim their equipment for the op.

"Hey, Tracy," Katie looked at the older woman, "how did Tiny get that nickname? He's anything but tiny. He must be at least six foot eight and three hundred pounds."

"Um, all I can say is: don't ask," Tracy replied with a chuckle.

Tracy drove Dean and Katie to Ned's office while Bill and Colleen stayed behind with Tom and Tiny. The office was located in downtown Freeport above the British American Bank on East Mall Drive. They pulled into the lot behind the bank and decided to take the rear entrance up to Ned's office, so they wouldn't arouse any curiosity or suspicion as they left with their cases of equipment. When they entered, an island woman named Corina had them sit in the outer office while she informed Ned of his visitors. Dean made a quick scan of the outer office and recognized several high tech security devices in the room, insuring the safety of the occupants. Spotting the hidden camera lens, Dean smiled into it and waved.

"Who are you waving at?" Katie asked as she looked around the empty room.

"I would assume, Ned and Corina," Dean replied, still smiling. At that moment, the door to Ned's office opened and Corina reappeared, followed by Ned and Art.

"I say, we can't put anything over on you, eh Colonel?" Art commented as he reached over for her hand. "Welcome to Grand Bahama Island." He turned to the local MI 6 representative and said, "Ned, two of these lovely ladies are the ones who saved my life."

The three visitors stood exchanging handshakes and introductions, then were led into Ned's office. The three cases of equipment were stacked in the corner of the office, still sporting their diplomatic pouch locks and papers. Ned indicated they should have a seat at the round table in the opposite corner.

"Any trouble with our equipment coming through?" Dean inquired as they sat on comfortable leather chairs around the conference table.

"Oh, no. Not at all," Ned answered. "It came in yesterday afternoon." Looking at the cases and the three women, he added chivalrously, "They're quite heavy you know. I can get someone to load them up for you if you'd like."

"Don't bother. We loaded them ourselves so we can handle them, but thank you."

"Is there anything else we can help with?"

"Well, I'm not sure what all we might need, but if we forgot anything, I'll give you a call," Dean replied appreciatively.

"A couple of friends of mine will be helping us out while we're here. You may know them," Tracy interjected. "Tom Zedos and Tiny Freeman. They work for Nick Davos."

"Ah, yes. Of course we know them. Mr. Davos is a good friend of the Minister, and we've had occasion to um, use the services of Mr. Zedos and Mr. Freeman on a few sticky drug smuggling cases." Ned looked over at Art and nodded. "Art here has an ongoing poker game with Nick whenever they meet at the casino."

"Yes, yes, that's right." Art reached inside his jacket pocket and pulled out a small note pad, flipping it open. "Right now, he owes me one hundred thousand pounds." The women raised their eyebrows at the huge amount of debt. "Of course, last year at this time," he flipped back through a few pages, "I owed him three million pounds." Chuckling he returned the note pad to his inside pocket. "Jolly good fun. No money exchanges, we just keep track for needling purposes."

"Bragging rights, huh?" Dean smiled at Art's pleased nod, then redirected the focus of the conversation. "Well, we'd better get this stuff to the condo. There are several items that will have to be reassembled. Thank you, Ned. Art, please say hello to Gwen for us." They stood and walked over to the cases as Ned produced a two-wheeled dolly from his closet.

"Here, this will help." He slipped it under the cases then gave Dean a business card. "This is my cell number. I always have it on. If you need anything, just give me a call. We have quite an impressive storehouse of equipment in the basement of this building, and if we don't have what you need, we can get it for you."

"Thanks," Katie responded as she gave Art a hug. "I hope we have time to get together after this is all over."

The older man blushed as he released Katie's hug. "My yes. Gwennie would love to have you over to the house for tea."

By the time they returned and stowed the equipment on the yacht, it was almost time to head out to monitor the arrival of the *Island Queen*. Even though the weather forecast for the night was for calm seas and a full moon, Dean wanted to be on location before sunset. Tom and Tiny had set up the stern with downriggers so anyone viewing the yacht would assume the group was out for some night fishing.

"According to the shipping charts, the *Island Queen* should be passing our bow about a quarter mile ahead." Dean was looking at the nautical charts in the pilothouse and working on an estimated time of arrival. She frowned as she refigured the arrival time, and rechecked the figures once more. "This isn't adding up. According to the Port Authority, the *Island Queen* should be arriving at 2000 hours, not 2300 hours. Let's head out a bit and see if we can find her."

It was about thirty minutes before they located their target on the yacht's radar screen and made some adjustments to run a parallel course. Turning on the TDSC unit, they were able to confirm the presence of the package. As they traveled along, it soon became apparent that the ship was veering out of the shipping lane and heading past the container port located on the west end of the island. Forty-five minutes later the big container ship began turning to head back towards the container port.

"Well, that explains the difference in arrival times," Dean commented as they watched the ship turn on the radar screen. "Now why did they come out this far past the port before heading back in?"

"That's why." Bill was pointing at the TDSC monitor as he observed a very stationary blue dot. "They offloaded the package."

"Where?" Katie came over to the monitor, and then checked the radar screen before checking the nautical charts. "There's nothing out there. Do you suppose another boat picked it up?"

"Nothing showing on radar." Dean shook her head as she rechecked the radar and TDSC screens. "Nope, it's just stationary." Dean turned to Tom and asked if the radar would be able to pick up small craft. Tom nodded, adding that if it were bigger than a jet ski, it would be on the scope. "Well, it just doesn't make sense that they'd just dump it overboard. Let's get a little closer and see what's there." Tom made the course adjustments and within minutes they were right on top of the blue dot.

"I'll be damned," Bill commented as he searched the sea around him. "What the hell is going on here?"

Just when they were about to drop anchor and find out, Katie called out that the dot was on the move. Dean moved over to the TDSC monitor and watched the dot slowly progress toward land, while Bill and Tom did visual and radar scans for any pick up boats.

"Start recording its progress," Dean told Katie as she walked back over to where Tom and Bill were standing. "Any visuals?"

"Nope," they both replied in unison.

"Well, obviously it's been picked up by a scuba diver." Heads nodded in agreement. "Any ideas where it might be going?"

Tom was the first to answer. "This area is noted for its underground caves." He pointed towards the shore that was outlined by white sand. "That area of the island is the Lucayan National Park. The little island you see in front of us has one of the two known 'wet' entrances to this underground system of caves. To date there are over ten kilometers of mapped passages. My bet is they're using that system to smuggle their stuff onto the island."

"Why not just use one of the deserted waterways? Wouldn't that be easier?" Katie asked, looking up from the monitor.

"That would work for one-time drops, but not drops on a regular basis. The risk of being caught would be too high. This way, nobody sees anything. The only reason we caught on, was because of the scanning chip," Dean explained as she realized the uniqueness of their drops. "Where do you think they're headed, Tom?"

"That's a tough one. Ben's Cave is the most well-known 'dry' entrance, but it's in the National Park, so I'd rule that one out. There are two others, but they're out in the open and they'd risk the possibility of being spotted. My guess would be that they found a new blue hole that no one knows about." As an afterthought he queried, "How far can you scan with this portable set up, Dean?"

"Unfortunately, not as far as we'd like. We can't use the satellite hook up since this is an unofficial op, so we're limited to the portable's range, which is about one kilometer, maybe less if they go very deep."

"That's a real possibility. Some of these passageways are three hundred feet deep." He was about to say something else when Katie called to them.

"Hey, the dot is getting fainter. It looks like it's going to fade out."

"Keep the tape going in case it comes up again." Dean turned to Tom. "Can you take us closer to shore? Maybe we can pick it up again."

"Sure thing," he replied. He started up the engine and began a slow troll towards shore. "Best you guys get on deck near the fishing equipment, just in case you're being watched from shore."

Tom took the boat in as close as he could. Unfortunately the tide was out, and this area was very shallow to begin with. Just before they headed back to the Grand Lucayan Waterway, a faint blue dot started to reappear on the monitor, but was soon gone from the screen. Its last position was noted on the chart at approximately one kilometer east of the national park, and still moving toward land.

Chapter
16

After a short rest at the condo and a quick breakfast, the trio boarded the *Lady Luck* and began poring over the charts. Bill and Dean spent the first hour transposing the tape-recorded course of the TDSC chip onto the ship's charts, including its last faded sighting.

"Now what, Colonel?" Bill asked as he traced the penciled line with his finger.

"Now, we go on gut instinct," Dean explained. "And my gut tells me they're probably headed here." She placed her index finger on a point on the chart.

"Makes sense," Katie spoke up. "We know one of the packages was a piece of a radar array, and what better place to use it than on a non-operational USAF missile tracking base."

Dean went over to the portable TDSC unit and selected a handheld monitor similar to the units the training team used in Las Vegas. "Anyone interested in a little ultralight sightseeing?" Katie and Bill looked at her quizzically, and then smiled as they stood to join her. "I saw an ultralight hangar at the airport when we landed. Let's go check it out. Katie, you'd better grab a lightweight jacket." Dean grabbed an old long sleeved T-shirt and her wrap-around glasses before disembarking from the boat.

Leaving a request with Tom and Tiny for scuba gear, the trio picked up Tracy and Colleen and headed to the airport. They all drove out to the airport where Tracy and Colleen dropped the trio off at the Bahama Buggies rental office before heading into town to pick up some groceries. Bill, Dean, and Katie went into the rental office to see if a buggie was available.

"Don't you think it would be better to get a regular jeep?" Katie asked Dean as they left the car rental agency.

"Nah, this is much more 'touristy' for ventures into the brush. We'll blend in better."

Katie looked around the small bustling airport and noted several of the open-air buggies loaded with tourists eager to explore off road. "Yeah, I see what you mean."

Once their vehicle was delivered, Dean instructed Bill to head to the gas station and pick up a five-gallon can and fill it with premium unleaded. Then he was to meet them on the Grand Bahama Highway, ten kilometers east of the Grand Lucayan Waterway, where an unpaved road met the highway.

Before he left on his errand, Dean gave Bill the duffel bag she brought from the condo. "We'll just walk over to the ultra-light hanger from here. That will give you a little extra time to get the gas and get out to the rendezvous spot."

"Okay, just follow my lead and let me do all the talking," Dean whispered as they entered the small hangar.

"I sure hope they have a double. I've never flown an ultralight." Katie's reply fell on deaf ears as Dean was already inside and striking up a conversation with the owner. Not wanting to interrupt, Katie wandered around the hangar inspecting the small aircraft that were in various stages of repair and maintenance. *Gee, these things are really cute. Not much different than a go-cart. Wonder what it would be like to fly one.* Walking over to the counter, she spied a souvenir rack and purchased two "Bahama Ultralights" baseball caps, figuring they would help keep their hair out of their eyes during the upcoming flight. Dean finished the negotiations for the rental and called over to Katie to join her.

"Here ya go, Dean." Katie said, handing her the hot pink ball cap. "Touristy enough?"

"Nice touch, and practical." Dean took the cap from Katie and put it on backwards, then reached up, and reversed the lime green one Katie had put on. When she got a quizzical look from Katie, she explained that the wind would take it off their heads if they wore it with the bill to the front. The two women then followed the rental agent to their waiting ultralight.

It didn't take long for Katie to get rid of the butterflies that had congregated in her stomach, and relax enough to begin enjoying the flight. Soon, the duo was slowly making their way towards the old USAF missile tracking base in a lazy serpentine path. From their moderate height of one hundred and fifty feet, they were able to see the majority of the width of the island, which was only sixteen miles at its widest point, and were almost to their rendezvous point just past the Grand Lucayan Waterway. It was now 1000 hours and traffic on the east side of the waterway was non-existent. Few tourists venture to Lucayan National Park their first day on the island. Most tended to gravitate to the hot spots of Xanadu Beach and Port Lucaya before they attempted the twenty-six mile journey to the park. Their ultralight had enough fuel to reach the tracking base, but they would need to put down and refuel to get back to the airport. Before they lifted off, they decided to make two pit stops to be on the safe side—one on the way out, and one on the way back. As they approached the rendezvous, Dean indicated to Katie with a hand signal that she was going to land. The colonel did another circle around the area, making sure there was no traffic in sight, before she came in for a landing.

"Wow. That's really a lot of fun," Katie exclaimed to a waiting Bill. "I never thought I would enjoy flying in an ultralight, but now I can see why people love it."

As Bill refueled the craft, Dean went over to the dune buggy and pulled the duffel bag out of the backseat, securing a set of com units, the portable TDSC tracking unit, digital camera, a small back pack, and her H & K Mark 23. She clipped the waistband holster at the small of her back before taking the other items back over to where Katie and Bill were discussing the flight. She put the tracking unit and the camera in the backpack before slipping it on. Handing a com unit to Katie, Dean told Bill they would use tack 3 for communication, and he should remain at that point unless directed otherwise.

"We'll follow this unpaved road toward the base. If we need help, stick to this road to find us."

"Got it." Bill helped steady the ultralight while the two women got settled and strapped in for take-off. "Just try not to get in trouble, Colonel. I don't feel like taking on any mercenaries today." The entire stop took only ten minutes. They lifted off and were back at their cruising altitude before Katie spoke into her com unit.

"I see you came prepared," Katie commented as she gently tapped the H & K in Dean's waistband. "Expecting trouble?"

"Nope, but I like to be ready for anything. We'll be coming up on the base in another ten minutes. Better turn on the TDSC unit now. I'm going to make two passes over the base. As we make the first pass, see if it's registering anything and look for anything out of order. If possible, see if you can pinpoint the location of the chips. I'll head out toward High Rock before turning for the second pass. On that pass, try to get in as many shots with the camera as you can without being obvious. I don't want them to think we're taking pictures of them." Dean continued on a lazy easterly course, flying toward the south coast then back inland before turning back to the coast once more. "Try to take your shots as I make the turn back toward the coast so they'll think we're going for a panorama of the coastline."

"Not a problem, Dean. The way the digital camera's viewfinder is set up, I'll be able to take the shots with the camera in my lap. They won't even know I'm shooting them."

As they finished their conversation, the old tracking base came into view. "Okay, here we go. Look like a tourist." Dean powered down the craft a bit so their flight time over the base was extended by a few seconds.

Dean concentrated on the line of her flight, while Katie tuned in the TDSC unit and conducted a visual scan of the base. For a non-operational base, it looked to be in good shape. The fencing surrounding the base was sound and secure with no breaks in its continuity, and the undergrowth was cut back from the fence a good fifty feet. This made it very difficult for anyone to sneak up to the fence without being observed. Even the buildings seemed to be in good condition. The tarmac showed the most evidence of disuse with tufts of grass growing in the cracks, and there were several trees down on the property. Most of those were probably due to the tropical storms and hurricanes that had passed the island since the base was deactivated. An area behind the main tracking station did show signs of use, as did a smaller barracks–like building. As Dean flew nearer the main tracking building, Katie noted the small blue blip on her miniature TDSC screen.

"I have a reading on the chip. It's in the main building." Katie attempted to fine tune the unit to get a precise location, but the movement of the ultralight made it too difficult to accomplish.

As they headed out towards the coast and High Rock, Katie caught a glimpse of a reflection bouncing off something shiny in one of the abandoned hangar buildings. She noted the approximate location so she could snap it on the return trip over the base.

"Alpha One to Tower," the lookout called on his com unit. "We've got company coming."

"What kind of company?" came the query.

"Airborne. Looks like an ultralight with two passengers. Coming in at one o'clock from my position."

Jerry Stockton picked up his binoculars and peered out of the airfield control tower in the direction given. "I've got them in view. Looks like a couple of women. Probably tourists from the way they're flying." He turned to a second man in the tower. "Better warn Scott. We'll need to pull everyone inside until they're gone." The second man hit a few keystrokes on the computer in front of him, activating a series of vibrating signals to the receiver attached to each man's belt.

As soon as the band of mercenaries felt the signal, all work stopped, and each man secured himself from view. Jerry and his partner, Joel, continued to watch the women approach from behind the special security glass that was installed in the tower. They could see out, but not be seen. As the ultralight approached, they confirmed that it was piloted by a woman and had another female for a passenger. He watched their flight over the base and held them in his sights until they headed out in the direction of High Rock before calling over to the command post.

Joel keyed in the "all clear" command as the ultralight disappeared from view. As a precaution, he next called Alpha Four, on the eastern boarder of the complex. "Tower to Alpha Four. Keep them in your sights and watch for a possible return."

"Affirmative. Alpha Four out."

"Did anything look out of the ordinary?" Dean asked as they flew out of view of the base.

"Most of it looked pretty abandoned, but there are a few places I'll focus on with the camera." Katie traded the TDSC unit for the camera in Dean's backpack. "I caught a glimpse of something in that last hangar farthest from the main building. Make sure you give me a full view of it on the return."

"Did you see anyone moving down there?"

"Nope. But it sure felt like someone was watching us." Katie slung the camera strap over her head and made sure it was secure before she fastened the flap on the backpack.

"I'm going to be a bit more acrobatic on the return trip so they'll get the idea we're really tourists." Dean looked over her shoulder at Katie. "Will you be all right with that?"

Katie smiled and nodded back. "Yeah, as long as you don't do any loops."

Dean just grinned and then put the ultralight into a tight loop and a few spiraling turns. The only comment from Katie was a barely audible, "Oh, no," and she felt Katie reach around and grab her tightly, then emit an "uuggnnhh" as Dean came out of the loop and into the spiral rolls, before steadying the flight path once more.

"When we get back, you're gonna pay for that." Katie relaxed her grip as Dean brought the aircraft into a more stable flight pattern.

"Aw, c'mon. That was milder than that roller coaster you made me ride last July."

"Maybe. But that roller coaster was at least attached to the earth." Katie shook her head and waited for her stomach to stop churning, as Dean made a wide turn over the ocean before heading back toward the base on a more meandering course.

"I'm going to fake a stall as I approach the base. That way I'll be able to glide down lower without seeming to do it on purpose." Dean looked over her shoulder at Katie to judge her reaction to the idea. "Don't worry, love, we'll come back out of it easily enough."

"Hey, you're the pilot. Wherever you go, I go." Katie reached forward and gave Dean's shoulders a squeeze.

As they came into view of the eastern edge of the building complex, Dean played with the choke to make the engine sputter. She did this three times before cutting the engine completely. The plane came down in a gentle glide, and Katie began covertly taking pictures of the surrounding complex. When they were only ten feet from landing on the tarmac, Dean switched on the engine and it came to life five feet from the concrete runway. As the engine sputtered and caught, Dean skillfully brought the ultralight back up to a comfortable altitude of 75 feet, barely clearing the hangar and control tower at the far end.

"Um, that was a little close, wasn't it?" Katie asked as Dean continued to put a little more altitude into their flight path.

"Nah. We had plenty of room." She grinned as she made a few half rolls from side to side as she headed back toward the rendezvous with Bill. "I just wanted to get a better look at the control tower, and that was the hangar you wanted to check out."

"Something catch your interest?"

"Yeah, the windows," Dean replied. "The glass was not the usual tinted glass you find in control towers. These were made of a special surveillance glass."

"Surveillance glass?"

"Yep. Lets you see out, but no one can see in." She smiled back at Katie. "They're definitely here. Now we have to figure out a way to get in without being noticed." Dean gave the little ultralight more gas and returned to their former altitude of one hundred fifty feet as they pleasurably zigzagged their way back to the rendezvous point.

"Alpha Four to Tower."

"Go ahead, Alpha Four."

"That ultralight is headed back our way. Sounds like they're having a bit of engine trouble," the lookout responded.

Jerry and Joel watched from the tower as the ultralight started to glide down towards the tarmac of the base. "If they land, we may have to send security out to meet them," Jerry commented. "Better warn Scott of the situation and ask him what he wants us to do."

Joel sat at the computer and typed in the message to Scott Gentry. The reply came quickly. "Scott wants us to wait and see if they land. If they do and can't get back up, that's when he wants us to send in the security team."

"Okay. Let's see what happens."

The two men watched the plane slowly descend as the pilot tried restarting the engine. When the plane was five feet from the tarmac, the engine kicked in and the little ultralight began to soar upward once more.

"Okay. Tell Scott, they've got it going again, and they're on their way out of the area."

Jerry picked up his radio and called to his guard on the west side of the base to keep an eye on the light plane as it left the base.

"That was too close," commented Joel. "We've never had an ultralight come right over us like that before."

"Yeah. Did you get a good look at them?"

"Sure did. I'd recognize them again if I saw them."

"I'm going over to the control room and talk to Scott about this. Stay here and keep an eye out while I'm gone. Let me know if they come back again."

Jerry took the stairs down from the tower and quickly crossed the tarmac to the main control building. Entering, he passed by the technicians putting together the last of the components for the Ares Array. Scott Gentry was sitting at the console entering code into the mainframe computer.

"Scott," Jerry called as he took a seat next to his boss, "the ultralight managed to get its engine restarted before they had to land. They're on their way back towards Freeport." Scott just nodded at the information, while continuing his data entries. "Do you want me and Joel to go into town to check them out?"

"Did they look unusual, or do anything suspicious?" Scott asked, turning in his seat to face his second in command.

"Not really, it just makes me nervous when something odd happens so close to a deadline." Jerry shrugged his shoulders as he waited for a reply.

"Me, too," Scott agreed. "We're too close now to let anyone mess up this op. Go ahead out to the airport with Joel to check it out. And, Jerry, don't do anything stupid. I'm already short one man on this op." He turned back to the computer and began entering information.

"Yeah, have you found out where Burt is?"

"Got a report half an hour ago." Scott stopped typing and turned to face Jerry again. "Our tracer found him admitted to George Washington University Hospital. According to the resident, a Dr. O'Brien, he was found outside the warehouse a couple of nights ago and is in a coma. Evidently somebody mugged him after the shipment went out. We're still trying to get a line on Roger, but no one's seen him since that night either."

"Well, if he was with Burt, and they can't find him, he's probably floating in the Potomac feeding the crabs." Jerry stood to leave, adding, "I'll make sure we stay out of trouble."

"Yeah, you do that," Scott agreed and returned to his keyboard, intent on completing his task. "We've only got a few days now to test all this stuff before we put it into action."

Chapter
17

1600 Hours, 12 November

"Hold it. Okay, enlarge that area," Dean said, pointing to a section of the photo from the morning's fly over. "Is that the hangar where you saw the reflection?"

Katie checked the number on the front of the hangar and nodded in the affirmative. "That's the one." She enlarged the section once more, then pointed to a section of interior wall that could be seen through the window. "See that reflection? It reminds me of the shimmer of an indoor swimming pool reflecting off a wall. Let me see if I can clear the image up a bit." Katie hit a few keys and watched as the resolution improved. "Yeah, that's it."

"Good catch, Katie. I think you just found our way into the complex." Dean stood and stretched before picking up her water bottle and draining half of it. "When we flew over the first time, I noted a trail of cracks in the ground that seemed to lead to that building. When we went back the second time, I could see water in those cracks. My guess is that a new blue hole opened up under that hangar, or Scott and his buddies opened it once they found the beginnings of the blue hole. It must connect somehow to the underwater caverns that lead to the national park."

"So, you're saying that our way in is through those caverns?" Katie asked for clarification.

"Exactly," Dean replied.

"And, out of the miles and miles of caverns, we're going to

be able to find the right cavern that leads to that hangar?" This came from Bill.

"Exactly," Dean echoed once more. "You have a problem with that?"

"Uh, no," Katie responded cautiously.

"Nuh uh," came the answer from Bill.

"Excuse me, Colonel. But I may be able to help y'all with this one." Tiny's thick Texas drawl caught them off guard since this was the first time he spoke. "I've been diving these caverns for nearly fifteen years with Dr. Samuel Withers. Went with him and his missus on most dives."

"Is that the Dr. Withers who died of nitrogen narcosis last month?" Dean asked, interested in what the quiet man was getting at.

"Same one. He knew these caverns like the back of his hand. But, on that last dive, he was checking out a new passageway that he hadn't explored before," Tiny continued with a shake of his head. "I was going to go with him that day, but came down with a stomach bug and had to stay home."

"Do you know which passageway he was exploring?" This question came from Bill.

"Yeah, we had gone over the map of the known ones in that area a couple of nights before. Wit was explaining how this new one developed. You see, most of this area is made up of limestone. It's pretty porous and gives way easily. It's not uncommon for a new passageway to open up."

It was Katie's turn to ask Tiny a question. "Can you direct us to this new one?"

"Only if you let me go along to the base." Tiny's normally unexpressive face was now very serious. "I've always felt something wasn't right about Wit's death, now I know it wasn't an accident. He was just too careful to wind up a victim of the bends. I want to help nail those guys for what they did."

"Anyone have a problem with this?" Dean surveyed her two partners' faces before agreeing with Tiny. "Okay, Tiny, you're in."

The group planned a checkout dive for Monday. Knowing how easily one could get disoriented on a cave dive, Dean insisted that each member of the group brush up on their cave diving techniques. Tiny offered to get the official permission forms for the checkout dive. The government had very strict regulations on cave diving, but with Ned's influence, they'd undoubtedly be able to get the required permit. They agreed that Tuesday's dive should take place in the Zodiac Caverns below Sweeting's Cay. That way, if Gentry had a watcher on Ben's Cave, they wouldn't bring attention to themselves. If all went well on Tuesday, they'd make the dive to explore the new corridor on Thursday. The day off in between would be necessary for their bodies to eliminate the build up of gases in their blood and body tissues.

"Now that we've settled the getting in part, how are we going to get out?" Katie looked around the room at her partners, who in turn looked at Dean. "We obviously won't be able to carry an extra set of tanks along."

"Uhh, well, hmm, let's take another look at those pictures you took," Dean replied casually.

Another two hours passed reviewing Katie's pictures before the group decided that they would need more information prior to any attempted excursion onto the base.

"Do you suppose Gentry will let any of his men off the base? You know, a little R&R before the big event?" This question came from Colleen who had been sitting quietly through the whole planning stage.

"If I were in charge, definitely not," Dean answered Colleen. "But then, I'm not running the show. Anyone have any ideas on the subject?"

"Well, if I were Gentry, and I just had an ultralight fly over my op area, I might be just a bit nervous, if not curious. Maybe I'd even send someone off base to check it out," Tracy chimed in.

"She's got a point there, Colonel," Tom commented. "How about if Tiny and I go and see if anyone was checking you out at Bahama Ultralights? We know the owner pretty well. He'll be straight with us."

"Sounds like a good idea. We'll keep a low profile here while you check it out."

Dean and Katie had just returned from the cove after a short snorkeling session in preparation for their checkout dive the next day. The air temperature was in the low eighties, and the water temperature in the mid seventies. They would still wear wet suits for the practice dive, but for the present, they were glad to get some sun. They were lying on the beach drying off when Tom and Tiny returned from Freeport.

"Colonel, it's just as we suspected. A couple of guys came around asking questions about the two of you after you left. Augie picked them out of the mug shots you gave us—Jerry Stockton and Joel Astin," Tom informed the two women.

"Ah, the elusive Jerry Stockton. Did your friend tell them anything?"

"Only that he was impressed with your flying ability, finding it very unusual for the normal run-of-the-mill tourist, and that you seemed to be pretty well off financially."

Dean smiled and nodded her head. "Did he happen to say anything else to them?"

"Yeah, I thought it was a bit strange, but he said that you two were planning on buying his place after you cleaned house at the casino tonight, and that you were planning a night out at Lucaya." Tom just shrugged his shoulders and looked quizzically at the two women. "Are you planning on going gambling tonight?" Dean was smiling broadly, and Katie was looking thoughtfully at her partner.

"So, you expected them to check us out, and you planted a little story to bring them to us. Pretty slick, Dean." Katie spoke with respect for her lover's creativity. "Guess that means we see a little night life tonight?"

"Yep, and Tom here, and Bill are going to be our escorts, okay?

"Be delighted to," Tom replied happily.

"Tracy and Colleen will go separately and watch our backs. And Tiny can keep an eye on the *Lady Luck*." She looked up at the two ex-Seals with a dazzling smile.

"I wish I were going along. I can't wait to get my hands on one of them," Tiny exclaimed.

"Ah, ah," Dean warned, waggling her index finger at him. "Not until we find out just what the hell is going on here."

"Yes, ma'am," Tiny responded in true military fashion, "but after we put a stop to them, I'll want a word or two alone with the one that ended Wit's life."

"Careful with your lust for revenge, my friend. I've been down that road, and it's easy to get lost," Dean cautioned softly, as she stood and gently placed her hand on the man's shoulder, peering into his brown eyes. Tiny read the pain in the sapphire eyes across from him, and nodded in understanding. Smiling once more, Dean suggested that they get changed and head to town for dinner. After that, they'd play a little game of cat and mouse at the Lucayan Casino.

Jerry and Joel nodded in unison. "That's what the guy said."

"So, they're a couple of seemingly rich broads, that you don't think add up to being just tourists?" Scott Gentry turned back towards the two men, contemplating the situation a bit longer.

"That one that piloted the ultralight seemed too calm and collected when she lost power," Jerry added. "I just have a bad feeling about this, Scott. I think we should check them out a little more."

"I don't like the idea of you guys going off base again. Every time someone leaves this compound, the chance of being spotted multiplies. It's too risky," Gentry replied shaking his head. "But then, I can't take the chance that they're more than they seem." He paused for a moment before continuing. "Go ahead and check them out. But be thorough about it. I don't want anyone leaving base again after tonight."

"Yes, Sir. We'll be thorough and careful," Joel offered.

"You'd better be. They've moved the live fire exercises up to this weekend, and I won't have time to come haul your asses out of trouble."

"No problem, Scott, we can handle them. They're just women." Jerry and Joel turned and left the control room. They headed to their quarters to change into clothes suitable for the casino, and to wait for the sun to go down before cautiously leaving the base.

"Just women. That's what I'm afraid of," Scott mumbled to himself as his two minions left on their assignment.

After discussing the plan for the evening and contacting Ned for support, Tom, Tiny, Dean, Katie and Bill decided to take the yacht to Port Lucaya to reinforce the "rich playgirls" storyline. Tom and Bill were assigned the role of escorts for Dean and Katie, while Tiny stayed on the yacht. Tracy and Colleen took the SUV and some miniature com units to be able to keep in

touch with the others once they arrived at the casino. Before
leaving, everyone familiarized themselves with the faces of the
two mercenaries that had been checking up on Dean and Katie.
They all hoped the same two men would be sent to check them
out at the casino. Just to be on the safe side, they also reviewed
the files of the other mercenaries thought to be involved in the
operation.

Tracy and Colleen left first to establish their presence prior
to the arrival of the others. The boat ride to the Port Lucaya
Marina & Marketplace took almost forty-five minutes from dock
to dock. Dean and company decided to eat at the Junkanoo,
where island dishes were the featured fare. Tracy and Colleen
staked out a table in the Corner Bar to watch the crowd filtering
through the entertainment section of the Marketplace. Their
location was advantageous, since it was diagonally across from
the Junkanoo and afforded a clear view for their surveillance.
As they sat sipping a Kalik beer, they watched the *Lady Luck*
enter the marina and dock at slip twenty-seven. The sun had
been down for nearly an hour, and the tourists were beginning to
gather in anticipation of the night's entertainment at the Count
Basie Bandstand. One of the local favorites was performing for
the evening, including a limbo show and contest. There would
be many faces to scan in the crowd when the foursome made
their way to the casino.

Dean checked out the entertainment square as the group of
four walked up the gangplank from their docking slip. A quick
appraisal of the square, and she spotted Tracy and Colleen at
their table, munching on conch fritters. The group walked casually around the square, checking the menus of each pub as they
passed by, finally entering the outside seating area of the Junkanoo. For all intents and purposes, they looked like typical tourists enjoying a night in the Marketplace. As Tom held the chair
out for Dean, he whispered that he had not seen any of the mercenaries as of yet.

"Well," she softly replied, "the sun's just been down for a
bit, and they probably had to wait 'til dark before they could
safely leave the base without being seen. Don't worry, we'll
make sure to get their attention before we leave for the casino."

Katie raised an eyebrow at her lover trying to decide just
how they were going to accomplish that, when Dean smiled at
her and told her to wait and see. Just then, "Little Joe and his
Band" started playing in true island fashion.

It was nearly an hour from the time they docked to the time they finished their meal, and the tourists were starting to crowd the area, much to the pleasure of Little Joe who was more than happy to see his tip bucket start to fill. The more dollars that made their way into his bucket, the more animated his performance became. Soon, tourists of all ages were up dancing in the square to his tunes.

Dean surveyed the crowd as she nonchalantly spoke into the miniature com microphone hidden in her watch. "Any sign of them?"

"Negative," came Tracy's response.

"Okay. We'll hang out here for another hour before heading over to the casino."

"Affirmative. We'll stay here and watch the crowd as you leave, then go to the casino."

"That's the plan," Dean confirmed before standing and taking Tom's hand, leading him to the square. Soon they were winding their way through the dance crowd, enjoying the music and revelers. As they danced, they both kept their eyes on the passing crowds looking for those familiar faces.

"Holy smokes," Bill whispered as he watched Dean undulate to the tropical tunes. "I didn't know the colonel had moves like that."

Katie's grin was getting wider as she grabbed Bill and headed to the dance square. "I didn't either. But, two can play this game," she commented as she began a wild dance with her awestruck partner. Soon, the crowd parted as they watched the two couples exhibiting their seductive dance moves across the open square. Even Little Joe picked up the tempo to aid their dancing performance. By the time the music ended, the entire crowd, including the band, applauded the four dancers. As they started to make their way back to their table, Little Joe announced the beginning of the limbo contest, encouraging the crowd to convince the foursome to enter. With the crowd voicing their encouragement, Dean winked at Katie and turned, walking back to the stage. Tom and Bill both begged off, but Katie eagerly joined her lover along with several other tourists. The limbo bar started out at a relatively easy height of five feet, but as it dropped, several tourists also dropped out. Soon, there were only three contestants remaining; Dean, Katie, and a young teenaged boy named Mac. When the bar was lowered to twenty-four inches, Mac fell to the wayside after losing his balance and landing unceremoniously on his keester, and Dean and Katie were the only contestants remaining.

"I'll get ya this time," crooned Dean.

"Wanna bet?" came Katie's challenge.

"You're on. Loser has to..."

"Has to be my personal slave for a week," Katie offered.

"A week. How about a month?" Dean shot back.

They both made the twenty-two inch bar and the twenty inch one. The crowd was on their feet cheering for their favorite, as the bar was lowered to eighteen inches.

"Wanna give up?" Katie asked, grinning.

"Nope."

Dean went first and nearly cleared the bar, but she lost her balance and hit the concrete with a grunt. Looking over at Katie she shrugged, stood, then waved her on, as the pole was reset for Katie's turn. Katie did a few stretches then approached the bar. The band began a slow island tune as Katie began to maneuver under the obstacle. The crowd started chanting as she slowly edged her way forward, then broke into cheers and applause as she completed the final height and stood, bowing to the crowd. After a brief conversation with Little Joe, and a presentation of Bahamas T-Shirts and caps, the two women returned to their table, arm-in-arm, waving at the crowd.

Tracy and Colleen had a hard time keeping their eyes on the crowd instead of Dean and Katie as they baited each other during the limbo contest. When it was finally over, Colleen said, "Pay up, partner. I knew Katie would beat Dean."

"Yeah, yeah," Tracy replied as she caught the attention of a passing waiter and placed an order for Colleen's winning beer. She then contacted Tom over her com unit and gave him the location of the two mercenaries they were seeking. "Tom, they're situated at eleven o'clock relative to your position. They have their backs to the square, but they've been watching every move through the mirror on the back bar. Never would have seen them, except for the fact that they were the only two heads not turned towards the square during the limbo contest. Joel's dressed in a black shirt and slacks, and Jerry's wearing tan dress shorts and a green golf shirt."

"Affirmative. I've got them. We'll hang here a bit after

Dean and Katie return to the table and then head across. Hang back and follow them."

"Jesus," Tracy whispered. "Just look at the crowd applaud those two."

"Nice try, sport," Katie said as they walked back to the table.

"Ah, well, it's a little harder when you're taller," Dean kidded.

"Oh, yeah." Katie agreed laughing. "The bigger they are the harder they fall," which elicited a round of laughter from Dean, too.

After they sat down, each eagerly took a large drink from their now tepid iced tea, then quickly requested a report from their friends on the crowd surveillance.

"Yep, they're here, and they definitely know we are too." Bill reported with a grin. "Nothing like making yourself the center of attention."

"Well, it seemed like the fastest way to get noticed." Dean looked over at Katie and smiled seductively. "Of, course we could have done something different to attract attention." Blue sapphires eyes pinned the emerald ones across from her in an intense, sensual stare.

"Ah, no. I think that was just right," Tom replied quickly, as he felt the animal heat rise from the two women that were locked in each other's gaze. "How about another round? That tea's got to be pretty warm by now," he offered feebly as he attempted to break their trance. "I'm sure a nice ice cold Kalik would go down better, but we do have to dive in the morning."

"Sure," Katie replied without taking her eyes off Dean. "Um, Dean, I think we're making the guys nervous," she mouthed silently to her lover. It was another few heartbeats before they broke contact, laughing. The four of them sat there for another fifteen minutes, finishing their round of drinks, before heading out across the marketplace for the casino.

"Wow," Katie muttered as she caught sight of the brand new casino. "I didn't realize it would be so, so..."

"Big?" Dean offered.

"No, so beautiful," Katie explained. "Most of the casinos I've seen on islands have been small and plain, but this one is gorgeous." She marveled at the marble columns that were dramatically highlighted by the precise placement of a low voltage lighting system. The whole appearance of the complex seemed to transport one back to the Greek isles during the height of their beauty. Even the reproduction statues between the columns were exquisite in their selection and location. The entire effect was warm and inviting, and more European in style and feel, unlike the architectural glitz and gaudiness of most American casinos.

"Yeah, the corporation that bought up this part of the island has spent millions making it a real classy resort. You should see it all in the daytime, it's very impressive," Tom informed the women. "They even cleaned up the beachfront. The sand is manicured daily at sunrise. You won't find a sliver of seaweed or a washed up jellyfish anywhere on that beach."

When they entered the casino lobby, everyone was impressed with the beautiful tile floors, Grecian architecture, and tropical plants. The gentle aroma rising from the multitude of flowering shrubs was pleasant, not offensive, as one might expect from so many flowers. Entering the casino proper, they were immediately struck by the lack of harsh noises, boisterous patrons, and smoke. It definitely had a European atmosphere, with the exception of the lack of cigarette smoke.

"I take it this place doesn't allow smoking?" Dean queried. Her escort nodded in confirmation. "Hmm, I like it."

After taking a casual walk through the casino to check out the other entrances and exits, the foursome settled down at the roulette table nearest the bar. In just ten minutes, Dean spied the two mercenaries sitting at the bar with their backs to them, and also Art and Gwen who were seated at the baccarat table. She found Ned and another woman chatting quietly at the bar. *Good. All the players are lined up for their roles.*

Whispering softly, Dean casually motioned to where the two men were sipping their beer. "You'd think they'd get tired of watching a mirror image."

As the two men and two women moved through the casino trying their luck at various tables, Tracy and Colleen watched discreetly, keeping an eye on the two mercenaries.

At midnight, Dean excused herself from the blackjack table, where they were now seated, and headed to the women's lounge, followed shortly thereafter by Tracy. When Tracy entered the room, Dean held her fingers to her lips in a silencing motion and nodded toward the far stall. Playing for time, Dean entered the first stall and waited until she heard the toilet flush before flushing hers and walking over to the washbasin. In the meantime, Tracy fiddled with her hair, while the other woman washed her hands before finally leaving the room.

"You know what to do, right?" Dean inquired as Tracy replaced her comb.

"Yep. We'll head out and get the SUV now. Give us ten minutes."

"Is Colleen ready with the syringe?"

"No problem. She's got the move down pat." Smiling at her friend she added, "Don't worry, I spotted Ned taking up his position near the entrance. Everything will go as planned."

"All right. Let's do it." Dean held the door as Tracy exited first without a backward glance, heading back to the bar where she'd left Colleen. Dean returned to her blackjack seat and nodded once as she placed her bet for the next hand.

Ten minutes later, the two couples were exiting the casino and casually walking down the sidewalk to return to the boat. Seconds later, they were followed by the two mercenaries. When they reached the street, Dean whispered to her companions, "Now," and they hurriedly crossed the road.

As they reached the other side, Katie caught sight of the two men beginning to sprint across after them. Fortunately, they both had their eyes on their targets, and never saw the SUV approach. Tracy executed the bump perfectly, sending Joel to the ground. As soon as he hit the pavement, Colleen jumped from the SUV and administered the injection, sending her victim into an immediate and harmless sleep, all the while calling for help from a conveniently stationed policeman.

A small crowd, including Gwen and Art acting brilliantly, gathered quickly as the policeman declared the man dead and began looking for the friend that had been crossing the road with him. Jerry hid in the shadows across the street, watching as the play unfolded. All the participants, even the gathering crowd, gave a very believable performance, thanks to Art and Gwen's lead. Tracy played her part to perfection as the distraught driver who didn't see the man dressed in black jump out in front of her vehicle until it was too late. As the constable continued to search for the victim's friend, Jerry silently slipped from view.

"Damn it, Jerry! Now we're short another pair of hands. Joel was my key radar technician, too." The anger in Scott's voice was palpable and made Jerry very edgy.

"Scott, it was an accident. We were so focused on following the targets, we didn't see the SUV come at us. Even the constable at the casino said it was an accident." Jerry was visibly shaken by his boss' fury, and stayed beyond his reach as a precaution.

"Did anyone see you?"

"No, Scott, no way. I hid in the shadows until I heard the cop say he was dead."

A calmer voice emerged from Scott as he paced the control room. "Are you sure he's dead?"

"Yeah, he's dead all right. I followed the ambulance to Rand Memorial, then called the ER a few minutes later." Jerry started to calm down as he realized his boss wasn't going to take any adverse action toward him. "Do you want me to claim the body?"

"No! Definitely not. I don't want him associated with anyone in our group. The less they know about him the better." Gentry continued pacing the room as he thought about his next problem. "Better get Sal in here. He's going to have to learn everything he can about the Ares Array before Saturday. The damned program requires two technicians, and he's going to have to be perfect or the whole op is down the tube."

Jerry jumped at this opportunity to leave the room and find Sal. He'd forewarned the young mercenary before he sent him to see Scott, knowing how hard a taskmaster his boss could be, especially when he was in a foul mood.

Dean approached her old friend in the secured morgue section of Rand Memorial Hospital and pulled her into a big hug. "That was the most perfect takedown I've ever seen."

Smiling broadly, Tracy blushed at the compliment from her friend. "Well, I just followed your directions," she demurred softly.

"And you too, Colleen. Just the right amount of panic to cover the injection." Dean looked around the room to find Ned,

Arthur, Matty, who was the island country's equivalent of a British MI 6 agent, and Katie. Tom and Bill were subtly keeping watch on the room from the staff lounge off the hallway. Dean approached the doctor who was injecting Joel with a stimulant that would bring him out of his induced sleep. "How long before we can question him?" she asked quietly.

"He'll be fully awake in about thirty minutes," the doctor responded, before leaving the room, not wanting to be there when the "official" interrogation began.

"Okay, folks, remember the plan. This is going to be a *Mission Impossible* type interrogation. Tracy, Colleen, you'd better duck out before he starts coming to." The two women left the room, joining Tom and Bill in the small staff lounge down the hall. The rest responded in unison, "Got it."

As they waited for Joel to come around, Dean and Katie commandeered the far corner of the small morgue prep room to discuss the interrogation. Matty, the local intelligence officer, and Art and Ned sat on stools near the patient.

"Do you think this will work?" Katie asked once more, hoping that they would finally be able to get to the bottom of the puzzle.

"I certainly hope so, or we're going to have to try to find our way through to that blue hole."

"He's beginning to come around," Matty's distinctive native voice called to them as Joel's eyes blinked open and closed several times.

Katie and Dean stood and walked over to flank the other side of Joel's gurney. They watched him struggle to consciousness and finally survey the room and his circumstances. He was dressed in a hospital gown, and his arms were strapped down to his sides.

"Wh...where am I?" His voice was slurred and his head lolled around limply as he looked at each face watching him. "Hey, I know you," he commented as he looked at Dean, then Katie, "and you, too."

"That's right Joel, and we know all about you and your buddies from the old tracking station. Too bad, you're the only one that made it out alive." Katie looked at the mercenary, nodding her head as she spoke.

"What d'ya mean? Alive... They're dead?" He was having trouble comprehending yet, and was fighting to understand what he was being told.

"Just what we said, Joel, and if you cooperate, maybe you'll stay alive." Matty leaned down, coming within inches of Joel's face as she did her best intimidation stare. "The Bahamian Commonwealth does not tolerate terrorists operating on its soil. And, our laws won't offer the kind of protection you would have in the United States."

"But, I'm a U.S. citizen, I...I demand to see an attorney." Beads of sweat were beginning to form on Joel's forehead as he looked around at the others by his bed.

As Matty straightened up, Dean leaned down into his personal space and spoke in a low menacing tone. "Sorry, Joel, no can do. Ya see, we reported your death with the rest of your cronies. You almost got yourself a toe tag, but you started to come to just in time. What'sa matter, Joel, you pass out from fright when you saw us hit the station?"

"No fuckin' way. I don't believe a word you say. How'd you get past our perimeter without being seen?"

"We came through the blue hole," Dean offered, hoping that he'd buy it. When he refused to talk any more, Dean shrugged saying, "Fine, Joel, we'll just let the Bahamian government put you away in some nice cell for the rest of your life."

"Unless, you want to cooperate and tell us the whole story from the top. Just fill in the blanks for us, starting with the contacts at the Algerian Embassy, and then finish with the radar array." Matty smiled sweetly at the sweating man as he seemed to be thinking it over.

"No, I don't believe you. You're just trying to get information from me." He shook his head, then spat out, "You know so much, you tell me."

Katie decided to try her hand at the interrogation. "Come on, Joel, we tracked all the pieces and parts through the warehouse in DC all the way to your little blue hole and the old tracking station. We'd been watching for a long time before we hit it. We just want to get at your sorry ass boss who let all your friends die for no reason. Don't you want to see him pay for letting your friends down?"

For just a moment, it looked like Joel was going to buy into Katie's logic, but then he just shook his head refusing to answer the question. "If you know about the blue hole, then tell me which entrance you use to get to it?" When no one responded, Joel laughed and said, "Yeah, just as I figured, you don't know squat, and I'm not saying another word."

They tried several other approaches to get the information, but Joel refused to talk any more. Matty called in her constables, and they took him out of the room and over to a solitary cell at headquarters.

Dean looked around the room. "Well, I guess we get to go diving," she commented.

"Our government will cooperate fully with your dive request. Unfortunately, we can't do more without specific evidence, and that man just isn't going to give us any. We'll keep up the interrogation pressure as well as keep him in solitary confinement for as long as possible. As you know, we don't have the capability to assault the site, and it still is under U.S. authority, so we can't be of much assistance, I'm afraid." Matty smiled sadly as she shook Dean's hand and nodded at Ned, Art, and Katie before exiting the room.

"Well, we'd better get some rest or we won't be able to function properly for our check out dive tomorrow. Let's get the guys and head home," Dean directed.

Chapter
18

The late night set back their schedule for the first dive. Needing to get sufficient rest before the ride out to the dive site, they opted to sleep in until 0900 before getting on the boat for the ride to Sweeting's Cay. By the time they left the dock, it was nearly 1000, but Tiny assured them there would be plenty of time for the dive. Tom decided to take the boat out a bit farther from the island, so he could open up the engines and make it to the Cay in record time. Dean, Bill, and Katie were in the cabin going over the plan for the late morning dive, while Tracy and Colleen kept their eyes out for any boats that may be suspicious.

The dive was going to be a refresher on cave diving techniques. Since they were all ANDI certified, it was a matter of land review followed by water practice. Unlike open water diving, cave diving required more equipment and expert techniques, in addition to specialized certifications. They were all National Association for Cave Diving certified, but the only one who had recent cave instructor certification was Tom. In addition to acquiring the NACD certification, they were also going to be practicing using closed circuit rebreathers. The rebreathers gave them some tactical advantages for sneaking up on their objective because they did not produce bubbles or noise, had on-board computers, and greatly reduced their decompression obligations. They were also more comfortable for the diver, their use reducing dehydration and maintaining a more constant body temperature. The first thing the dive team did was to review the precautions for CCR use.

The other objectives for the morning were to practice guide line and reel use, buoyancy control, body positioning, and propulsion techniques. For use inside the caves, these skills had to be mastered to near instructor level perfection. All it would take would be one careless kick to stir up the silt and their vision would be obscured until it settled again. With their vision impaired, it would be too easy to get disoriented and lose their way. That's where the guide line and reel came into play. On the off chance they lost their lights or the bottom was stirred up, they would still be able to find their way back to the entrance. Horizontal hovering and the helicopter turns were also on their task sheet for the morning dive.

As they eased into the cay, Tom cut the engines and Tiny set the anchor. The morning was clear with only a slight breeze skipping across the water. It was perfect weather for open water diving. Where they were headed, the lack of choppy waves would help in the approach to the entrance, but after they were in, the weather on top would not be a factor for them. Tiny, Tracy and Colleen would remain on board, while Bill, Tom, Katie and Dean headed out for the cave.

"All right, let's go over it from the top." Tom was elected to be the dive leader since he was an instructor and was familiar with the cave. "Training, experience, ability and fitness are the keys to safe cave diving. I know we don't have to worry about your fitness and ability, but this morning, I'm going to drill you on techniques until you feel you've been diving every day since you were born. I'm going to throw everything I can at you to make up for your lack of recent experience." He scowled at his three students who were dutifully standing at attention, listening to his words.

Tom pointed towards a bright red and blue buoy, fifty feet off the port side. "The cave entrance is about twenty feet below that buoy marker. Before we get there, I want you to make sure everything is on snug, the weights are at the right amount, and you feel comfortable. We'll practice our buoyancy control, hovering and helicopter turns before we enter the cave. Once I'm satisfied with your skills, I'll head toward the entrance. Before we enter, I'll wait for your thumbs up signal indicating that you're ready. I'll handle the guide line on this trip, but we'll each take a turn before the day is over."

He inspected each one of them, making sure their gear was on properly, pulling on straps, and checking their rebreathers. They were all carrying lights, dive knives, message pads with a cave layout on the back, and a diving model GPS unit. Although the water temperature was still in the seventies, they were wearing special lightweight dive suits designed to protect and keep them warm once inside the cave. "Ready?" Three heads nodded in unison. "Let's go." On that command, the four divers headed to the aft platform, slipped on their fins and gloves, and entered the water.

Dean waited for the bubbles from their entry to clear, then swam to where Tom was waiting, floating at a depth of fifteen feet. Bill and Katie quickly joined her, and they waited for Tom's signal. Once his three students were floating motionless, he gave a flat, palm down hand signal indicating he wanted them to assume the horizontal hover position. As each diver completed the task, Tom would approach and adjust their body position until he was satisfied. They returned to vertical then assumed the horizontal position once more, waiting for Tom to assess their technique. This continued for several minutes before Tom gave the signal for the helicopter turn.

They practiced these two skills for what seemed like an hour, but in actuality was only thirty minutes. Finally, Tom gave his charges a thumbs up, indicating he was satisfied with their performances. He turned and effortlessly made for the cave opening. As he reached the entrance, he attached the carabiner at the end of the guide line to the ring located to the right of the mouth of the cave, then waited for the three others to join him.

As they approached, each diver gave Tom the thumbs up, indicating they were ready to enter the cave. He tapped his dive watch and held up one finger to let them know they would be practicing and exploring for one additional hour. Because they were using CCR's, it allowed them hours of bottom time, and the equipment was smaller and lighter to allow them more maneuverability if the caves started to close in on them. He lifted his CCR gauge and indicated that they all should check their supply. Satisfied by the three thumbs up, he nodded and led the way into the cave, turning on his light as the cave roof cut off the sunlight that had been filtering down through the water from the sky above.

As they entered the Zodiac Caverns under Sweeting's Cay, the four divers were mesmerized by the beauty of the cavern hidden from view in the depths of the ocean. The limestone cavern had obviously once been above sea level, as stalagmites and stalactites were in evidence on the floor and ceiling of the cave. They slowly traveled farther inward, occasionally stopping at Tom's command and assuming the horizontal hover position, or practicing a helicopter turn. After traversing the cavern for about thirty minutes, Tom gave the signal to return to the entrance and finally, topside. As they broke through the water and climbed aboard the dive ramp, Tom looked at his charges, who were all sporting huge grins.

"Wow. That sure beats the fresh water caves in Florida," commented Katie as she stripped off her weight belt, BC vest, and tank.

"Yeah," Bill added. "I've been to the blue holes in the Yucatan, but this one's pretty cool, too. Did you see that one set of columns just before we turned back?"

"They'd been forming for thousands of years before the ice cap melted and put those caves under water," Tom informed the trio as they finished stripping out of their gear and wet suits.

Tiny greeted them as they entered the cabin, ready for a light lunch and rest before attempting their second dive of the day. "How'd it go?"

"Better than I expected. These three aren't half bad cave divers." Tom looked over his shoulder at his students, smiling. "If all goes as well this afternoon, we'll be able to tackle the Lucayan Caverns on Wednesday."

"That's good, because we received a message from General Carlton while you were down. The live fire exercises have been moved up to Saturday." Tiny nodded at Dean as she registered the news. "Tracy has the info for you on the sundeck. I'll bring lunch up in a minute."

"Damn. Why did they do that?" Dean mumbled to herself as she took the ladder to the sundeck. Bill and Katie followed her closely, as they too were anxious to hear the particulars of the news.

They finished toweling off while Tracy filled them in on the change in plans. "General Carlton said the joint exercises were going so well, that the powers that be decided to end them a week early. They thought it would be a nice reward for the crews to be able to return to their home ports in time for some Christmas liberty."

Dean paced the deck as she thought about her team's agenda

for the next couple of days. "Did she say if the targets for the live fire have changed?"

"No changes as far as she knows." Tracy flipped through her notes on the call from General Carlton. "She also said the Joint Chiefs are confident that the 'concerns' she had about a possible threat have no foundation. You're supposed to call her ASAP with an update. I filled her in on the latest, but she wants your take on the situation."

Dean nodded and headed to the pilothouse to make the call. Katie and Bill stayed on the sundeck and related their experience to Tracy and Colleen, who were not certified for cave diving. By the time Dean returned from making her call, Tiny had brought up a light lunch of fresh conch salad, sliced mangos, papayas, bananas, and assorted cheeses and breads. After lunch, the seven shipmates gathered in the pilothouse to review the maps of the Zodiac Caverns to plan the afternoon dive. The tasks for review in the afternoon dealt with safety issues: more reel and guide line practice, lost diver, loss of lights, and out of breathing gas drills. They would also practice with the propulsion units that Tiny had procured the day before. These propulsion units would help them to make the best time possible through the caverns, thus extending the distance they could cover with their air supply. It would be a full and taxing afternoon. At 1400, the four divers returned to the waters to recommence their exercises, and by 1600 they were back on deck and looking forward to a good night's rest. By the time they docked the *Lady Luck* in the waterway behind the resort, the sun was beginning its downward plunge into the sea, turning white puffs of clouds into beautiful dollops of oranges, reds, and violets.

After showering and changing into shorts, no one felt like fixing dinner, so they opted to eat out at Bananas on the Bay, the one and only restaurant located on their road. It was a warm, breezeless evening and they decided to walk the mile to the restaurant.

"Y'all'll like the food at this restaurant, but y'all'll probably be surprised at the service," Tiny chuckled. "They definitely believe in 'Bahama time.'"

"Bahama time? What's that?" Katie asked inquisitively.

"Well, let's put it this way...if you're a Type A personality,

as soon as a waiter comes to the table, be ready to order everything at once—appetizers, drinks, and main meal," Colleen
informed the young agent. "If you don't, you'll be waiting at
least a half hour between visits by the waiter. It's a rather slow
pace on these islands; no one is in a hurry."

"Oh," Katie replied as the ramifications of the slowed pace
hit her, "Guess I'd better get in my order for appetizers then,
'cuz I'm starved. Maybe I should order two, just to be safe."
Everyone laughed in agreement, knowing that Katie's voracious
appetite might not be able to withstand Bahama time.

After dinner, the group decided to take the beach route back
to their resort. The tide was out making the walk a bit easier,
particularly around the point leading to their cove. As they
walked, Dean set out the assignments for the next day. Tom and
Tiny would get the dive equipment refilled, and the rest would
take a tour of Lucayan National Park. Dean was 99.9% certain
that Scott would not chance any more of his men in a surveillance effort, especially with the live fire exercises being moved
up. She had a gut feeling that those exercises were part of Gentry's plan, but what role they were to play was yet to be determined.

"I wish we could have gotten some information out of Joel.
I'd certainly like to know more about that radar set up." Dean's
comment wasn't made to anyone in particular, but at the mention
of the radar set up, Katie let out a groan.

"Damn." The expletive was out of Katie's mouth as she
reached up and gently smacked her forehead. "I forgot to give
you the serial numbers off the computer parts we tagged on the
container ship. I was hoping General Carlton could run a check
on them and maybe they'd shed some light on the radar array."
Dean stopped walking, then asked Katie if she still had the numbers. "Yes, I entered them in my palm pilot as soon as we got
back to land. I was afraid I'd forget them. My palm's on the
dresser."

Bill offered to send them on to the general as soon as he got
into the apartment. Katie gave him the location of the information on her palm pilot and apologized once more for forgetting
about them. Bill, Tracy and Colleen headed back to the condo,
sensing that the two women needed some private time to talk.

"Hey, don't worry about it," Dean offered as she placed her
arm around Katie's shoulder. "It's not like we haven't had other
things on our mind."

"Yeah, but, I should have remembered. That could turn out to be vital information."

"Yes, it could, and if it is, we'll still have time to act on it. It won't take the general long to get the info for us." Dean turned Katie around to face her, then reached out to lift Katie's chin. She smiled at the still frowning young woman, then bent her head to place a gentle kiss on the pouting lips. "C'mon. It's a nice evening. Let's take a walk on the beach before we call it a night."

The moon was still fairly full, and it shone brightly on the calmer waters of the cove. Dean and Katie walked to the inlet for the waterway then turned and headed back toward the beach. Leading Katie over to a large piece of driftwood, the taller woman sat with her back braced on the log and patted the sand between her legs. Katie settled down there and leaned back against the warmth of her companion's chest. They sat there quietly for several minutes, enjoying the feel of each other's body while watching the gentle waves lap up on the shore. Finally, Katie tipped her head to the side and peered into the eyes of her lover. "Thank you, Dean."

"For what, love?"

"For not being angry with me about the serial numbers."

Dean smiled and increased the pressure of her embrace around the young woman. "Like I said, we still have time to get the information and act on it. Besides, I could never be angry with you, love." She bent her head and placed a gentle kiss on Katie's mouth. "I nearly lost you last year, and I vowed that if I were given a second chance with you, I would never let anything come between us."

"Really?"

"Really." Dean sealed the promise with another kiss that started gently before deepening and opening the door of passion once again. As they broke the kiss, Dean marveled at the ease with which the young woman in her arms was able to penetrate her soul and release her desires. She covertly scanned the beach for any other late night strollers, then slipped her hand up and began a loving caress of the beautiful woman in her arms. Lips replaced caressing hands, as buttons were opened to expose Katie's suntanned skin. Soon they were in a world where no one else existed, concentrating only on each other.

Chapter
19

0615 Hours, 14 November

Katie followed Dean quietly through the condo and into their front bedroom. They slipped off their sand covered clothes, exchanging them for running shorts, tops, and Ree-boks. Just as they were opening the door again, a voice cleared its throat behind them.

"Ahem. Coming in, or going out?" Bill whispered from the hallway.

"Um, going out," Katie whispered back.

"Yeah, lazybones. Wanna join us for a run on the beach?" Dean lifted an eyebrow and gave Bill a feral grin.

"Nope. I already had my run this morning." A dazzling smile was on the young lieutenant's face as he continued. "And you'll never guess what I saw over by that piece of driftwood log on the beach."

"Busted," Katie whispered in Dean's ear as her neck began to take on a nice shade of pink.

"One word, Lieutenant, and you'll be assigned to the most remote duty station I can find." Dean attempted an intimidating posture, but it was very difficult with Katie's arm firmly wrapped around her waist.

"Aw, I thought it was pretty cute, all..." He was interrupted by Tracy's sleepy voice behind him.

"What was cute?"

"Oh, you know," he grinned at Dean before turning to face Tracy, "those little puppies outside by the beach. They were all snuggled up when I went out for my run this morning."

"Oh, yeah. Colleen's been feeding them every night. They are cute." Tracy moved into the kitchen and filled a kettle with water for tea as she spoke over her shoulder. "So, where are you two going?"

"Out for our morning run. Want to join us?" Katie asked politely.

"Nah. You two go ahead." She came out of the kitchen smiling at them. "Oh, next time you two decide to sleep on the beach, better take your towels. That sand is going to be a bitch to get out of your long hair, Dean."

"Busted again," Katie said softly as she pulled Dean out the front door.

At 0930, packing coolers, beach towels and snorkeling equipment, the five "tourists" set out for Lucayan National Park in the rented SUV. It took them a little under thirty minutes to reach the park, pulling into the parking area on the cave side of the road. Dean noted that there were only four cars in the parking lot, but that was not unusual as it was fairly early yet. A Bahamian constable, whose duty for the week was to patrol the park grounds, greeted them warmly. As they presented their admission tickets, he led them to the path for Ben's Cave. The tour was self-guided, with many trail signs highlighting the variety of ecosystems they encountered along the way. When they arrived at Ben's Cave, Dean, Katie and Bill, began to pay very close attention to the layout in case they decided to enter the underwater cave system from this point. Tracy and Colleen made excellent tour guides as they related a large amount of information about the system that they had picked up over the years. After checking out Ben's Cave, the group moved on to Burial Mound Cave, inspecting that as a possible entry site also.

"We'll have to talk to Tom and Tiny, but my guess is that we will probably use Ben's Cave for our entry. If we try the water entrance out in the ocean, it will take too long to find the right cut-off toward the tracking station." Heads nodded in agreement with Dean's speculation.

"Is Tiny certain he'll be able to find the right corridor to take?" Colleen asked as they returned to the car to retrieve their beach supplies.

"He seems pretty certain. He'd been diving with Professor Withers for several years, so, he'll lead us on the dive tomorrow." Katie offered this bit of information as she hefted the bag with the snorkel gear over her shoulder. "One of the things he and Tom are doing today is making an overlay of the cave system map, with the approximate coordinates we recorded when tracking the package Saturday night."

The group crossed the road and started down the path toward the beach. They traversed through mangrove swamps, crossed the pristine Gold Rock Creek and sand dunes, and finally came through a strip of pinelands onto the beach. The sand was snow white and contrasted sharply with the deep blue of the water. The beach itself was very wide, and there wasn't another soul in sight.

"Wow." was the single word uttered collectively by Bill, Katie and Dean, as Tracy and Colleen just nodded in agreement.

"That's exactly what we said the first time we came here," Colleen commented.

"Where is everybody?" Bill asked as he surveyed the beach from one end to the other.

"You'll get a handful of people here, but usually it's pretty empty. Most tourists opt for the excitement of Xanadu Beach or the beach across from Port Lucaya. It's too dull here for most folks." Tracy kept speaking as she led the way to her favorite spot. "The people that drove the cars you saw in the parking lot are probably on one of the kayak trips on Gold Rock Creek. They'll be on the beach when they get back around 12:30. Until then, we'll probably have the place to ourselves."

They set their coolers in the shade of some pines, then spread their blankets out in the sun. Dean and Katie were the first in the water, followed shortly thereafter by Bill. They had their snorkel gear and decided to take a swim out to the island just off shore where the wet entrance to the caverns began. It was a long swim, and by the time they got back to the beach, they were pretty tired.

"Well, I sure hope we'll be going through Ben's Cave. That was quite a workout," Bill offered as he collapsed on a blanket.

"Don't forget we'll have some assistance tomorrow," Katie reminded Bill.

The group spent the rest of the morning and early afternoon on the beach resting up for their next dive. At 1500, they packed up their gear and headed back to the parking lot, eager to get back and check out the map overlay that should be completed.

"Yep. That's the way to go in." Tiny was pointing to a route that was using the entrance at Ben's Cave. "It'll save us time and air. It's also closer to the corridor that Wit was going to explore the day he died. I'll bet my ranch in Texas that this corridor leads to the tracking station, and that's why he was murdered."

Tom turned to the group and set out the schedule for the next day's dive. "We'll have to go in before the park opens. You'll have three hours of time on the rebreathers and can only use one hour for exploration. The authorities are going to shut down the cave to visitors from 1100 to 1300 hours to cover our exit, if necessary."

"Why only one hour? Couldn't you use a half hour more to explore?" This question came from Colleen as she noted the others nodding in agreement with Tom.

Dean elected to answer the question, explaining that most cave diving deaths occur from three basic reasons: failure to use a guide line, diving deeper than one hundred thirty feet, and failure to keep two thirds of your air supply in reserve for your exit. She further explained that the two-thirds rule was necessary in case of emergencies, like a snapped guide line, or one of your buddies running out of air, loss of lights, and so forth.

"Guess I'll stick to open water diving," Colleen said softly.

Tiny jumped into the conversation to ease Colleen's fears. "Don't let that scare you out of cave diving, Col," Tiny drawled. "The beauty you can find in an underwater cave is amazing, and as long as you are certified, and have a healthy respect for the element you are diving in, it can be just as safe, or even safer, than open water diving."

"Tom, you, Tracy and Colleen will be on land during this dive, maintaining the communication equipment. Tiny will lead us to the corridor and, hopefully, the tracking station. If we make it that far, we'll go directly into plan A." Dean continued to issue assignments as the group went through plan A. This involved the land team taking up a ready position at the southwestern edge of the station on the main road, ready to forge across the terrain to the fence line where there was an old gate for the sewer system lines. It was small, but they could access it on their bellies and be ready as back up if needed. They would have to be extremely careful not to be detected by the security team that Gentry surely had in place. The dive team was not going to perform a daytime exploration because it would be too risky. If everything went well, their job would be to mark their course, so a night insertion could be made on Thursday. With all assignments made, they had a light dinner and turned in early, eager to face the challenges the morrow would bring.

Chapter
20

The gear was tightly packed into Tom's panel van. Four sets of tanks and propulsion gear, plus masks, fins, BC vests, and weight belts, taxed the space to the limit. He had brought the van to the resort the evening before so that he and Tiny, and all the equipment could be transported to the park. The rest of the group would ride to the park in Tracy's rented SUV, which would also be the back-up vehicle to reach the outskirts of the tracking station. Each of the divers would be wearing a TDSC chip so Tom could track the twists and turns of the underwater system, and as a security measure, in case they were detected when they reached the blue hole in the hangar. By 0700, the two vehicles left for the park as the dawn began to break on another beautiful day.

It didn't take long for them to reach the park. At that hour of the morning, there was very little traffic on Grand Bahama Highway. Pulling into the parking lot, Officer Matty Soule and two constables greeted them, helping to carry the dive equipment up to the cave. Getting the equipment across the wooden platforms and down the narrow stairs in the cavern was a slow and laborious project, but by 0800, the team was suited up and heading out the passageway into the bowels of the system.

"How are you reading us?" Dean questioned as they ventured further into the cave's tunnels.

"Loud and clear," came Tom's reply. "And you're showing

up perfectly on the TDSC, too. Colleen did a great job integrating the map overlays into the TDSC's GPS program."

"Good, we'll be able to review the route later when we download the information to the laptop."

Progress through the underwater system went better than expected. Within fifteen minutes, Tiny had led them to the new corridor that Dr. Withers was going to explore on the fateful morning that proved to be his last. Before entering, Tiny held the team up with a raised hand as he proceeded cautiously, checking for any trips or traps that might have been set by Gentry's men. The area looked clean and unexplored as they continued through a narrow crack. They were all glad they were using the smaller and lighter rebreathing systems. If they had been using regular cave diving equipment, Tiny would have had to take his off and hand it through the opening in order to get through. Once they were all through the small crevice, they continued forward carefully. Fifteen minutes after entering the new passageway, the divers found it gradually expanding out until it opened up on a large cave that had rays of sunlight coming in from the ceiling. Adding the light that emanated from their dive lights, they hovered in awe of the highlighted columns of stalactites and stalagmites that had grown to enormous size.

"I'll go up and check the opening in the ceiling," Tiny called through his com unit as he slowly swam to the surface. Noting the blue sky visible above, he cautiously broke surface and looked around, realizing that he was still in the bay near the Lucayan park beach, but quite a distance to the east. Submerging, he returned to the others giving a thumbs down signal. They spread out examining the huge monoliths, marveling at the eons of growth represented in each prior to their resubmersion.

"Okay team, we had better get back on track. We only have twenty-five minutes left before we have to turn back. Let's see if we can find another tunnel to follow." Tiny made a circular motion with his hand indicating that they should check the outer walls for an exit.

"I've got it," called Bill on his com unit, immediately followed by another "got one" from Katie. As Dean searched her area, she too found another tunnel leading down into the floor of the cave. "I have one too, leading down."

"Okay. Which one do we want to explore?" Tiny asked as the group returned to the center of the cave. "We don't have enough time to tackle them all."

"I remember Joel asking which entrance we used when we interrogated him. I wonder if this is what he was talking about?" Dean commented to no one in particular.

"Yeah, I remember that, too," Katie contributed.

"So, which one do we choose?" Bill asked.

"The one that goes down," Katie suggested. "When we were tracking the package, the TDSC signature faded out for a bit indicating it was out of range, then came back again before it moved out of range completely. I'll bet it faded the first time because of depth, not distance."

"Our depth right now is thirty meters. If we go much deeper, we'll have to consider some decompression stops for safety when we start to rise." Tiny paused as he looked at each diver. "Even though we're using rebreathers, I'd rather play it on the safe side. That's going to cut into our timetable by ten minutes." Tiny waited for each diver to nod before adding, "If that's the one you want to explore, let's do it."

With that, the four divers headed for the passageway in the floor of the cave. It turned out to be fairly broad, making it easy for the divers to maneuver. The tunnel bottomed out at ninety-three meters, before turning upward again at a fairly steep angle. Unfortunately, the upward swim took more time than they had hoped since it contained a maze of tunnels. Most of them were dead ends, and others turned out to be too small to traverse. Factoring in the decompression stops they had to take, they had five minutes left to find out if they had chosen the right tunnel. When they reached a depth of twenty-three meters, they noticed columns of sunlight entering the corridor from the ceiling of the passage. Forty more feet and they came to a section of ceiling with a rough opening that allowed light into the passage, but no sky was to be seen.

"Let's check this out," Dean called to Tiny as she pointed up. "Katie, Bill, stay down here." Bill and Katie took the propulsion units from Dean and Tiny as they cautiously kicked up toward the opening, staying under the ledge to cover their approach. They didn't have to worry about tank noise or bubbles, since the rebreathers did not produce either. As they touched the ceiling, they crawled forward using their hands to control their forward movement. At the lip, they noted that the top layer of the opening was made up of concrete. They could even see some of the rebar protruding from the concrete at different intervals. Cautiously, they broke the surface and surveyed their surroundings, relieved to see the inside of an airplane hangar above their heads. It only took a second or two to confirm that they had found their way to the tracking station before they returned to the depths of the blue hole, giving their fellow divers a thumbs up.

In the dim light of the blue hole, Bill, in turn, held up a piece of broken concrete flooring with one hand and returned the thumbs up with the other. "Looks like it was a natural cave-in from the way this concrete is broken," Bill commented as he gently put the piece back down, not wanting to stir up the fine layer of silt on the bottom.

"Okay, let's get back to the park," Dean ordered. Turning and retracing their movements, each diver experienced a feeling of relief at the success of this dive. The trip back did not take as long as it would have, since they did not reel in the guide line, choosing instead to leave it in place to mark the course through the maze for the next dive. They just hid it around the rocks and coral as they went back over their path. When they arrived back at Ben's Cave, the smiling faces of Tracy, Colleen and Matty greeted them.

"Sounds like a successful dive," Tracy commented as she helped Dean take her equipment off. "We turned around as soon as you headed back to the park."

"See anyone suspicious along the way?" Dean inquired as she slipped out of her wet suit.

"Nope. Not a soul passed us as we ate our breakfast along the roadside. Speaking of which, you guys must be hungry?"

"Nope," Katie commented as she came up behind Tracy. "We're starved."

Dean just raised an eyebrow and grinned as the rest of the group broke out in hearty laughter that echoed across the small cave. "Guess we'd better get you fed then. Let's get this gear out of here so these fine constables can re-open the park."

Brunch was served on the deck of the *Lady Luck* and included a fantastic fare of island favorites and good old down home Texas style cooking. Tiny outdid himself as chef, all to the delight of a certain young blonde who was now stretched out on a chaise lounge with a very satiated grin on her face.

"You should open a restaurant," the blonde commented to

Tiny as she sipped her third glass of orange juice.
"Been there, didn't like it. Too time consuming, too many
worries. Besides, a customer like you would eat me out of business in no time flat." Tiny chuckled as the rest of the group nodded in agreement. "Never saw so much food packed away by
such a petite little thing." Shaking his head, Tiny walked off,
followed by Tracy and Colleen who had volunteered for clean up
duty.

"That big cave was really something," Katie spoke, eyes
closed, enjoying the warming rays of the sun.

Dean was in the lounge chair next to her in pretty much the
same state of enjoyment. "Just imagine how long it took for
those columns to grow to that size. I wonder if Dr. Withers ever
saw that cave before..." She let the sentence trail off as Tiny
rejoined them.

"I hope he did," Tiny offered quietly. "They found his body
on the shore east of the park. I'm guessing it was just about
across from where the blue hole into that cave is."

Trying to change the subject, but not completely, Dean
asked if he thought that Gentry used that entrance instead of the
corridor Dr. Withers found in the cave system. "That passageway entrance would have been too small to lug his contraband
through."

"Never thought of that. You're probably right, Colonel,"
Tiny admitted. "So where do we go from here?"

"I've got a call in to General Carlton. As soon as she gets
out of her Joint Chiefs meeting, she'll be calling on my satellite
phone. Until then, let's just relax a bit while Colleen does her
voodoo with the laptop."

"Aye, aye, Colonel," Tiny replied, then stood. "Tom and I
are going to get the equipment refilled at UNEXSO. Wanna stay
on board while we cruise over to Port Lucaya?"

"Sure," came the immediate response from Dean and Katie.

"What do you mean someone's been in the hangar?" Gentry
bellowed angrily.

"Well, maybe not in the hangar, but definitely in the blue
hole." The young mercenary recovered from his boss' ire, then
went on, "I did my usual inspection dive, checking for any sign
of intrusion, when I spotted this guide line tucked behind some

rocks. I went ahead and checked it out, but didn't find anyone. Someone had left that guide line there purposely though, so I checked in with Jerry and he had security do a search of the base, but they didn't find anyone."

"What did you do with the guide line?"

"Um, I...uh, I...left it there," the young man managed to stammer out.

"Good. Don't touch it...just leave it the way it is. Send Stockton in here on your way out." A gleam of evil was in Gentry's eyes as the young man hurried out the door. He spoke out loud to himself as he waited for Jerry Stockton to arrive. "So, someone's come knocking at our back door? Guess we'll just have to have a welcome party there to answer the knock next time."

"Hey Dean," Katie murmured softly as the *Lady Luck* docked and they felt the engines shut down.

"Mmm?"

"It's going to take them a while before they're ready to head out. How about we stretch our legs and do a little shop...um, go for a little walk?"

Dean tried to think of a way to get out of shopping, but she knew it was one of Katie's favorite things to do, so she gracefully stood and offered her lover a hand up. "Sure, I'd love to do a little...shopping." *Hey, maybe I can find something for Dirk and Tibbets,* she consoled herself, as they walked into the main cabin. "We're going to stretch our legs for a bit. Anyone care to join us?"

Knowing heads nodded and smiled.

"Nah, you two go ahead. I'm going over to UNEXSO with the guys. I need a new purge valve on my snorkel mask." Bill looked over at Tracy and Colleen. "How about you two?"

"Nope, we're just going to enjoy lying out on the deck, playing rich tourist for all the passersby," Colleen offered with a wink and waved the two away. "Have fun."

Dean rolled her eyes at the "have fun" comment and received a light slap in the abdomen from her lover.

"C'mon, it won't be that bad," Katie purred. "Besides, I saw a couple of ice cream places the other night." Katie knew exactly how to entice the tall woman at her side, and Dean's eyes lit up at the mention of the confection.

"Ah. Now you're talking."

Dean was first off the gangplank, eagerly looking for the aforementioned ice cream parlor. Katie picked up the pace a bit, catching up to her lover, and her quest for ice cream. Bill, Tom, and Tiny loaded the air tanks on two carts and headed off for the Underwater Explorers' Society dive shop.

Within thirty minutes, Dean's arms were full of purchases made by her young lover. They were just heading into Candy's Ice Cream and Hot Dogs when her cell phone chirped.

"Damn." Dean cursed the timing as she quickly walked over to an empty bench and dropped the armload of bags. She reached for the phone on her belt clip and flipped it open. "Peterson." Katie joined her as she listened intently, eyebrows furrowing as the caller continued. "Yes, ma'am. Yes. I'll contact him right now. Understood." She flipped the phone shut and replaced it on her belt before speaking. Letting out a deep breath she started to fill in her partner. "Those serial numbers you picked up off that piece of equipment spell trouble. Let's get back to the boat. I've got to call Ned and Matty." They hurriedly picked up the packages, all thoughts of ice cream banished as they briskly headed back to the *Lady Luck*.

As soon as they boarded, Dean explained to Katie that the serial numbers matched a control component for an Ares Array radar computer, only that particular board was supposedly defective and destroyed at the component lab.

"That's probably how they got a lot of their equipment without anyone catching on. Label the piece defective and instead of tossing or destroying it, sell it to the highest bidder. Pretty slick." Tom's analysis received concurring nods from the group settled around the table.

"I called Ned as soon as I got on board. He's going to call Matty and alert the local authorities."

"Excuse me, Dean, but, just what is an Ares Array?" Colleen asked the question Tracy and Katie were about to ask.

"An Ares Array is the newest development in remote control missile targeting. It not only targets launched missiles, it can intercept and redirect incoming missiles from the enemy. That's one of the things they're doing in the live fire exercises.

Testing the ability to control enemy missiles and render them harmless...or redirect them back on the enemy," Dean explained.

"So, if the task force ships have them, wouldn't they be able to redirect any missiles that Gentry might have tampered with?"

"You would think so, but unfortunately, no. Once they're redirected, the Ares Array also shields them from further redirection or allowing the original sender to send the self-destruct signal to the missiles."

The next question came from Katie. "Well, if General Carlton knows Gentry has an Ares Array, why don't the Joint Chiefs stop the exercises?"

"It's too late. The Joint Chiefs gave the go ahead for the live fire exercises to begin Thursday morning at 0600 hours. Seems there's a tropical depression building, and they want to end the exercises earlier, in case it intensifies. As of 0230 this morning, the entire task force is under radio silence. Any attempt to break that silence will be viewed as enemy transmissions and will be totally ignored."

"You have got to be kidding." Colleen inhaled sharply as she spoke. "There's no fail safe, no way to stop the exercises?"

"Nope." Dean stood and paced. "We're going to have to go in tonight. General Carlton will be sending in a Delta Force unit from Fort Bragg, as soon as she can get the green light from the Bahamian government, but they won't be able to get here until morning at best. The tracking station is still technically under U.S. control, but the land in between isn't, so it's a tricky situation. We're going to have to go in and try to neutralize Gentry and his mercenaries before they can activate the Ares Array against the first flight of missiles launched by the combined forces."

Asking the obvious question, Tracy spoke next. "What if he activates the Array before you can stop him?"

Dean's jaw grew rigid, then her expression softened into a menacing smile. "Then we'll have to convince him to enter the code to redirect the missile coordinates, won't we?"

Chapter
21

After docking back at the resort and eating a quick dinner, the group was gathered around the table in the dining room of the condo. Dean and Katie had devised a plan earlier on the yacht and were now going over it with the rest of the group. "Gentry must have at least twenty guys on the base, maybe more. That makes the odds five to one, in their favor, but I've been up against worse." She pointed at Tracy, Colleen, and Tom. "That's not counting the three of you on back up. I don't want to have to use you three, but if push comes to shove, we'll need someone to show the Delta Force team how to get in."

"At least you'll have the element of surprise," Colleen offered.

"That's what I'm counting on," Dean confided. "Okay, let's go over it from the top one more time." She checked her watch before pointing at the map. "In approximately two hours, at 2230, the *Lady Luck* will pull out of the Grand Bahama Waterway on its way to the coordinates Colleen gave us. That will hopefully place us over the opening in what we're calling the 'cave of columns.' Katie, Bill, Tiny, and I will enter the water at that point and head for the cave opening, and then the tunnel leading to the tracking station. Once we're in the cave system, I'll give one click on the com unit, and the *Lady Luck* can head to the dock at High Rock to await the arrival of the Delta Force unit. We'll maintain radio silence once we're on our way to the hangar. We should reach the hangar by 2400. Once we get into the base, we'll locate the radar array, plant the C-12, and detonators. We won't blow it until 0600. When you see the fireworks, bring in the Delta Force unit." Dean paused, looking around the table as heads nodded in agreement. "Give us a plus or minus leeway of ten minutes for the fireworks. If you don't hear them within the time frame...well, you can assume we've been compromised. You'll need to apprise the Delta Force unit, then get them in ASAP."

Colleen raised her hand, student fashion. "But, Dean, they won't arrive in High Rock until 0500 or later. Won't that be too late?"

Dean smiled broadly. "Not for a mop up operation, but if we're caught, well...we'll just have to do our best tonight. We need to disable that Ares Array one way or another. And, we need to do this as quickly and quietly as possible. Make sure the Delta Force unit silences their guns. I don't want any curious Bahamians showing up and getting blown away."

"Why not just cut the computer leads to the array instead of blowing the whole thing? Wouldn't that be quieter?" Tracy suggested.

"Yes, it would be quieter, but I want us to be far enough away from the unit when it ceases to function. If we cut the cable, we'd be too close to it and could get caught if they're still checking out the system and notice it doesn't respond. Besides, they can always replace the cable, but wouldn't be able to replace the whole array," Dean explained.

She reviewed her notes as she began mentally calming herself in preparation for the night's op. "Any more questions?" No one spoke as each participant registered the importance of a successful operation. "All right, we'd better get our gear ready and into our waterproof bags, then get it on board. Tom, you and Tiny get the yacht ready. We'll be on board shortly."

Bill and the four women went silently about their business, readying themselves for action. Dean and Katie pulled out the equipment bags that had been sent through the British Embassy, and took an accounting of the weapons at their disposal. After some deliberation, they opted to travel as light as possible. In addition to their dive knives, they each added to their waterproof bags their silenced H & K's, ten clips of ammo, and one dose pack syringe that was packaged to look like a fat grease pen for writing underwater. Dean also packed two separate bags with C-

12 explosive gel and detonators. This explosive was as powerful as its putty-like C-4 counterpart, but came in gel form so it could be squeezed into tight areas, making it difficult to find and remove. She also slipped a couple of pairs of razor sharp throwing knives into the specially-lined slots of her wet suit at the wrists and ankles. When the bags were packed, they were transferred into duffels to take on board the *Lady Luck*.

Dean paced the living room of the condo as she waited for their departure time. Finally, at 2200, she gathered her group and the duffels and headed out to the yacht. "Let's get on board, and we'll recheck the computer coordinates on the boat's computer with the one's on Colleen's laptop." The quiet group exited the condo, passing by a bunch of late night revelers in the swimming pool, who tried to entice them into trying the several flavored rums on the bar. Tracy and Col, knowing the gang from previous years, waved and promised to join them another night.

"We might as well head out," Tiny suggested as Dean came aboard. "We can take our time heading to the dive site."

Dean nodded her approval as they stowed their gear on the main deck. The women took the ladder to the pilothouse while Bill helped Tiny cast off the bow and stern lines. It took a bit of maneuvering to get the big yacht turned around, but by 2230 they were right on schedule—exiting the Grand Bahama Waterway.

"Good job on the overlay, Colleen. We should be able to find the blue hole in the roof of that cave easily." Dean called over the coordinates to Tom, allowing him to make the course adjustment.

"We should be over the coordinates in about an hour if we continue to cruise at this speed. That should leave you thirty minutes to get to the hangar," Tom informed Dean.

"Perfect. Give us a ten minute heads up so we can get into our gear. I don't want the *Lady Luck* staying in this vicinity too long, just in case they have someone watching."

"Aye, aye, Colonel."

The next fifty minutes went by too slowly for Dean as she went over the station's layout in her head, confirming her mental images with a review of the photos Katie had taken. When Tom gave the signal, Tiny, Dean, Bill and Katie donned their wet suits and gear. They each slung their weapons bag over their shoulders, and Dean and Tiny carried the C-12 bags. At precisely 2330, they slipped off the aft ramp into the dark waters, waiting until they were submerged to turn on their lights. It took them three minutes to locate the opening in the underwater cave, and another minute before they headed into the lower tunnel. As soon as they headed in, Dean gave one click on the com unit, pausing to hear the faint sound of the yacht moving off towards High Rock. The divers followed the guide line down through the tunnel and then on an upward course again, dousing three of the underwater lights as they made the approach to the opening under the hangar. Dean looked at her watch and read the time, *2354, not bad. Now let's just get in and get this over with.* Nodding at her team, she gave the thumbs up signal, doused her light, and proceeded toward the opening.

"There," whispered the mercenary, pointing. "A glint of light in the water. Get ready." A team of eight mercenaries spread out, hiding behind a variety of boxes that were scattered around the hangar.

"Make sure they're all out first. Wait for my signal," ordered Jerry Stockton.

As Dean lifted out of the water, she removed her waterproof bags, tank, and BC vest and waited for the others to join her. They were squatting on the concrete floor, reaching in their weapons bags, when a series of bright lights came on, temporarily blinding them.

"Just drop the bags, and put your hands behind your head," Stockton ordered.

Shielding her eyes from the bright lights focused on them, Dean recognized Stockton as he leveled his weapon on her. "Do what he says," she commanded as she stood to her full height. Immediately her team stood, slowly raising their hands and placing them behind their heads.

"Wise decision," Stockton commented. One by one, their hands were jerked behind their backs to be tied up with disposable, plastic, flex-cuff restraints. "Now, move." The mercenaries with Jerry surrounded the four divers and herded them toward the base of the control tower. "Lock them up in the storeroom while I get Gentry."

The guards opened the door and led them to the storeroom as ordered, giving each a shove into the dark room. As the metal door slammed shut and locked behind them, Dean cursed as her shin hit an object in front of her. Even with her hands tied behind her back, she was able to maintain her balance and keep from falling over the obstacle. "Damn. It's pitch black in here. Watch where you're going, I just hit something," she warned.

"Oww. So did I," Katie added.

Dean wryly addressed their predicament. "All right. So much for the element of surprise. Let's see what we've got here." She slowly made her way around the room to get her bearings and a feel for the size of their prison. "No windows, so this may be an interior storeroom. I'm guessing, about ten by ten."

"Yeah, with a bunch of crates in it," Bill offered as he bumped against another one.

"Well, we might as well get comfortable while we wait for Gentry to show up," she sighed as she felt for a nearby crate and sat down on it.

"Now what, Colonel?" Tiny finally asked as he sat on the next crate over.

"We'll wait and see what Gentry has to say first. Then we'll continue with our plan, after we've made a few necessary changes," she added with a teasing tone, in an attempt to keep up morale.

Although things had definitely not gone according to plan so far, they all had complete faith in the woman they followed. "Right," three voices chimed confidently in unison.

At that moment, Dean heard a hissing sound coming from somewhere above them. "Gas," she warned her companions. Hoping it was a heavy gas like the KO237 they had used in New York, she ordered them to get on top of the crates and hold their breath for as long as they could.

Five hours later, Dean woke with a pounding headache. She slowly maneuvered into a sitting position. "Everyone okay?" she asked groggily. From the moans and groans she realized that they were all accounted for, but still somewhat disoriented. After a few minutes, they all seemed to return to the land of the fully coherent. "Anyone have an idea what time it is?"

"Step over here Dean, and we'll check your dive watch." Dean slid over to Katie who blindly felt for the watch on Dean's wrist, depressing the light button once Bill was in position to read it.

"It's 0530," Bill informed the group.

"All right," Dean began, "here's what we're going to do. First, we need to get out of here."

"Um, Dean. Haven't you forgot something? Like our hands are bound?" Katie reminded her.

"No problem. I have..." she stopped talking as she heard the key turn in the lock. The lights went on as the door opened, admitting Gentry, Stockton, and three others.

"Well, well. What do we have here? Everyone have a nice nap?" Gentry spoke as he entered, surveying the prisoners. "We waited to see if anyone else was going to pop out of that blue hole, but no one came. Pity, I do so love an audience. So, which country do you belong to? Not that it's going to matter." He walked over to Bill and looked him up and down, then went over to Tiny, before checking out Katie and then Dean. "Ah, you two must be the ones that Jerry and Joel were worried about." He started to walk away then turned back, quickly raising his hand and striking Dean with a vicious backhand across her face, splitting her lip in the process. The guards held Katie, Bill, and Tiny back, as they all attempted to lunge at Gentry. "I really don't like it when someone messes with me...or my men," he growled. "And I especially don't like it when they kill one of my men." He reached out and grabbed Dean by her wet suit, and struck her across the face again. Dean's head snapped to the right with the impact, but she turned her head back around slowly to face Gentry with a feral sneer.

"And I don't like it when a piece of shit like you thinks he can mess with my country," Dean countered in a low menacing tone.

Gentry laughed at the insult as he stepped back. "Oh, let me guess, an American, huh? Too bad, because about ninety minutes from now I'm gonna fuck with the United States really good. You see, I'm going to take over a flight of ballistic missiles as soon as they leave their ships, then send them off on a different set of target coordinates. Care to know where they're going?" He released Dean, laughing once more as he walked over to Katie and ran his hand down her face and under her chin. This time, Dean had to be held back, as he continued to caress

Katie's face with a gentle touch. Katie tried to move her head away from his hand, only to find his fingers sliding to cradle her neck with his thumb pushing her chin back. "Wish I had some time to play with you," he whispered in Katie's ear, before letting her go, "but, I have to get to work now. No time to dawdle. Maybe later." He winked at Katie as he turned to leave, pausing to look back at Dean. "Oh, do you think the Cubans will like a missile or two landing on their island?" Shaking his head he smiled at Dean. "Hmm, probably not, but then, the President won't like them landing on his vacation either. Oh, don't worry. I'll make it look like a retaliatory strike from the Cubans." He laughed again as he headed for the door. "Saddam is just going to love this. He only wanted the President and Vice-President out of the way so he could carry out his little plan, but I'm feeling generous, so maybe I'll scatter a few more missiles about." The guards followed Gentry and Stockton out of the room, locking the door behind them.

"At least they left the lights on this time," Tiny observed, as he took in his surroundings in the artificial light.

"Good, all the better to get my knives out." Dean walked over to Katie and held her hands out away from her back. "Along the inside of the wet suit by each wrist you'll find a throwing knife. Be careful taking them out, they're razor sharp."

Katie turned around and reached for Dean's wrists. "Um, could you bend down a little?"

Dean did as requested and soon Katie was in possession of one of the knives, carefully cutting at the plastic restraints on Dean's wrists.

"Just a bit more," Bill estimated as he watched. The next stroke cut through the tough plastic and released Dean's hands. She removed the second knife herself and cut through Katie's bonds, then the two women freed the men.

"Now, let's see if there's anyone outside the door." Crossing to the door, Dean kicked it with her foot and yelled that they need to go to the bathroom. There was no response. She kicked it again and again, with the guys joining in to give her neoprene booted foot a respite. Again, there was no response.

"Hmm, guess they're all busy," Katie surmised.

"Yeah, they all probably have duties to perform during the operation," Dean agreed. "Okay, let's see if we can jimmy the door." She reached down first and extracted the other two throwing knives from the slim ankle pouches and gave one apiece to Bill and Tiny.

"Allow me," Katie offered magnanimously, as she stepped up to the door and unzipped the front of her wet suit. Reaching into her cleavage, she removed a small bottle containing four black earrings.

"That's my girl," Dean purred as she watched Katie remove one and crush its contents onto the knife blade.

Katie slipped the tip of the blade between the door and the frame, tapping the powder onto the bolt. Looking around the room, she shrugged then turned back to the door and spit on the powder.

"We'd better talk loud just in case there is someone out there. We don't want them to hear the sound of the powder working." They followed Dean's directions and began yelling for the bathroom again. It took two doses of powder to eat through the sturdy bolt before they were ready to leave the store-room. "We'll need to get our weapons first. Let's hope they're still in the hangar. Ready?" Three heads nodded, knives held at the ready.

Dean shut off the room light and slowly opened the door. Only emergency lighting fixtures at each end of the corridor dimly lighted the hallway, and no guards could be seen. She silently waved her team to follow as she noiselessly retraced their earlier steps. "Better check the tower for any watchers." She motioned for Bill and Tiny to ascend the stairs and carry out this assignment while she and Katie waited below. After a span of three minutes the two men returned, sporting a pair of 9mm Glocks, a two-way radio, and a set of keys. Dean raised an eye-brow in mute question, and received a shrug and a guarantee that no one would be watching from the tower for a while.

Dean checked her watch. "It's 0556. We don't have enough time to get the C-12 and set the charges on the radar array. If we blow the array after he's reprogrammed the coordinates, we won't be able to regain control. We're gonna have to take over the control room. Let's get to the hangar and get our weapons," she whispered as they quickly but cautiously left the tower building.

Chapter
22

0600 Hours, 16 November

Dean and the rest of her team made it back to the entry hangar without incident, unfortunately, their weapons bags weren't beside the blue hole where they'd left them. "Damn. Where the hell did they take the stuff?" she mumbled to herself.

"Over here," Katie called quietly, pointing to a locked cage area. "Our stuff is in there."

Flipping through the keys he had taken off of the mercenary in the tower, Bill started trying all the Master lock keys he could find. With the fifth key, the padlock opened. Tiny was first into the cage, retrieving the silenced Glock he had brought, along with several clips of ammo. Bill, Katie, and Dean retrieved their weapons too, and two of the com units.

"Team One is in need of assistance. Go to plan Beta," Dean whispered into the unit.

"Roger," came the barely audible response. "ETA approximately fifteen minutes."

"Too long. Make it sooner," she replied, checking her watch and noting that it was already 0600. "Birds are probably in the air."

"Copy that. Will do our best to comply."

"All right, let's see if we can find that control room," Dean growled as they swiftly left the hangar.

The morning light was going to make it more difficult to keep their search unobserved. Staying to the perimeter of the tarmac, they began a scan of the buildings, looking for the radar array they had pinpointed on the pictures Katie had taken during the ultralight flight.

"There." Tiny pointed at a low cinder block building that was only partially visible, with the rest of the building hidden behind another hangar. "There's the top of the radar array."

"Got it. Bill, Tiny...you two circle around from the north. We'll swing around from the south." The two men nodded and quickly sprinted back the way they had come before heading around to the other side of the tarmac. "Ready?" Dean looked into Katie's emerald eyes hoping that this wouldn't be the last time she gazed into them.

Katie nodded, then reached up and brushed Dean's cheek with her left hand. "Be careful, love."

Dean reached up and held Katie's hand to her lips, giving it a quick kiss before responding, "Always, my love; you, too." Dean looked across the tarmac and caught a glimpse of Tiny and Bill slipping behind a barracks building. "Let's go."

"Five minutes to launch," the mercenary called out.

"All right everyone, you know what to do." Gentry surveyed his makeshift control room as he finished entering the target coordinates. "That little trip to see our prisoners just gave me a few new ideas." He tapped the keys a few more times as he entered the coded password for the operation. "There. No turning back now." He turned to face his security commander, Jerry Stockton. "So, have you figured out who we have in that storeroom yet?"

"Four minutes to launch," came the warning.

"No. Not yet. I've got Ted over in the control tower trying to access all the files he can. So far, they're not FBI, CIA, NSA, or any of the military we've accessed so far. We've got the Navy and Army left to go, plus a few other agencies like Treasury, DEA, Secret Service, and the like."

"Well, no matter. In three minutes we'll have control. We can eliminate them after the op is underway." He turned back toward his computer screen.

"Two minutes to launch."

"Sal...get ready. Everything's loaded in the computer. Just watch your screen. Remember, at an altitude of five thousand,"

Gentry reminded his replacement radar man.

"Yes, sir. I can do it in my sleep," Sal replied.

"One minute to launch, fifty-nine, fifty-eight..."

As calm as Gentry tried to appear, sweat was beginning to show on his brow. He concentrated on his computer screen, tension building in his shoulders, fingers poised over the keyboard, ready for action.

"Missiles launched. Sixteen birds are airborne. Climbing to one thousand feet, fifteen hundred feet..."

"On my mark, Sal," Gentry commanded.

"Thirty-five hundred feet, four thousand feet..."

Gentry waited anxiously, finally giving the "mark" signal at five thousand feet. Fingers expertly tapped the keyboard in a flurry of activity, as Scott Gentry and his technician entered the final keystrokes taking over the flight of the launched missiles. It took less than sixty seconds for them to complete the transfer of control and lock in the Ares Array.

"Missiles locked, new coordinates accepted," Sal informed his superior.

"How long before impact in Havana?" Jerry inquired.

Scott looked at his watch and mentally estimated the time. "It's 0606 hours now, impact in Havana will take thirty-four minutes, then, a ten minute delay before the birds land on the President and Vice-President in the Keys. The main missiles will have delivered their payloads by 0640 and 0650, the others at 0710 and 0725."

"Just out of curiosity, where did you target the others?"

"Besides the four to Havana and four to the Keys, there are four heading to Pensacola Naval Air Station, and the last four are headed to Red Stone Arsenal in Alabama. Rather poetic, don't you think?"

The two women kept to the fading shadows as they made their way towards the control building. There were two buildings left to go when they turned a corner and ran into two of the mercenaries heading towards their barracks from their night duty. For a split second, no one moved, then Dean darted forward and caught the taller one's arm with a vicious kick as he raised his weapon toward them, sending the weapon spinning out of his hand. Katie, following Dean's lead, went after the second man, deflecting his weapon but not before he was able to release a spurt of automatic weapon fire into the air. She followed through with a series of punches and jabs that sent him to the ground for the rest of the engagement.

"That's the second surprise party spoiled," Dean mumbled as she finished dispatching her man.

"Sorry," Katie replied as she kicked the weapon into the brush.

"Just makes things a little more interesting," Dean responded with a grin as they continued toward their target, scanning the areas around them and expecting more adversaries along the way. "Better get on each side of that door. We're about to have more company."

Gentry, laughing at his last minute decision to send four missiles into the heart of the Missile Defense Command Center at Red Stone, did not hear the automatic weapons fire at first; when he did, the laughter was cut short. "Get out there and see what that's all about," he ordered Stockton. "The rest of you, stay on task, but get your weapons ready." Gentry stood and surveyed his men for a moment as they each concentrated on their task—monitoring the flight of the missiles, then he ducked into his private quarters just off the main room. Once in his room, he armed himself, grabbed a set of keys, and headed out his side door. Slipping unremarked past mercenaries running into the fray, he entered the vehicle hangar.

The gunfire also alerted two other guards in the barracks building. Grabbing their weapons, they ran out of the barracks door and right into two fists, the impact causing them to stumble backwards into the building.

"Oww. That hurt," Katie called, shaking her hand as she followed Dean into the building. The two men were trying to get up, but went down for the count when the butt of Dean's pistol connected with their heads.

"Grab that uniform and slip it on," Dean ordered as she did the same. "Maybe we can save time, and just walk in the front door."

Within ninety seconds, the two women were exiting the other end of the barracks and fell into step behind three other mercenaries headed toward the control room. When they were at the building's door, Dean tapped the shoulder of the man in front of her while Katie did the same. As the two men turned, blows to their abdomen, followed by knees to their heads, leveled them. The third man, turning as he heard the grunts, was taken out by a chop to his neck delivered by Bill, as he and Tiny rejoined the small group of intruders.

"Nice work, Lieutenant." Dean complimented the young man as she opened the door. "Now, put your hands behind your head and pretend you're a prisoner. You too, Tiny."

The men complied, effectively hiding their captors behind their bodies as the foursome entered the control room. As they walked down the corridor, Tiny whispered that they had taken out Stockton and four more guards on their way over. "Good. Let's hope the cavalry gets to the rest, before they get to us." Turning the corner, they came into the control room and were met by Sal who had a pistol aimed at them.

"Whoa," Tiny called out. "We've already been had."

Sal put his weapon back in his holster and sat back down at the console, eyes intent on the radar images once more. "Good work, Jerry."

Tiny and Bill stepped to the side, allowing Dean to step up to the console and place her H & K at Sal's temple. "Sorry, but the name's not Jerry." The young mercenary froze as he felt the cold steel at his temple. Tiny, Katie, and Bill trained their weapons on the rest of the technicians, ordering them to place their weapons on the floor and their hands behind their heads.

"Now, where's Gentry?" Dean asked in a low growl. Gulping, the man barely shook his head, indicating that he didn't know. Dean responded by turning Sal's chair around to face her, pinning him with a cold, steel blue stare. Again, the young mercenary gulped and shook his head once more.

"I...I don't know. When he heard the gunfire he told us to arm ourselves but stay with our tasks. Then he got up and went to his room. Haven't seen him since."

"When do the missiles impact?" Dean asked urgently as she grabbed a handful of the man's uniform.

"The first ones will land in Havana at 0640, then the Keys at 0650."

"Damn it! The President and Vice-President are in the

Keys. Can you recall those birds?" Dean asked as she checked her watch. It was now 0612.

"Not by my myself. Gentry has the other set of code numbers."

"Can you send the destruct signal?"

"Not without the codes to release it." The young man was now visibly shaken by the fact that he would be spending the rest of his life in Leavenworth, if not worse. "Look, I'll help, but I have to have the rest of the codes. I didn't know Gentry was sending them to Cuba and the States. No one did. We all just found out a few minutes ago." The heads of the other mercenary's nodded in affirmation. "We thought he was trying to ruin the combined exercises by taking them over. You know, playing games with them."

Dean looked around the room at seven other men who were now sweating profusely at the prospect of life in prison, all nodding vigorously in agreement. All eyes suddenly turned to the doorway as they heard running steps coming down the hall. Turning her weapon toward the door, Dean and her team readied themselves for the attack.

"Colonel." Tom shouted as he turned the corner. Lowering their weapons at the sound of a friendly voice, they retrained them on their control room captives who were still sitting with their hands behind their heads in complete cooperation. "It's Gentry. He's headed out to sea."

Tracy and Colleen entered the room right behind Tom. "The Delta Force unit reported a submarine about ten miles out. He's headed for it," Tracy informed them.

"Colleen. Grab that com unit and sit at that console. You," Dean pointed at the young technician, "tell her what has to be done. I'm going after Gentry. I'll radio in the codes."

She grabbed another com unit, and Tracy, as she ran out of the room. "C'mon, you're gonna fly me out there." The two women ran to the hangar next to the control room where Dean had seen a small helicopter. "You said you could fly one, right?"

"Right." Tracy answered out loud as she mentally scolded herself, *but only on the simulator program on the computer.* Tracy got into the pilot's seat, strapping herself in, while Dean did the same in the co-pilot's seat. Scanning the instrument panel, Tracy went through the procedures required to put the helicopter into the air. Breathing a deep sigh, she began concentrating on the techniques that she'd learned from the simulator program. After a jerky start that had Dean's eyes wide, Tracy barely lifted off, slipping the 'copter out of the hangar, then powered the craft upward, heading over the treetops towards the bay. From their aerial vantage point, in less than two minutes they spotted Gentry speeding towards open sea.

"There he is." Dean shouted as she pointed to the boat. "Get me down low enough so I can jump in."

"Are you trying to kill yourself?" Tracy asked as she tried to maintain the minimal control she had over the 'copter.

"No choice," Dean shouted, again indicating to Tracy to lower the 'copter.

Gentry did not hear the approaching helicopter over the roar of the speedboat until it was almost on top of him.

Oops, a little too low, Tracy thought as she bumped the side of the boat. Before she knew it, Dean was hanging from the landing runners, ready to jump. When the mercenary realized that she was about to board, he turned to face Dean and aimed his Glock at her, squeezing off a round as she released her hold on the runner and stepped neatly into the craft. The round missed her, entering the fuselage of the 'copter instead. He fired again as Dean reached him, kicking his weaponed hand upward just as he squeezed off the shot. The bullet ripped through the cockpit of the 'copter hitting Tracy's left shoulder before it continued through the roof, lodging in the main rotor. The helicopter pitched and swerved before hitting the ocean, bobbing helplessly in the water as it slowly began to sink.

Dean grabbed viciously at the hand with the gun, slamming it into the frame of the windscreen, causing it to jar loose and slip into the ocean. She grabbed the collar of Gentry's uniform with her left hand, cocking her right hand and delivering a blow to his head. As it snapped back, his head hit the dash, sending him unconscious to the deck. Dean slipped into the driver's seat and turned the boat around, aiming it at the sinking helicopter. As soon as it reached the spot where the 'copter was barely visible below the surface, Dean cut the engine, slipped off her com unit, and dove into the water. Swimming to the sinking aircraft, she could see Tracy struggling to open the pilot's door with her one uninjured arm. Aiding her friend with opening the door, she grabbed Tracy by the collar and kicked hard to reach the surface, breaking through in time for a sputtering Tracy to catch her breath.

"Damn. You really know how to show a girl a good time,"

Tracy sputtered as Dean towed her to the boat and secured Tracy's hold on the ladder with her uninjured arm.

"Do you think you can hold on while I get the codes out of Gentry?" she asked, conscious that time was slipping away. At a brief nod from her friend, Dean hoisted herself into the speedboat, replaced the com unit on her head, and grabbed a bottled water from the drink holder next to the throttle. She twisted off the cap and doused Gentry with the water to bring him back to consciousness. As he blinked himself awake, she grabbed fistfuls of the mercenary's collar and pulled him up to within an inch of her face. "Now tell me the codes, you piece of shit," she growled, "before you make me hurt you some more." Gentry was refusing to talk, so she reached down with her right hand and snapped his left wrist back, effectively breaking it. He screamed in pain as she changed grips and grabbed his right wrist. *This was the one with which he had caressed Katie's cheek.* Eyeing it malevolently, she threatened, "Just give me an excuse, Gentry. I'd love a reason to..."

"No, no. I'll tell, I'll tell. It's 4A37066Z989C001. That'll get you control of the birds again." He clutched his broken wrist to his chest and tried to squirm away, only there was no place for him to go.

"You'd better be telling the truth, or so help me..." Dean shoved him back on the deck and called the code in to Colleen. She then tied Gentry up, pulled Tracy onboard, and attended to the wound in Tracy's shoulder. Waiting anxiously for a report from the computer room, they headed the craft back toward High Rock. Her watch read 0632 hours.

As the codes were repeated aloud by Colleen, Katie jotted them down on the pad next to the computer. Mindful that the initial contact would occur in less than 8 minutes, Sal quickly directed Colleen through the process of gaining manual control over the sixteen missiles. With the clock ticking towards impact, the two computer technicians entered their codes in the required alternating series, finally regaining control at 0636. Next, Sal led Colleen through another series of commands to program the missiles to soar to an altitude of forty-five thousand feet before self-destructing. A collective sigh of relief went through the room as the sixteen blips on the radar screen disappeared.

"That was too damned close," Katie said as she picked up a com unit to inform Dean. "Dean, we got them in time. The Delta Force team has everyone rounded up, and the base is secured. Everything okay with you?"

"Yeah. Lost the helicopter, but Tracy is okay. We'll need to get her some medical attention though."

"What happened?" Colleen interrupted impatiently.

"Just a couple of stray shots that hit the 'copter. One hit Trace in the shoulder, but she's okay, don't worry. We'll be at the dock in about ten minutes. Have a medic standing by."

"Roger. We'll meet you there." Katie and Colleen removed their com units and stared at each other for a brief moment before breaking into wide grins, relief washing over them.

"Just like those two. Getting to have all the fun," Bill said as he walked over to the two women. "C'mon, I'll get the medic, and we'll go meet them at the dock."

As they drove over to the tiny village of High Rock, Katie asked Colleen how long Tracy had been flying helicopters.

"She's never flown one to my knowledge. Well, not an actual, real one, that is."

"What do you mean?" Katie questioned. "She told Dean she could fly it."

"She's only flown computer simulations, not real helicopters. And, she can fly the simulated ones...she just can't land them. She can get them up, and fly them around, but crashes every time she tries to land."

"Does Dean know that?"

"Guess not, or she wouldn't have grabbed her to be her chauffeur. I had no idea where they were going in such a rush until I heard the thing taking off."

"How did you manage to sit there so calmly then?" Katie asked, completely astonished.

"Katie, sometimes, you just gotta have faith." Colleen reached over and squeezed Katie's hand, smiling at the flabbergasted look on the young agent's face.

Chapter
23

The U.S. Army transport plane was taxiing to a stop on the tarmac at the eastern edge of the tracking station. Waiting on the border of the tarmac were the Delta Force insertion team, twenty-two handcuffed prisoners, Ned, Art and Gwen, Matty, and Dean's small island contingent. Tom and Tiny were waiting with Colleen and Tracy, who was protesting being relegated to a wheelchair. The MI 6 faction and Matty were conferring with Dean and Katie, going over the clean-up tasks left for the arriving Delta Force unit.

"We really appreciate your government's cooperation, Matty. I'm sure the mop up detail will have everything taken down and off the island by the end of next week. One of our intelligence officers will be in charge of the operation," Dean was explaining as Major Fellows stepped off the rear ramp of the C-130 and headed in her direction. "This is Major Fellows, he'll be in charge of the clean-up unit." Introductions were made, then Matty and the major walked back over to the C-130 as his troops lined up.

Art reached out to shake Dean's hand. "I dare say, that was quite a bang-up job you did."

Ned duplicated the gesture with Katie's hand, "Yes, our governments are grateful for your timely intervention. We could have had quite a bit of trouble trying to explain that it was all part of a terrorist plot and not a botched exercise."

"My, yes," interjected Gwen. "Imagine Saddam wanting to assassinate the President and Vice-President. I can't picture, for the life of me, what he hoped to accomplish by that."

"Well," Katie began, "it seems he wanted to invade Kuwait before the New Year, and he felt that if he did that with this sitting president, he would wind up in another Desert Storm situation."

"Why not wait until the new president is sworn in then?" Art questioned.

"He's an unknown as far as what his political response would be. Saddam figured with these two out of the picture, he could count on the temporary successor waiting until the new president was sworn in. By then, he'd be firmly entrenched, and the chances of the U.S. routing him out would be slim."

"Faulty thinking if you ask me," Ned put in. "After the last time, other countries, England especially, would be at the top of the list working to get him out again."

"Ah, but that's why he chose the Combined Forces exercises to make his move. The chaos and political fall-out that would have resulted would have decreased the Brit's ability to lead. At least that seems to be what he was thinking," Katie concluded as heads shook in disgust.

Dean reached up and gently grabbed Katie's elbow to lead her away. "Excuse us, but we'd like to say good-bye to Tracy and Colleen." They walked over to where Tiny was pushing Tracy's wheelchair towards the waiting C-130. As he saw them approach, he stopped. "Hey, Trace," Dean smiled as she spoke to her old friend. "You take care now, and do what the docs say, all right?"

"Yeah, yeah."

Colleen placed her hand on Tracy's good shoulder and gave it a gentle tug. "Don't worry, Dean, she'll behave."

Dean smiled at Colleen in complete understanding. Bending down to be face-to-face with her friend, Dean said, "I've got to hand it to ya, Trace. I never knew you could handle a helicopter so well. Where on earth did you learn that dipping maneuver that let me just step on board? That was sweet." In answer, Dean heard three people clear their throats and cough.

"Umm, well, I...oh, hell. You'll find out eventually," Tracy stammered. "Today was the first day I flew a real helicopter."

"Huh?" The dumbfounded look on Dean's face was a true Kodak moment, and Katie wished she had the digital camera in her hands to capture it.

"Yeah. I've only flown computer simulations before today."

"You..." Dean's wide-eyed look was interrupted by giggles coming from Colleen.

"Yeah, and she always crash-landed them," Katie managed to get out before she burst into laughter, too.

"Damn," Dean whispered softly as she stood. "That was amazing."

The four women finished their good-byes, and Tiny wheeled Tracy on board the C-130. Within fifteen minutes, the small cargo plane was lifting off the runway, heading back to the States.

"She'll be all right, Dean, won't she?" Katie asked as they walked toward Tracy's SUV.

"Yeah, no problem. The bullet went straight through. When I called General Carlton with my report, she said she'd take care of Tracy personally. She'll be admitted to Walter Reed as soon as they can get her there. The general said she knows just the doctor for her case."

"Oh?" Katie raised an eyebrow in question.

"She didn't say. She commended us on our success and said that she's really enjoying watching the Joint Chiefs eat crow. Um, she also said something about having to see the President when we get back from the rest of our vacation. She'll expect a full report when we get back after Thanksgiving."

"Hey," Katie perked up at the vacation word. "You mean to say we don't have to do the clean-up, or rush back, or..."

"Nope. We have the use of the condo, the SUV, and the yacht for the next eight days."

"Whoo wheee!" Katie shouted. "Well, what are we waiting for?" She grabbed Dean's hand and ran for the SUV.

Epilogue

1330 Hours, 24 November

Seven days had gone by, and the old missile tracking station was devoid of any indications that Scott Gentry and his group of mercenaries had been there at all. The Delta Force unit had made a clean sweep of the base, even to the point of securing the blue hole that had developed in the floor of the hangar. Dean and Katie had checked in on the progress from time to time, but left Major Fellows to do the dirty work, while they took advantage of the rest of their vacation time.

Bill's partner, Dirk, had flown down a day after the round up of Gentry and his men, and the foursome toured the island from one end to the other. There wasn't a cove, or bay, or little fishing village that they did not explore. They even spent a day at some of the local wreck diving sites. Their evenings were spent enjoying the bands that played nightly at Count Basie Square in Port Lucaya, and in long peaceful walks on the islands' beaches. Today, they had helped with the final loading of the last C-130, and said goodbye to Bill and Dirk, as they hitched a ride back to the States on the cargo plane. Tonight, Dean and Katie were left to themselves for their final night on Grand Bahama Island, and they were looking forward to it.

"So, where or what would you like to have for dinner tonight?" Katie asked as Dean drove the SUV back to the condo. It was starting to get dark, and Katie's mind was now on feeding her grumbling stomach.

There wasn't any traffic on the road, so Dean took the opportunity to take her eyes off the road and allowed them to roam seductively over her partner's beautiful body. "Hmm, you mean I have a choice?" Eyebrows lifted and lips curled into a crooked grin.

Katie felt a blush creep up her neck and color her cheeks as she reprimanded, "Keep your eyes on the road, Colonel."

"Oh, I have great peripheral vision," Dean replied in a sensual voice, as she resumed her normal driving position. "In fact, right now, I can see your blush deepening."

"C'mon, Dean. Seriously. I'm a bit hungry, especially since we didn't stop to eat lunch today." The young blonde squirmed, as Dean raked her body with another disrobing look.

"Okaaay," she drawled out. "And, what are you hungry for?" Dean asked relenting a little as she focused her eyes back on the road.

"How about we take a run into Port Lucaya and hit that great Greek restaurant one last time?" Katie was nearly drooling at the thought of the gyro sandwiches they'd had two days before. "I can almost taste one of their gyros right now."

"What, no veggies?" An eyebrow raised in question.

"Oh, yeah...and one of those Greek salads, and umm, don't forget the yummy desserts." The mention of the Greek desserts got Dean's interest, and the SUV picked up some speed as it took the turn heading for Port Lucaya. Ten minutes later, they were walking through the marketplace with their destination in sight, oblivious to the covert gaze of a tourist hiding calculating eyes behind a gnarled hand. As the two women passed the jewelry store window the tourist was viewing them from, an icy shiver crossed its way up Dean's spine, setting her nape hairs on edge. Dean glanced quickly around the gaily-decorated walkway trying to focus on the source, but shook off the feeling, attributing it to a cool breeze that slipped from the opened door of an air-conditioned shop.

Gustatory appetites satisfied, Dean pulled the SUV into the parking lot at the resort and turned off the engine. "Interested in one last walk on the beach?" she asked as she removed the key from the ignition.

"Sounds good to me, but let me run up to the room first."

Katie exited the vehicle and jogged to the room, planning her next course of action. She returned in a matter of minutes carrying a beach blanket, a bottle of wine, and two wine glasses. Smiling at Dean's questioning look, Katie offered her excuse with a beaming smile and a twinkle in her eye. "Thought we'd finish the cabernet from last night's Thanksgiving dinner."

They walked in silence to the beach, slipping an arm around each other's waist. As they came to the beach, they slipped off their Tevas to enjoy the feel of the warm sand. The night was exceptional. A light breeze played in the air, and the temperature was a very comfortable eighty degrees. The moonless sky was perfect for star gazing as they settled into the sun-warmed sand in front of a large driftwood log. There wasn't a soul on the beach in the resort's private cove. The majority of the guests were either packing for their trip home, or getting in one final dose of nightlife in town.

"This is a perfect ending for our vacation," Katie sighed, as she poured a glass of wine for Dean and herself. "I really prefer vacationing on a beach. How about you?" she asked her lover as she sipped her wine.

"Mmm, I really don't care as long as it's with you." Dean looked over the top of her wine glass at her young lover, drinking in her beauty. "You are the most beautiful thing in my life, Katie. Everything else is muted next to you." She reached up with her right hand gently caressing Katie's cheek before slipping her hand behind the golden head, pulling the young woman into a soft kiss. Even in the darkness of the night, Dean could see and feel her lover's blush, as the heat of it rose to her face. Lifting her head from the kiss, lips barely touching, Dean added, "I'm so lucky to have found you."

"I'm the lucky one," Katie insisted, as she leaned in for another kiss that was gentle but more insistent. As they broke from it this time, Dean set her wineglass down, and pulled Katie into an embrace as she settled them back on the blanket. Katie likewise, set her glass to the side, preferring the intoxication of her lover to the fruit of the vine. Her hands now free, she began an earnest exploration of her lover's body. "I can't think of a more perfect ending for these last few days, than to make love with you right here on this beach."

Katie straddled her lover, lowering her head to meet parted lips as her hands slid along Dean's sides, garnering a soft moan from the woman beneath her. The kiss lingered as tongues explored the soft wetness of each other's mouth, finally submitting to gentle nips as Katie pulled on Dean's lower lip before moving to her neck. The searing kisses were working their magic as Dean moaned again before beginning her own exploration of her lover's peaks and valleys. Hands danced over muscled backs, flowed along ribs, and sought sensitive breasts, stopping to tease alert nipples before repeating the ballet once more.

On the next trip, Katie slipped her hands down to Dean's shorts, skillfully unbuttoning them and lowering the zipper. Dean responded with a feral growl as Katie eased questing fingers past the bikini underwear, sliding them down along with the shorts. Next, Katie lowered her head to Dean's abdomen as she placed kisses on every inch of exposed flesh, while her hands were nimbly removing the clothing that was covering the upper torso.

Achieving her goal, Katie sat up, slipping off her tank dress to expose her naked body. She took in the beauty of her lover lying nude beneath her, caressing her with her eyes. "I love you, Dean, with all my heart and soul," she whispered as she lowered herself once more to begin her ministrations in earnest.

She began at Dean's earlobes, lightly kissing and sucking them before running her tongue across her ear. She trailed kisses across Dean's long neck as she moved to the other ear, giving it the same tender attention, and concentrating on her actions as Dean's hands roamed her body. Her breasts gently slid across Dean's, eliciting a moan from both women and lighting a fire that reached to their very cores. Katie continued her kisses across each collarbone, slowly making her way down towards Dean's firm breasts. Reaching the right breast, she allowed her tongue to tease the nipple taut, as her hand massaged the left breast in synchronization.

Dean purred Katie's name through clenched teeth as her lover steadily moved south, stopping at the crest of each hip before making the final dive for her lover's sex. As Katie pleasured her partner with deep thrusts, she heard Dean cry out to her, begging to be taken. Heeding this call, Katie poured her soul into her actions and took Dean to the brink of her orgasm, pushing her over the edge with one final thrust. As the waves of pleasure coursed through Dean's body, Katie's body reacted in kind as she held on to her lover with strong arms, sliding up easily along sweat soaked skin to rest her head on Dean's chest.

Minutes passed as the lovers remained locked in each other's embrace, enjoying the after-glow of their lovemaking. Katie reached over and covered their intertwined bodies with the beach towel that was wrapped in the blanket, lest someone stumble upon the naked lovers in the starry night. "Hmmm, definitely a nice way to end a vacation," Katie whispered as she kissed Dean's neck, enjoying the salty tang of her lover's skin.

"Good thing you brought a blanket. It would take us forever to get the sand out of, um, all our exposed places. Needless to say, it could have hurt a bit, too," Dean acknowledged as she cupped Katie's chin, placing a kiss on the young blonde's lips.

"Oooo. That would have definitely hurt." Katie shuddered at the thought. Looking up and down the beach and seeing no one in sight, Katie suggested they go for a quick swim before going back to their room.

"You mean, without our suits?" A raised eyebrow teased the young woman.

"Nah, we've got suits on...at least the ones we were born with," Katie giggled.

"Yeah, and I really like yours," Dean teased as she ran her hands over the naked body lying next to her.

Katie flipped off the beach towel and pushed up to her feet. "Last one in is a rotten egg," she shouted as she sprinted for the water. Dean just shook her head as she stood, then raced to catch up with her partner, best friend, and lover.

Author's Note

My partner and I have been vacationing in the Bahamas for several years, and have found the people of the Bahamas warm and friendly, and the island beaches stunning. Lucaya National Park is a breathtaking panorama of white beach that stretches for miles and can be seen on the back cover of this book. It is also the location of the blue holes used in this story.

For those of you that are interested in learning more about the Bahamas, Lucaya National Park, cave diving, and the blue holes of the Caribbean, there is a wealth of sources on the internet that you can explore either by using your favorite search engine or going to some of these sources:

The Blue Holes Foundation: http://home.swipnet.se/blue-holes/start_640.htm

Grand Bahama Island: www.grand-bahama.com/

Cave Diving: www.Cavediving.org
www.cavediving.com
www.divernet.com/technol/stef1197.htm

Finally, every author hopes to pen a story that is thoroughly enjoyed by the reader. I hope that my books do that for you. If you wish to contact me with comments, please email me at: tkocials@nycap.rr.com I hope to have a website in the near future so I can keep you informed of my latest projects, where I may be doing a book signing, or other events I may be attending.

Trish Kocialski resides outside of Albany, New York. Although she is a New Yorker by birth, she also claims the states of Missouri and Kansas as her "other home" having lived in the greater Kansas City area for twenty-two years. Trish taught school for eighteen years and worked as an advocate for comprehensive school health education and wellness for another nine years. She wrote her first novel while working as the Director of Parks and Recreation for the Town of Liberty in the beautiful Catskills of New York. Trish has now returned to work in the field of education

Printed in the United States
743600003B